Haymaker
in Heaven

Also by Edvard Hoem in English

Ave Eva
The Ferry Crossing

Haymaker in Heaven

a novel

EDVARD HOEM

❄

translated from the Norwegian by TARA CHACE

MILKWEED EDITIONS

This translation has been published with the financial support of NORLA

Published 2022 by Milkweed Editions
Printed in the United States of America
Cover design by Mary Austin Speaker
Cover artwork: photochrom print, Molde, 1890. Public domain.
Author photo by Paal Audestad
22 23 24 25 26 5 4 3 2 1

First Edition

ISBN 978-1-57131-129-0
Library of Congress Control Number: 2021943841
CIP Data has been applied for

Milkweed Editions is committed to ecological stewardship. We strive to align our book production practices with this principle, and to reduce the impact of our operations in the environment. We are a member of the Green Press Initiative, a nonprofit coalition of publishers, manufacturers, and authors working to protect the world's endangered forests and conserve natural resources. *Haymaker in Heaven* was printed on acid-free 100% postconsumer-waste paper by McNaughton & Gunn.

For my family in North America, who told me the stories

CONTENTS

Do not let them fool you!
There is no way back home.
Day's on the point of going
Already the night wind's blowing.
No dawn will ever come.
—BERTOLT BRECHT

Haymaker in Heaven

The Turning Point

I

The haymaker's name was Knut Hansen Nesje, but folks just called him Nesje and they called the farm he leased on the hillside above the small town of Molde on the west coast of Norway "the Nesje parcel." Nesje was my great-grandfather, and during my childhood I heard many stories about him from my grandfather, Edvard Hoem, and my father, Knut.

But, although I know the key dates in his life and have a few documents about how he lived, when I went to write about him, it was not enough. I had to invent him out of air and nothingness, out of the light over Molde and Rekneslia, out of the wind that tousles my hair and the rain that falls over the fields and the people, both in his day and in mine.

On June 17, 1874, he woke up earlier than usual in the house he had built below the horizon. The pocket watch on the chair beside his bed said five o'clock. His heart beat erratically the way it did when he was short on sleep, and he thought, as he usually did when it thumped like that, that our minds bear many a worry that we do not comprehend.

He lay still a while before it dawned on him that today was his birthday and he would be thirty-six. Two years had passed since his wife Guri had died. For the first time, he now felt that time was easing his pain and longing.

He swung his feet over the side of the bed, descended the steep attic stairs, and went out behind the house to pass water. The summer morning was waking up with floral scents and steaming sod. He heard birdsong farther up the hillside—at first a thrush, then a chorus of starlings, chaffinches, and willow warblers.

He went back inside and drank his fill from the dipper that stood in the rainwater bucket before pulling on a pair of wadmal pants that had once been his Sunday best, a linen shirt, a vest, and a neckerchief. The window was open. A pair of starlings reared a brood of chicks in a nest under the eaves. He buttered a heel of bread and drank a mug of milk with it. He didn't usually make coffee on weekdays, but if Claus Gørvell's servant girls should offer him a cup later in the day, he wouldn't turn them down. In his youth he allowed himself a dram on his birthday, but he hadn't tasted the stuff since he became a widower. A tenant farmer had no time for drinking or idleness. Summer days at the Gørvell farm were long and hard, and when the haymaking was finished he still had to do his six days of contractually obligated mowing for Reknes, from whom he leased his land. In addition to this seasonal farm work Nesje also made tools at the workbench and in the forge, and he took care of those Danish draft horses Claus Gørvell loved so much.

During the haymaking, he always led the line of five scythemen. He set the pace for their mowing. His work at the Gørvell farm meant that he mowed his own parcel at night, and during the busy season in the summer that usually meant no more than three or four hours of sleep. In the winter he worked in the woods for Gørvell. He worked for a half *dalar* a day, or sixty *skilling* as people called it, which was less than a day's wages for a day laborer. But Nesje worked on the Gørvell farm year-round. In the spring and fall he spent every free moment clearing, sowing, and harvesting the four acres of land he had leased in Rekneslia. In only ten years he cleared and plowed two and a half acres. He had one and a half to go. He tilled the soil with a spade and a mattock. Only for the plowing did he borrow a horse. By his fortieth birthday, he would have all the land under his control converted to hayfields and cropland. That was his plan, at least, and so far he had stuck to it.

2

Before Nesje left the house, he yelled at the attic to wake his fourteen-year-old son, Hans, who worked as the errand boy at the Gørvell family's mercantile for the summer. Nesje heard no response. He grabbed his ax and pounded on a rafter with the ax handle until the boy came stumbling down the stairs.

"Stop, I'm awake!" mumbled Hans from a rung. He ladled water into a small basin and headed out the door to wash the sleep from his eyes. Then he came back in and put on his clothes, which were sitting on a chair. Then it hit him.

"Happy birthday, Pa."

"Thank you."

Nesje looked at his son. He had shot up really nicely the past couple of years. He had curls in his hair that he tried to flatten in the morning with water. He had a gentle face, almost delicate, and like so many other members of the Nesje family, he tended to his hands and fingernails well. Hans would be confirmed next spring. It's often said that children are only ours on loan, but Nesje hoped the boy would settle nearby when he grew up. It was just the two of them, after all, and who knew what the future would bring. So many people were setting out across the Atlantic to America in those days, without any regard for their parents, who were left behind in misery and destitution.

Nesje's voice caught a little as he reminded the boy, as he had every day of his life, to be on his best behavior. The boy eyed his father carefully and, quietly, placatingly, he replied, "I will, Pa."

Nesje picked up his whetstone from the table and secured a sheathed whittling knife to his belt. Then he walked down the big stone steps and paused for a moment in front of the house. The mountains on the far side of the Molde Fjord were an incomparable sight on this misty morning. The view of the mountain range was a major reason why he'd decided to settle so high on the hillside. Some of the mountains across the fjord were near the water, others farther inland, but they were all spectacular from here, like one contiguous chain of more than seventy peaks. There was still snow on most of them. And the surface of the fjord was smooth and still. In the early morning, the islands and islets looked as though they floated on the water.

Nesje jogged down the hillsides and didn't stop until he reached the top of the hill at Rekneshaugen. He paused there, giving some thought to his age. I'm an adult, he thought, but not yet old. He looked out over the landscape. He lived here, and this was where he would continue to live. He was a thin man with a full beard and hair that curled when he sweat. He always wore a hat in the field, so his face wasn't too sunburned, but his forearms and hands were dark brown. There was nothing a laborer could do about that.

Below him lay the little town of Molde, which had grown up on the land belonging to the Reknes estate and, just across the Molde River, Moldegaard Manor. A row of houses lined both sides of the old carriage road between Reknes Hospital and Moldegaard, and each year new buildings were added.

Nesje walked down the path to the right of the *Humlehaven*, the large "hops garden." This was all fields and no buildings on the outskirts of Molde, which was technically still a part of Bolsøy, the neighboring town. The hillside was fenced in to keep animals out, with several hundred plant species that now, in early summer, were in peak bloom. The garden was called Humlehaven because Judge Advocate Koren, who at one time owned the large Reknes estate, raised hops for brewing beer. Humlehaven now belonged to the Dahl family, and the skippers of Nicolay Dahl's ships, who sailed many oceans, had instructions to bring home all the exotic seeds, rootstock, and cuttings they could find, to see if these would grow in Molde. In its floral splendor Humlehaven was a wonder to behold so far north. The Dahl family's arched and columned gazebo stood atop the hill, and the steep slope below was covered in rosebushes, clematis, and honeysuckle. Through the garden, wind rustled the crowns of larch trees and stone pines.

Nesje inhaled as he walked by. The course of life is like the cycle of the seasons, he thought.

He came down onto the lane lined with ash trees that Claus Gørvell planted a couple of years earlier, after the birch trees that had grown there since the time of Judge Advocate Koren were chopped down. The ash trees were not yet head high, but even so, people referred to the unfinished lane as Gørvell Allée.

3

When Nesje got down to the Gørvell house, he saw a woman standing down by the water on the dock. She wasn't especially young, perhaps in her early thirties. She had a black headscarf and carried a gray canvas travel case. She wore a white apron over her skirt, as if she were about to cater a wedding.

Since there was no one else around, he thought to go down and talk to her. She was following something out on the water with her eyes and looked over at him when he grew near.

"Do you see the pollock?" she called.

A huge school of pollock was passing right in front of the dock, moving up the fjord. The surface was choppy, the water turgid with swiftly moving fish, and a flock of seagulls followed and dived down frequently to try to snatch one out.

"If you had some fishing line and a boat handy, we could row out and catch a passel!" she said.

Nesje remembered there was a net in the boathouse.

"Well, come with me, then," he replied. Gørvell kept a small, two-man *faering* moored to the dock, and Nesje pointed to it. There wasn't much time for conversation.

"Pull that boat in," he said.

He yanked open the boathouse door. The net was in a crate. He pulled off his neckerchief and his good jacket and grabbed it. By the time he returned, she already had the boat to the dock, where she removed her apron, rolled it up, and stuck it in her travel bag, tossing it up into the little loft in the boathouse. Out of the corner of his eye he noticed a slight limp as she maneuvered the boat beside the dock and untied the mooring. He hopped in and held the boat steady for her. They flung the two sets of oars into place and rowed so the water churned and even frothed. The sea glittered. And she was as eager as he was. It didn't take long to reach the seething school.

"You've got them!" she exclaimed. He stood up and cast the net as far as he could. It fell right past the school of fish. Then she rowed as hard as she could to the shore, and the fish swam straight into the mesh, pulling against her efforts with tremendous force. He hauled it in. There were at least twenty good-sized fish in the net. Once the net and the fish were in the boat, she used the oars to hold the boat steady, despite the current, and laughed.

He was smiling too.

He plucked the fish from the net, cut their gills, and broke their necks. Then they rowed back as she laughed.

"You know they're my fish," she said to him.

"Where did you come from?" he asked. "And how did you get here?"

"My brother Ola dropped me off."

She pointed to the fjord, and in the far distance he could see a larger *faering*. These were a common boat in the outer district, bigger than the standard two-man version because they were used for both fishing and hauling freight, but still manageable for one person. In a *faering* out on the Molde Fjord, Nesje could just make out a man hoisting the sail. The sail went up, the man found the offshore breeze, and the boat darted away.

"Why did he drop you here?" Nesje asked.

"Well, I suppose he didn't want me hanging around home anymore. I'm Serianna. You?"

She held out her hand. It was small but calloused.

"They call me Nesje," he said.

"Then I guess I'll call you Nesje too," she said.

He figured she was probably looking for work, though he didn't expect her to find any.

"If you are looking for work you should have come on Moving Day," he said. "I think Gørvell has all the servants he needs."

"You know, I thought I might smoke a pipe with Gørvell," the woman said. "I figured then he'd realize that he needs me! You wouldn't happen to have any tobacco, would you?"

She placed her oars in the boat, pulled a pipe out of her shift, and popped it in her mouth.

Nesje was tongue-tied. He had heard of women who smoked but he had never seen one with his own eyes. His breath caught in his throat.

"I haven't tasted tobacco in years," Nesje said. "But you can go to Gørvell's mercantile when they open. They stock that kind of thing."

He rowed to the dock and she hopped out. He passed her the box of fish and straightened out the net before mooring the boat.

"Take the fish," she said.

"I'll bring them to the kitchen," Nesje said. "It *was* Gørvell's boat and Gørvell's net."

"But we were the ones who caught them," she said. "Where can I find this Gørvell?"

"Gørvell's not up yet, I don't think, and I don't know if he'd have time to talk to you anyway," Nesje said.

She started up toward the house, so he asked her to wait by the servants' quarters while he brought the fish to the kitchen door.

Nesje was wrong. Claus Gørvell wasn't asleep. He was standing on the front steps, squinting at the sun.

"Who's this you found, Nesje?" he said.

"She was standing on your dock," Nesje said. "You can have pollock for dinner tonight if you'd like. We spotted a school of them, and if can you believe it, we caught quite a few."

"You go ahead and take the fish, Nesje. Just make sure you get them out of here before my mother sees them," Gørvell said with a laugh.

This was no joke. Claus Gørvell's mother, Mrs. Anne Margrete Gørvell, was seventy years old and ran her bachelor son's household with a firm hand. Nesje rarely saw her, because she didn't come outside unless she had good reason, and he rarely went in. But he was around the Gørvell estate all year and caught a glimpse of her every once in a while through the window.

He wanted to say something more, but Gørvell gestured with his hand to say the matter was closed. Gørvell strode down his front steps.

"I suppose you're looking for work," Claus Gørvell said to Serianna, holding out his hand to shake hers, which he glanced at. "You look like you're accustomed to work. I don't know if Sina will be staying on. If Sina stays but Anna leaves, we'll need an indoor girl. We already have enough outdoor help."

He spoke as though she was familiar with everyone and everything at the Gørvell estate.

"I prefer to work outdoors," Serianna said.

"An indoor girl is what we need," Gørvell said. "You could inquire over at Moldegaard Manor."

Nesje had a thought.

"Maybe Sina would stay if she could work inside," he said. "Then this new one could take Sina's place in the field."

"Really?" Gørvell asked thoughtfully.

"Just a thought," Nesje said.

Gørvell contemplated the stranger.

"I suppose you have a child or two?" he said.

"I had a daughter," Serianna said.

"Where's your daughter now?" Gørvell asked.

"In heaven," Serianna said.

"Ah," Gørvell said. "That is where our longing lies!"

Though you certainly have an interest in more earthly pursuits, don't you, Gørvell? Nesje thought.

"All right, you can put Serianna to work," Gørvell told Nesje. "I think Sina's getting a fire going in the cookhouse, and there's some baking to be done before the haymaking."

"Baking is a skill I've mastered," Serianna said.

"You'll get by on fourteen *spesidalar* a year, like everyone else."

"Plus food," she stipulated.

"Yes, plus food," Gørvell said.

"Do you have any tobacco?" she asked. "You probably do, right, since you sell pipes in your store?"

"Yes?" Gørvell said, clearly stunned. He went back inside, grabbed his tobacco pouch, and pressed a wad of tobacco, pinched between his fingers, in the palm of her hand. She had her own matches! And just lit up her pipe and started smoking away! Gørvell watched her, motionless, then suddenly chuckled and went back inside. But he returned again just as quickly, remembering something.

"We need to cut a few loads of peat before haymaking begins," he instructed Nesje. "Can you spend the rest of the week up in the bog?"

"What about the haymaking and the tools?"

"We won't start for another two weeks."

"I should have brought a boy with me to haul peat to the drying field."

"I'll send someone up," Gørvell said.

"How much peat should I harvest?"

"Fill up the barn in the far field," Gørvell ordered.

"That'll take a week, I think. Is there a peat spade in the barn?"

"I think so. And don't forget to take that fish with you," Gørvell said as he turned on his heel and left.

Nesje walked up toward Rekneshaugen. Mrs. Louise Dahl was standing out in Humlehaven with Ole Gjelden. She was sixty years old and absolutely old-fashioned, but she didn't think so highly of herself as to avoid speaking to Nesje. Ole Gjelden was digging and didn't notice the haymaker.

"What is that you're carrying there, Nesje?" Louise Dahl inquired.

"A school of pollock swam by," he explained. "So I went out with the net."

"Would you care to sell me some, Nesje?"

There was no point in being difficult.

"How many would you be requiring, ma'am?" Nesje asked. He could sound educated when necessary.

"All you've got," Mrs. Dahl said. "My son Bastian is coming home from Christiania today. He has earned his degree in philology now, just twenty-four years old."

"It is well known that Bastian Dahl has a rare gift," Nesje said.

A few years earlier, Bastian Dahl had received top marks on his university entrance exam at Molde Academy. Few people were unaware of that.

Nesje was looking forward to his meal, but he sold the fish to Mrs. Dahl. He walked back to his house in Rekneslia, went inside, drank some water, and put on a heavier shirt. There was no need to wear a dress shirt up in the mountains.

But he didn't regret wearing his good shirt to town that morning. Now he was to collect thirty *skilling* from Mrs. Louise Dahl the next time he passed Humlehaven. That little boat trip was worth half a day's labor.

4

It took nearly a half hour to walk to the peat bog. The summer day was hot and Nesje was damp as he arrived. He hung his shirt on a nail in the barn and walked to the peat trench with his torso bare and a spade in his hands. He pared off the heather and the top layer of soil. The rich, glistening peat appeared, remnants of many leaves and plant debris from ages past. He worked a few hours without a break and thought he might be able to go home around four and cook for his boy.

When he finally looked up from his work, it was because he smelled tobacco. Serianna stood by the barn, watching him. She came over to where he stood, waist-deep in the peat trench.

"Gørvell told me to come up and help you."

"Weren't you supposed to help with the baking?"

"They have enough people. Where's the wheelbarrow?"

"In the barn."

She fetched the peat barrow and a pitchfork and started loading the pieces of peat he had set up on the edge onto the barrow. Then she wheeled the load to a dry spot on the hill a ways off and stacked the pieces for the sun to dry them. She had done this before. There were only two ways to do it. You could lean the tops of four pieces of peat together so they formed a pyramid, or you could arrange them in a square, first two north-south, then two east-west, and then alternating, so the air and the wind got to them. She knew both ways, and did it first the one way and then the other for the sake of variety.

They worked for hours this way. He cut the peat and she stacked big loads before grasping the handles of the peat barrow and pushing it to the hillock. He tried to focus on what he was doing and avoid looking at her, but that just made things more obvious, because he tried to sneak peeks at her when he thought she wouldn't notice. It was no better after she took off her blouse so that she strode around in her shift with bare arms. Then she went down to the stream a short distance away and arranged rocks into a sort of a firepit before lighting twigs and filling a pot with water. Was she making coffee? He leaned over by the stream and rinsed himself to put his shirt back on. There came the smell of good coffee brewing. It didn't take long for the pot to boil. She had two lathed wooden cups and poured coffee into both. Nesje drank his in cautious gulps, then ate a crust of bread he drew from his pocket. The stream trickled before them.

"I suppose you'd like to see how things look around here," he said, standing up.

"Look?" she said.

"There's a nice grassy area behind the barn," he said, and then showed her.

"Ah, a person could just lie down right here!" Serianna exclaimed.

"Sure, but then you nod off and you don't do the things that need doing," he said, walking back to the peat trench. So she grabbed the wheelbarrow and followed.

After they returned to their work, the mood changed. What transpired between them was fragile and delicate. Her eyes had a sparkle as she talked about her siblings, six of them all together, three sisters and three brothers. Then he told her about his family and the place he was from, that he was the youngest of ten siblings, and that his father had died when he was only two.

Then the conversation quieted, and they looked at each other.

He turned away and focused again on his work. He had never dug so much peat so fast, and she had never run any faster. As she watched him there was something inviting about her, as though she were waiting for him to stop and talk to her again, but he kept on working. He wasn't going to give in to something he couldn't condone, he thought. But what was she thinking about as she looked at him that way?

Serianna talked about her youngest sister, Gjertine. She was worried about her. Gjertine had become involved with the devout in the village, the ones called Readers who held prayer meetings in their own homes and didn't attend church to listen to the pastor. They had been operating like this since the time of preacher Hans Nielsen Hauge, but now, fifty or sixty years later, the preaching came from people with a darker view. They believed pastors took too casual of a view of the true conversion, the renunciation of all worldly desires, that was necessary before one could receive God's grace.

"I went to the Readers when I faced grief," Serianna said, "but I didn't attend many sessions."

"Why not?"

"I had enough when one of them suggested that God took my daughter because I had not converted in my heart."

"Some thrive off of adding stones to another's burden,"
he said.

"I cannot believe in such a harsh God."

"How old were you when you had your daughter?"

"I was twenty-four."

"And the child's father?"

"He didn't want to marry me."

"Why not?"

"He was only seventeen."

Nesje felt he was being intrusive, but he wanted to know
everything.

"How old is your sister?"

"Gjertine will be sixteen just after New Year's. She goes
before the pastor this fall."

"There's a lot going on with people at that age," he said,
thinking of his own son.

5

Nesje and Serianna went to the peat bog all week and worked
there. They were alone on the mountain; people rarely went
there. It was no one's business, what happened. But one afternoon, after they finished and washed up in the stream, he
said, "I suppose we could sit behind the barn for a bit."

So they did that.

"I think I might lie down for five minutes," he said, and
lay down.

"I feel like I got up early today," she said, and she lay down too. "But what if I fall asleep?"

"I don't suppose there's any danger of that," he said, moving closer to her.

"But what are you doing?" she said. "You're putting your hand on my shoulder?"

"I guess I'll give you a rub as well," he said as he undid a button on her bodice.

"You're certainly in a hurry!" she said.

"Well, we don't have all day, do we?" he said.

She said take it easy, but then he heard her lovely laugh. And then she was quiet, but breathing hard. She smelled of tobacco with a hint of sweat. He thought of oar strokes, and surf striking the shore. He thought of the school of pollock and the boat rocking.

When he came around, she was lying there watching him.

"Well, aren't you something," she murmured.

"There was no getting around that today," he said.

"What came over us?" she said.

"That was full-grown folks' longing for love," he said.

"Oh, is that what it was?" she said.

6

It was late in the day when Nesje said enough. The peat barn would be more than full with what he cut and she set out to dry. When the haymaking was done the peat would be dry. Maybe they would get to work together then too? He thanked her, she smiled, and they walked down the mountain together. But when they passed his house, he didn't ask her in. His son was there. Maybe it was wise to wait.

"You have to talk to him about it," she said.

There was no getting around this.

That night Nesje told his son he had met a woman he liked better than the others.

The boy said, "You mustn't forget Mother."

"I will never forget your mother," Nesje said as the words caught in his throat.

"You can't think about two women at once, you know," Hans said.

"One is on earth and the other is in heaven," Nesje said meekly. "I'm thirty-six years old. I can't spend the rest of my life alone."

"No, maybe it would be good for you have someone after I leave," the boy said.

"Where are you planning to go?"

"I thought I would do what you suggested."

"What was it I said? I've said so many things."

"You said you'd write to Hans Olsen at the Trolla Brug Foundry."

Ah, yes, he had said that. Nesje had been an agent for Trolla Brug at one point and had met Hans Olsen, the manager, at a mission meeting in Molde. Hans Olsen, who founded Trolla Brug, had approached Nesje and asked him if he would sell woodstoves for them. When Guri was alive Nesje traveled around a fair amount, convincing people to order ovens and stoves. But when he was left alone with the boy he set that aside to work closer to home. His agency wasn't officially terminated, but it had been on hold for a long time. Nesje didn't know what, if anything, would happen with it. Two years earlier the Trolla Brug Foundry had merged with Throndhjems Mekaniske Værksted, and now Hans Olsen was in charge of the whole thing. All Nesje knew was that the oven factory part of the business was going to carry on as before.

"Write to Trolla Brug in Throndhjem and ask if they have any work for me this summer," Hans begged.

"You need to be confirmed first," Nesje said. "And there's almost a year to go before you can be."

"I want to go work in Uncle Hans's carpentry shop in Kringstadhagen until I'm confirmed. Uncle Hans says it's best I live there too."

"Why aren't you going to live here, where you belong?"

"I reckon a new lady is moving in."

"There's been no talk of anything like that," Nesje said.

"I'm sure it will come up," his son said.

Nesje felt his son was pulling away. Why hadn't he waited a while before mentioning Serianna? Things might have worked out better.

"Is this how I'm going to lose you?" he asked weakly.

"You're not losing me," the boy said. "Uncle Hans is my godfather and my uncle, after all. In one little year I'll be confirmed, and then I'll go."

Nesje said no more. But when Hans went to bed, he was overcome with despair and lay down pondering, eyes open to the dark.

The haymaking was in full swing, and Nesje and Serianna weren't able to meet every evening.

On the morning of the day they thought they would finish with the hay, she waited for him as he walked down the path.

"I have to tell you something," she said.

"I know what it is," he replied.

"You'll have to think it over, but if it sounds good I can cook for you and warm your bed."

"I have to think about it," he said.

"Take all the time you need."

At the Gørvell farm the servants were gathered in the hall, where they buttered lefse and drank warm milk.

"We have to finish today," they said to each other.

It was like every other year. Gørvell would walk down to them at some point and ask the same old question, "Did we do it?"

"Yes!" they would chime.

Because it had to be done.

Soon the first two haymakers walked to the grindstone behind the storehouse, where one turned the stone as the other sharpened the scythe. The stone wobbled and spun, and they poured water onto it to whet the edge.

How will it all go, Nesje wondered.

Once the first two sharpened their scythes, the next two came. This didn't take long, and then it was their turn to wait until every scythe was sharp. Then five guys grabbed their scythes, five girls fetched their rakes, and they all walked down to the fields by the fjord. There the men tipped their scythes upside down, resting the snaths on the ground so the blades jutted out from their shoulders. Then each man honed his edge with a scythestone, moistened in a little bucket made of hollowed-out wood. The stones made a light, nimble sound. For the last time this summer the scythestones swished, chiming almost out of step, almost on the beat.

My own child, Nesje thought. What will become of Hans? Do I have to lose him to gain her? That is a high price.

The five scythemen lined themselves up as they had done every day for three weeks, each beside and slightly behind the next.

Nesje, the lead scytheman, walked at the front of the mowing line, swinging his scythe in a wide arc, and the others followed through the final section of field by the fjord where they mowed, the field that ran down to the waterline. Nesje saw they would finish when the sun was still high. So they would have time to cut around the perimeter, too, and they would have time to cut between those big trees over by Reknes Hospital, the part they always did last. It would be the last day of the season.

The grass lay flat in long bands. The raking girls worked, even the two indoor girls. Everyone helped with haymaking. The girls didn't rake the grass together into windrows. They were tedding. They shook it up, spread it out so the hay didn't lie in clumps and bunches but in a thin layer so the sun could dry it—so that, if it was hot and windy enough, it could be brought indoors that evening.

Nesje swung the scythe again and Serianna walked behind him in the swath he cut. She wore a long under-shift of checked fabric and a white kerchief on her head, but she didn't hold back when she spread the hay. No, she didn't. Not an hour into their labor she snapped two tines on her rake. Nesje shouted to a boy standing by the fence to run the damaged rake to the carpenter and bring another. Serianna observed, wryly, that he seemed to know what to do most of the time.

Yes, he did. He thought back on the summer they shared. He had told her about his life over their breakfast in the servants' hall, and she had told him, quietly, about the child she had lost, and he had shown her his genuine compassion.

I need to propose to her before someone else does it, he thought, as Claus Gørvell came into view and said what he always said as the haymaking drew to an end: "Did we do it?"

"Yes," Nesje said, "we did."

"What time will you finish?"

"In a couple of hours."

"Haying porridge tonight, then?" asked Gørvell.

"Yes, eight o'clock," said Nesje. "The haymakers need time to clean themselves up."

"Should we bring the wagons down around six?"

Yes, that was how it would be.

So when everything was cut right up to the fence, and the mowers stood leaning on their scythe snaths and exhaling through their nostrils like horses, as though they couldn't believe they'd got it all done, and the girls spread the last of it to dry, there on the far side of the fence they saw four wretches from Reknes Leprosy Hospital, two men and two women, who waited to have a little conversation—from a distance. The men didn't have fingers and the women's faces were big, open wounds. They didn't come all the way up to the fence, but they could see the last of the haymaking was done, like every other summer.

"Congratulations on your haying success!" the wretches called out in unison. "Congratulations!"

"Yes, thanks! No more haymaking this year!"

It was only five o'clock. The hay wagons wouldn't come for another hour. The five mowers hung their scythes from a tree while the raking girls scattered hay. And then they all stood there as Nesje pulled out his pocket watch. Not everyone had a watch.

"It's almost six," he announced.

Then they heard a clatter of wagons from behind the farm buildings, two horse-drawn wagons. The wagoner rode on one and. . . if that wasn't Gørvell himself on the other one. Gørvell had lost his jacket and tie and wore a white shirt. He knew he was about to sweat. They pulled up to the fence so the mowers could load the hay onto the wagons with forks.

"Hey, I want to stomp it down!" Claus Gørvell declared, and they helped him up onto the hay wain. He was no spring chicken. Wasn't he almost fifty? But he liked to stomp. It was easier to joke with him when he pretended he was one of them. There was Gørvell stomping down the hay. One would think there would never be enough stomping, but then one of the haymakers tossed a scoop of hay high into the air so that it fell on Gørvell's head like snowflakes. He just laughed, and then they all laughed as he waved his head in the air.

7

They still had an hour before the porridge would be ready. One of the guys said, "Well, we'd better go for a dip!"

They headed to Reknes Beach, into the grove of trees by the fjord, where they couldn't be seen by anyone passing by. Then they tore off their clothes and stood there buck naked. No one had swim trunks and the womenfolk weren't there, so they jumped in, shrieking and squealing, five guys.

After a moment the wagoner came. He was wearing some kind of strange pants, and they laughed at him. The fjord water was bracing, even after a beautiful summer. The snow on the peaks across the fjord was almost gone. The water was never truly warm, because the glacial meltwater kept it cool.

Nesje and one other were the only ones who could swim, and they swam far out. The others splashed around closer to shore. They couldn't believe it when Claus Gørvell drove up. He had harnessed up the shay. He gave the horse free rein to wander and graze, ran down to the beach, and tore off his clothes! That skinny man, with skin so white you'd never believe it ever saw the sun. And they couldn't help but notice it—his tool. Man, they couldn't help but talk about it. He had a general's tool, that Gørvell, it was probably true that he came from an ancient family in Finland. Why was he a bachelor? Why had he never found himself a wife? And he could swim—like a seal. They stood and watched. He swam unbelievably far out. Was he planning to swim all the way to Reknesholmen Islet? Everyone knew that Gørvell recently lost a court case. He had lost the entire Molde Archipelago and had only Reknes Islet left. Maybe he wanted to make it to shore and stake his claim again!

But it was a long way out. Did he lack the sense to turn back?

"Get the boat, Lars!" one of the guys yelled to the wagoner. "Master Gørvell is swimming out too far!"

Then they saw him turn around and return with powerful strokes. As he walked onto shore and dried himself off with a big towel, they saw that his nethers had shrunk away to almost nothing.

8

As the storehouse bell rang at the Gørvell farm, the guys yelled to each other, "You hear the bell, don't you, boys? They're serving the porridge!"

"You'd better hurry, fellas," Gørvell said. When he was in the mood he talked like anyone else, as if it were completely natural.

It was time to don their duds. The sun was far in the west. As they came into the yard the women stood waiting. Many were changed into their best skirts and bodices. There were almost a dozen around Serianna, who had put her white apron back on. She looked at Nesje but didn't come over. Gørvell, on the other hand, walked up to Nesje and said something in Finnish that the lead haymaker couldn't understand. He suspected it was not a Bible verse.

"*Perkele*! You'd better make up your mind soon, man!" Gørvell said. "Because the haymaking is all done."

Then Gørvell walked over to Serianna and said something, and she followed him to the steps and into the house. The others stood elbowing each other a little. No one wanted to be the first to go in. But then Lars the wagoner went in, and Nesje.

Nesje was curious to see if the old lady would come greet them, but she didn't make an appearance. In the parlor the cook stood ready with two wenches to help. Lars called out that they ought to sing grace and launched into *Our Plate and Cloth Are All Laid Out*. Not everyone sang. Gørvell sat down with Serianna, and the porridge was brought to the table. When they finished the first helping and were waiting for more, Gørvell stood and gave a speech that thanked everyone who helped with the haying. True, there were still a couple of loads outside, but that was the nature of farm work, Gørvell said. It was never completely finished. In particular, he said, he wanted to thank his lead haymaker, Nesje, for his efforts. Did everyone realize Nesje had been his lead haymaker for thirteen years?

When Gørvell asked whether Nesje wanted to say anything to the haymakers, Nesje saw his moment to say something. Everyone knew what this was about; now was his chance to say how things were going to be.

So Nesje stood up and said that he had been thinking about his father a great deal lately. Not that he could remember his father, who had died when he had been a baby. But his father had left him some words that his mother had taught to him when he was old enough to understand, and they were what a man should say when he went to woo a woman.

The chatter in Gørvell's parlor died.

Nesje deployed his finest formal language as he said, "I hereby request of you, Serianna Eriksdatter: Will you be the joy of my youth and the comfort of my old age?"

It was quieter in Gørvell's house than it had ever been. Serianna changed color, smoothed her white apron with her hand, and said yes.

Enough commotion followed to raise the roof. They hollered and laughed and shouted to each other, and Gørvell yelled the loudest of all. But he was the one who asked the question that silenced the room again: "When is the baby due, Serianna?"

"After Christmas," said Serianna. "But before Easter," she added.

The room erupted in pandemonium.

A Restless Family

I

When the fall evenings grew dark, Hans moved his things to his uncle's place in Kringstadhagen and Serianna moved in at Rekneslia. But when a message came from Frænen that her youngest brother, Botolv, who was only eighteen, had contracted pneumonia, she went home to her parents' house.

Nesje's house felt as empty as it was. Hans occasionally stopped by in the evening, but never spent the night.

"I don't want to sleep in two beds," he said.

"What do you do after work?" Nesje said to his son. "Don't the afternoons get long?"

"I'm in the woodshop, and then we go fishing. Uncle Hans has a boat, you know."

"I wish you hadn't left so suddenly," Nesje told his son.

"I haven't left you. I'm just living with my uncle," Hans said. "So let's not discuss it anymore. But I did go to the post office earlier today, by the way, and they asked me to tell you that there's a letter there for you."

"I picked it up this afternoon," Nesje said, "but I haven't opened it yet. I'm afraid it's bad news about her brother."

"I can stay until you've read it."

Nesje ripped open the envelope. For some reason his hand was trembling a little.

The letter from Serianna said that Botolv was dead. Nesje thought it had happened very quickly. She wanted him to come to the funeral. He explained that to Hans, who said: "You have to go, Pa."

"But who will feed the cows? Who will milk them?"

"I'll take care of it. Uncle Hans will help me."

"But then you'll have to sleep here."

"So I'll sleep here. Get going!"

Because the snow had arrived and there was no going over the mountains, Nesje borrowed a boat from Gørvell and rowed to Serianna. He rowed in the rain and wind for four hours and was soaked to the skin, shivering, as he walked from the water, following the instructions she had given him, to the farm where Serianna waited. It was dark, but Nesje could make out farm buildings against the storm clouds: two storehouses, a cookhouse, and a barn.

He went to the door and knocked. No one answered. He lifted the latch and walked in. Seated around the table was a family of what was now only seven. The parents were easy to make out. He greeted them first, Ingeborg and Erik, then said his name and bowed his head, as was customary. They were old, he saw. But they were still in charge, though their eldest son, Ola, did all the work. Serianna was pleased he had come. She stood up and said, "Ah, there you are!" But he didn't embrace her. He had to greet the others first.

"Are you Ola?" he said to the dark-haired man at the end of the table.

"That's what they say," said Ola, and took his hand.

Ola was thirty, Nesje knew, but he didn't yet have a wife. He had a reputation as a fun-loving guy, Ola did, but Nesje found himself looking into a face that revealed a sensitive soul in a powerful body. The other brother, Erik, who had studied carpentry in Molde, wasn't married either. He sat at the other end of the table, so Nesje walked around. And who was who among the sisters? Ane-Martha and Gjertine were nineteen and fifteen. The one with the sharp eyes was Gjertine, no doubt. So he greeted the older one first.

"You must be Ane-Martha," he said.

Nesje had an excellent memory, and Serianna had told him about all of them. At the moment, however, she was quiet and happy.

He was offered a place at the table, but he was wet as a dog and asked to go sit by the fire until he dried out. They poured him warm milk and offered him some porridge. He was hungry.

Ane-Martha was friendly, but Gjertine—she was something! She got up from the table and stood in the corner where she could watch him as he tried to warm himself back up. She was tall and slim, but a looker, as they said, and also old, he thought. She had open buttons at the top of her dress so you could glimpse the curves of her white breasts when she leaned forward.

She laughed abruptly. He asked, was she laughing at him? No, she wasn't, but then she laughed again and confessed that she hadn't expected him to be so old. Then she remembered that her brother's body was in the room, and burst into tears because she had laughed while death was visiting. In a flash she was gone, as though she became invisible, and just as suddenly she came back again with a book that engrossed her: *Om Forholdene I Amerika* the book was called—*On Conditions in America*—she held it up when Nesje asked. After a minute of reading she began to stare at him again, and when Serianna asked her to quit staring, she asked: "How do things stand with your Christian beliefs, Nesje?"

"Could you leave people be, Gjertine?" Serianna said.

"Do you believe in the crucified and risen Jesus Christ? Yes or no," Gjertine asked Nesje.

"No, honestly," Serianna said firmly. "Some things are Nesje's own business."

"I have my childhood faith, and that's enough for me," Nesje said.

Once again Gjertine left the room for a bit, only to return and read again, but she couldn't concentrate. She had been reading to Botolv when he fell asleep for the last time. What would happen to them now? Was there any assurance that more wouldn't die?

"Knock it off, Gjertine!" the others said.

This was a different breed of people, Nesje thought. They had a restlessness, something he noticed in Serianna. Shouldn't they spend this energy on work so they could have some peace? They all got up as soon as they sat down. They went out the one door and came in the other. They asked him again about things he had already told him, as if they hadn't heard. Their vast grief made the house too crowded; they could hardly breathe. This seemed to pain old Erik, but he didn't seem to quite understand it either.

"Who's come?" he asked. "Is this that cotter from Rekneslia, Serianna?"

"His name is Knut Hansen Nesje, and he came from Nesjestranda," Serianna said.

"He is a tall and handsome man!" said ld Ingeborg.

"He must marry Serianna. I understand she is heavy with child," Erik Olsen said. And then he was off in his own thoughts, grieving his youngest son.

Nesje didn't know how there would be room for him, at the table or to sleep. Ola slept in the *kårstua*, the cottage meant for retired owners of the farm, with Erik the cabinet-maker, and the sisters slept up in the loft. Why were they all still living at home? Wasn't it time that Erik and Ane-Martha went out into the world? And Gjertine, who talked back to the pastor, and lost her spot at the front of the confirmation line, where would she go!

Serianna had told him about that, that everyone in the family was proud of what Gjertine did. What was it that she had done? She told the Readers that she was going to tell off that pastor!

It was pandemonium. The pastor sent the other confirmands home to set Gjertine straight. When she wouldn't relent the pastor said that she couldn't stand at the head of the line of girls, as was the plan, unless she took it back.

Gjertine didn't take anything back, so the pastor paid a visit to her parents. They asked her to be reasonable, but Gjertine wouldn't relent. And now Nesje was going to hear about it. In the middle of this conversation with the pastor, they heard a roar from Ola, out behind the barn sharpening a scythe. He had cut himself and blood was gushing from his wrist. The servant girl went running with a strip of cloth diaper and wrapped it, but the bleeding wouldn't stop. Then Gjertine asked everyone to step out so she could stop it. She had a spell from the Readers, a gift for her having stood up to the pastor.

Everyone withdrew, confused, including the pastor. Gjertine mumbled the words that staunch blood, and the bleeding stopped.

"The pastor was speechless," her mother, Ingeborg, said proudly.

"You said it," the old father agreed. "The pastor was speechless, and then he left."

Gjertine was ninth in line, but she was confirmed.

"What words did she say?" Nesje asked. "What sort of spell makes the bleeding stop?"

"There are words that can accomplish wonders."

"But what words were they?"

"That I cannot say, because they would lose their power," Gjertine said.

"Is it a dark art or the Christian faith?" Nesje asked. He hadn't expected this young girl to wrap him around her fingers.

"It includes His name, He who hung on the cross," Gjertine said, "so I doubt the devil was a part of it. But they're powerful words, and the pastor understood that too. He couldn't do anything other than let me be confirmed."

Nesje wondered, What was the point of all of this? Nobody cared that Gjertine moved back in the line.

"She'll get married anyway," her brother Ola said.

"Ninth in line was just fine, Gjertine," the mother said. "You answered best of all of them! People will talk about it for a long time to come, about how you put that pastor in his place!"

Nesje tried to steer the conversation in another direction. At New Year's the same pastor was going to marry him and Serianna—this is what the family decided, here and now. Nesje said it was time for people to be looking ahead and working to ensure that the country of Norway continued in the right direction. Surely this would mean that they would have to work together, the pastors and the farmers. He thought better times were coming, he said, with more work for young people, with roads and railroads being built. Everyone knew, he said, that a prosperous era was coming.

"Things are only getting worse in Norway," Gjertine said. "Anyone who wants a better future needs to get out of here as soon as possible. Have you heard of Lars Stavig?" she said to Nesje.

They began to talk over each other about this man named Lars Stavig, who lived across the fjord. He was a relation of old Ingeborg's, and he knew what was needed. Lars Stavig experienced firsthand that Norway was no up-and-coming place. He watched his mother marry a younger man and, after his mother died, his stepfather marry a younger woman, so now Lars was responsible for supporting this couple. The farm's former owners, practically his own age and only related to him through some younger half-siblings, were living in the cottage on the farm with his support.

He didn't want this! It wasn't right that he had to feed these people who were of no concern to him. Lars Stavig wanted to take his family and go to America. He only needed the money for the tickets, and then he would be off.

"After some leave, it will be better for the rest of us," Ola said.

How could he believe that, Nesje asked. Didn't the country need all the working hands it could get?

"Mother Norway isn't able to feed all her children," Ola said. "Some of them do need to go out into the world. Everyone here on the farm has to work now. Bortegard cannot feed us all."

Ane-Martha had been at home for the fall, but she was about to go into service. And Gjertine needed to find a position as well. Then there was the brother Erik. He had a lot of work in the village now. They were building a school, and he was making a lot of furniture. The parents would move into the cottage when the snow melted, and Ola would borrow five hundred kroner from Norges Hypotekbank, the government mortgage lender, to build a new addition on the house. The kitchen where they sat would be divided with a panel wall, and the new room would have a bedroom loft above it. Then Erik would have a half kitchen, living room, and a bedroom to himself.

"But everything will have to be paid back at some point, right?" Nesje asked.

The others stopped eating, afraid of Ola's anger. The potatoes got cold and the herring sat untouched. Ola gripped his fork and said well, people were welcome to have opinions, but he was going to live the way he planned. And he was also thinking about buying a new woodstove. A man shouldn't scrimp on what it took to live comfortably. How was a man supposed to persevere in the weather if he couldn't get warm when he came home? How could he expect to find a wife if all he had was an old iron hook to hold a pot over a hearth! Could Nesje tell him what a stove cost?

Nesje realized that Serianna must have told them that he was an agent for Trolla Brug, and he realized he needed to handle Ola gently.

"You should have a model TMV Number 217," Nesje said. "Or a Number 208. There's a little more room in the 208s for bigger splits of wood."

"It's the 208 for me," Ola said. "How much does it cost?"

"The stove can be had for ten *spesidalar*," Nesje said, "or forty kroner, as they say now. And I'm not making any money on that."

A twitch in Serianna's lip suggested she thought differently, but she didn't say anything. Ola grasped Nesje's hand and said they had a deal. Nesje announced he would slaughter a cow for the wedding, he would pull out all the stops. They needed to marry before the baby came, Ola said. Serianna was fit to burst.

Then everyone turned off the lamp and went to bed, and Nesje finally held Serianna.

2

The next day they welcomed the neighbors. People sat in á silent circle around Botolv's open casket. One by one the neighbors rose to stand by the casket to say goodbye. Then the family drove the casket to the cemetery with the horse and cart, and bells were rung over Botolv's body, though no pastor came. That would have to wait until there were more dead to bury.

Nesje expected Gjertine to break into tears and lamentations, but he was wrong. She was the one who imparted comforting words to others as their grief carried them away. She patted her mother, and she patted Ola when he was overcome. Serianna grieved, too, but she had a baby in her belly to consider. It was difficult for everyone until Botolv was finally in the ground.

There were still three weeks until Christmas.

Nesje went home, and Hans came to stay with him. Nesje walked to the tailor and ordered a new suit that he would pay for in three installments. The suit cost forty kroner. It was a stretch, but he would manage. He picked up the suit three days before Christmas, and on Christmas Eve wore it for the first time when he and Hans walked to Molde Church together.

Nesje slaughtered and salted a calf that fall. They had gone a long time without eating meat. Now they had veal on Christmas Eve. Nesje read the nativity story from his mother's Bible, as he always did, but they didn't sing.

Nesje and Serianna held their wedding at Bortegard on January 3, 1875. Nesje felt young and handsome in his new suit. The bride was in her seventh month. Ola called the shots now and he spared no expense. He brewed big kegs of beer that sat cooling in the cookhouse. He slaughtered a bull, bigger than a cow, and fiddlers were invited in from three neighboring villages. The guests squeezed in until you could hardly turn around. None of the Nesje's nine siblings came, not even his brother Hans, and his son Hans didn't attend either.

"I don't belong with people I don't know," Hans told his father.

"It is too far to travel to Frænen in winter," his siblings said. "We'll get to know her when she comes to Rekneslia."

Nesje was deeply hurt but said nothing. He danced the wedding dance with Serianna, who barely moved as he tried to swing her around. He would have liked to see a more sober wedding, but maybe this was how things were done here. One man stood out on the steps, trying to collect his thoughts. When another man came out, the first one said: "Hey, do you see the moon? Behind the mountain there? It just jumped like a foal!"

"And now I'll jump!" shouted cabinetmaker Erik, and he jumped into the air, fell flat on the floor, and lay there until someone threw cold water on his face.

3

The next day they left Bortegard. Since Serianna was too far along to go by boat, Ola sailed the Gørvell boat back to Molde, and Nesje drove his bride using Ola's horse and sleigh. When they reached town they saw Ola in the boat out by Reknes Islet. By the time they reached the dock, he was ashore and waiting.

Hans was at Rekneslia too. He saw to their coats once they were inside.

"Couldn't you stay here with us?" Serianna asked. "I'll try to be a mother to you."

"That's nice of you to say," Hans said, "but I had a mother and I can't have a new one."

"You could let me try," Serianna said.

"When will my brother be born?" Hans deflected.

"How do you know it will be a boy?"

"I can tell by how you're carrying the baby," the boy said.

"Where did you learn that sort of thing, you wise young man?"

"From my grandmother. She was a midwife and she delivered more than a thousand babies."

"You Nesje folks are wiser than other people," Serianna said, and that cut Hans, who didn't say anymore.

But when the time came, Hans happened to be over for a little visit, and he was the one Serianna sent to fetch the midwife.

The midwife put Hans to work. He fetched the wood and hot water because Nesje had to work at the Gørvell farm, just like every other day.

On March 7, before the soil had thawed, Serianna had a son with bright eyes, feisty from the start—very different from Hans when he was a baby, Nesje said.

The snow was a meter deep, and the new mother couldn't get anywhere. She wanted Nesje to stay home for a few days, but there was no one at the farm to feed the cows. So Serianna said, "Could my sister Gjertine come and stay with me?"

"I can't pay her," Nesje said.

"She just needs food," Serianna replied.

Gjertine hadn't found a job yet. Word was out about the mouth she had on her. People didn't want a proselytizer in the house, especially a proselytizer in a skirt.

Nesje said that Gjertine should come, if that's what Serianna wanted.

Five days later Ola brought her over by boat, and Gjertine walked up the hills to their house. There was a steamship now, but this way they saved the fare, Gjertine said. They could hear Ola's voice in much of what she said, but then there was all the rest of it that was uniquely hers. She had a wooden suitcase Erik made for her and set it on the coffee table to unpack, as if there were no problem with Nesje seeing that she had two pairs of underpants, two cotton undershirts, and one pair of dress shoes. Nothing in the world seemed dangerous to Gjertine. She looked around.

"Who did all this?" she asked. "Two living rooms? And it's not a big house."

Nesje was pleased by her question. "Who do you think?"

"Was it you, Knut?" Gjertine asked her brother-in-law.

Serianna didn't like that. "Call him Nesje like the rest of us do," she said sternly.

"But wasn't he christened Knut?"

"In this house he goes by Nesje," Serianna said.

"So was it you, Nesje?"

"It wasn't anyone else, as far as I know," Nesje said.

"Even this lovely trim?"

Yes, he planed the wood himself. Did he own a lot of fancy tools? Oh, he had done this at the Kvam farm. They had a woodshop there, with edge-trimming planes, two-man planes, tonguing and grooving planes, fillister planes, and rabbeting planes. Why all this work? She asked. Well, Nesje said, he had always dreamt of building his own home, the way his brother Hans did in Kringstadhagen.

"And then when the day came that Guri was ready to give birth," Nesje said, "I felt like we had to have a real home."

"So Hans arrived before you could get married?" Gjertine asked astutely.

Nesje chose not to answer.

"I spent three years building this house," Nesje said, "and while I did we had to live apart. Hans and his mother lived at Bjørset, and I stayed at Kvam while I designed it. It didn't need to be big, but we wanted two living rooms, a small bedroom, and a kitchen on the main floor with three attic rooms upstairs. At first we didn't have lumber to build the house or land to put it on! But I had to keep Guri's spirits up, so I designed a plan with all the measurements that showed how I wanted it to be, outside and in. Once the money was there, all I had to do was plane the moldings before the house was built."

That was when he went to County Governor Leth, owner of the Reknes estate, Nesje explained, and asked to build a home in Rekneslia and lease the surrounding land. Sixteen *mål*, about four acres, of nothing but pine forest, and he wanted to build the house out of that!

And Leth said, "All right, you can have it, but you can't buy it. I'll only lease it to you."

This impressed Gjertine, and in fact it seemed like she was more impressed than Serianna had been when he told her the same story. Serianna was more tight lipped, but that didn't mean that she had any less of a mind! Be that as it may:

he built the house after logging the big heartwood pines in Rekneslia the summer when Hans was one. When the snow arrived, he put the logs onto a sled and hauled them in many trips to the Årø sawmill. He sawed the boards and beams and rafters and then took it all back with everything marked for cutting. He calculated what was needed to build the house, and when he was done about six months later there was hardly a stump of a board left over.

Nesje added that he wasn't saying this to puff himself up but to show how important it was to plan for the long term. In just two summers he had built his own home, and while his son was a baby.

"And your first wife was alive then?"

"Yes, that was while Guri was alive," he said.

"I bet she was happy when the house was done," Gjertine said.

"Yes, you bet she was."

"She was lucky to have a husband like you."

"Well, I suppose others will be the judge of that."

"And now Serianna is the lucky one! Right, Serianna?"

Serianna didn't respond. Serianna kept her own council. But she didn't manage to keep her irritation to herself.

"Does everything have to be said out loud?" Serianna said after a pause. "It's too hard to be with others when anything can be discussed! People want to walk around with their hearts on their sleeves and share everything they think about whenever something pops into their heads. Can't a person keep something to themselves?"

"I don't understand you," Gjertine told her sister. "We can be open and honest in all our conduct."

"Where does it say that in the Bible?" Serianna asked.

Gjertine couldn't answer.

"It says, *Let your communication be, Yea, yea; Nay, nay,*" Serianna said. "Do you want to have supper now, yes or no?"

What could they say to that?

"If you're going to eat, then I will too," Nesje told Gjertine.

"I must confess that I'm starving . . . where will I sleep, by the way?" Gjertine said, looking around.

"In the loft," Serianna said.

"But shouldn't I take the baby when he wakes up?"

"Prepare the meal for Nesje! There is only one thing that matters, and that's that Nesje gets the sleep he needs," Serianna said. "Clear away your things so I can set the table."

Then the baby woke up, as if on cue.

"God's peace and blessing on this house," Gjertine said. She tossed her clothes back into her suitcase and then held the newborn as Serianna cooked the evening porridge on the stove.

Nesje had to admit there was something kindhearted about Gjertine. She didn't seem to have any ulterior motives. She sat with the baby while Serianna set the table, and as they ate Nesje inquired after the news from Frænen.

Well, the brothers at Bortegard had divided the kitchen with a panel wall, as they planned, and Ola took the side where the new woodstove would go. Erik made do with the old hearth. Next summer they would add on a new living room with a loft that would extend the house by more than ten *ells*, about twenty feet. This had been the plan for almost a hundred years, since the house was first erected. To qualify for a mortgage loan, as they called it, there had to be a living room on both sides. Until now, there had only been one, but Gjertine wasn't sure it was a good idea for two brothers to live together and run the farm. As long as they were bachelors it would work, but about when you added a woman or two?

What did Gjertine know about how life was on a farm with two ladies? But she understood more than her years would indicate, from the books she had borrowed from the pastor Josef Jervell's library, now in the public library in Frænen.

Nesje sat lost in his thoughts while the two sisters made amends. Then they discussed everything going on in the world and across the ocean.

Nesje didn't like the way this conversation was going, but he didn't get angry because it clarified his views. He realized that he wasn't going anywhere. He had put his stakes down, as they said, and here he would remain.

"For I have found my Canaan!" he said.

Gjertine looked at him, startled, and they laughed.

"I can't see the milk and honey," Gjertine said.

"Then you don't have the eyes to see it with," her brother-in-law parried.

"O, Jesus, open thou mine eyes so I can see how rich I am," Gjertine sang.

The song was written by someone named Lina Sandell in Sweden. Gjertine learned it from some preacher or other. She sang the same song every night, and the tune was catchy, Nesje had to admit. But his eyes had been open for a long time. They didn't need to be opened again.

"This is where I put in the sweat of my youth," Nesje said, "and I'll take my last breath here."

Serianna stood up abruptly and began to clear the table.

"Bring in more wood," she asked sharply. "The fire's almost out in the stove."

"Aren't we going to put them all out soon? I mean— shouldn't we get some sleep?" he asked her. "I have to be up in six hours."

"Then make sure we have wood inside," Serianna said.

Nesje thought she was unreasonable, but he didn't take the bait.

"I haven't lost my faith that life will be good here one day," he said to Gjertine as she stood up. "I have faith that I will receive my mortgage, and the farm will be mine one day."

"The Lord watch over your coming and going," Gjertine said, and went upstairs to settle in the loft.

Hans stopped by more often after his brother was born. Maybe he was curious about Gjertine, who was less than a year older than he was. But their conversation didn't flow smoothly, at least not when there were others present. Might they take a stroll into town? Or couldn't they stay home and watch the baby while Serianna took one? Isn't that why Gjertine was here?

But Serianna didn't want to go anywhere, no matter how many people offered to watch the baby.

"I don't feel well enough to show myself out among people yet," she said.

"What do you mean? He's three weeks old already!"

But Serianna didn't want to go out at all. She was terrified that something would happen to the baby. If she could share this with her husband, everything would be easier. But she was least willing to confide in him of anyone. When Gjertine asked her why she didn't talk to her husband about what weighed on her, Serianna said he was struggling enough.

Gjertine said, "That's not how it's supposed to be between married people!"

"Oh, you're one to tell me that!" Serianna exclaimed. "Dry off behind your ears before you give other people advice about life."

She had already lost one child before and she was terrified of losing another. When he woke in the night she wouldn't let Gjertine get near him. Without sleep Serianna was short tempered. Gjertine did the housework, and Serianna took care of the baby.

4

Hans came one day in spring when Gjertine wasn't home. Gjertine had gone to town with the milk before Nesje came home. Hans stood by the kitchen window looking out at the fjord, still wintery gray beneath the disappearing snow. He didn't know if he should wait for his father or bundle back up and leave. Serianna was more than taciturn, and he couldn't think of anything to say either.

It's terrible how long the snow has lingered, he thought. Down in town the ground was clear and would soon be green, but up in Rekneslia there were still drifts around the house.

He heard the lid of a chest bang shut and the water ladle hit a wall. He turned around and saw his stepmother's tired, furrowed face.

"Some spring cleaning?" he asked, picking up the ladle.

"Something came over me," she said.

"What came over you?'

"I feel like I'm trapped. I haven't been out in a month."

"I've said many times that I can watch my brother, and Gjertine is here to give you a break when you need one. But I never see you put on your coat."

"I can't deal with this long winter!" Serianna yelled. "Why doesn't spring ever arrive up here? And why doesn't your father come home?"

"He's just down the hill."

"And why are you always against me?" she yelled again.

Then she slumped over the table.

"I'm not a good person," she said. "What will happen to Gjertine?"

"You're only human, like the rest of us," Hans said.

"I'm a troubled soul. I get mean when I can't get out and breathe."

"Go take a walk. Maybe he'll sleep until you come back."

She pulled herself together, realizing how silly it was that she didn't let the baby out of her sight. She looked for her shoes. She hadn't worn them in weeks. She saw they needed to be waxed, and so she started polishing her shoes instead of going anywhere. At least she would have her footwear ready the next time she had a chance to get outside.

"Your father is so sensitive," she said as she polished her shoes. "Everything worries him, even the littlest things."

"What do you mean?"

"I suggested that maybe we could move to another place, since there are more of us now. That offended him. He doesn't want to move. I said that he could apply for that position that was in the newspaper, as manager of Gørvell's farm, and I said I didn't know anyone better suited to manage it. I meant that as a compliment, but it hurt his feelings. He asked what would happen to his house and the land, to which he gave his best years."

"That's how Pa is."

"The baby will be unhappy because I am," she wailed.

"It's not uncommon for women to feel down after giving birth," Hans said.

"What do you know, you ninny?"

"My grandmother told me," Hans said. "She delivered a thousand babies, all told."

"I don't ever need to hear that again," Serianna said.

"You haven't found your way back to life yet," Hans said.

"Where do you get these strange expressions?"

"The wind brings them to me," the boy said.

Then Nesje walked in.

"Can you close the window?" he said, peeling off his wet clothes. "I had to work in that rain. Could you bring in some wood, Hans?"

Serianna shut the window and Hans went to get some firewood.

"You've got to get out into the spring air," Nesje said.

"I don't have anyone to see," she said.

"You owe the neighbors a visit."

"They could have brought some food during recovery," she said. "People do that in other places. But I'll go and we'll see how they receive me."

She fetched a shawl and wool sweater and, finally, went out. Nesje saw her stand outside the Sættem house before she knocked and went inside. Was the worst of it now over?

Gjertine came up the hill, her cheeks flushed and pink. She was not unhappy when she saw Hans, and she clapped her hands when she learned her sister had finally gone for a walk.

"There, we see that God hears our prayers!" she said. "I feared she would never cross the doorway again."

A month had passed before Serianna put on her shoes and gone out to see that spring was on its way. When she returned she was a changed woman. She had seen the lady next door and then gone down to the dock. She had smelled the scent of rain and dirt and seen the bare ground, finally free of snow.

She was a new woman. She beamed.

"Nice people, the Sættem family," she said. "They're pious enough, but they care about their neighbors. Julia knit this for our little boy." She held up a little white hat.

The mood of the whole house eased.

Hans said, "Bastian slept the whole time."

"What did you call him?"

"I call him Bastian when I think of him."

"Are you the one who gets to name him?"

"I just meant it in fun."

Gjertine clapped her hands loudly.

"I'll change him," she said. Serianna hadn't taken off her shawl and sweater when she suddenly laughed her first laugh in a long time.

"Bastian?"

"Yeah, why? What were you thinking?" Hans asked.

"I thought we should baptize him Georg."

"Doesn't the father usually have some say?" asked Nesje, who to that point was lost in thought. "Bastian and Georg, where do you get all these names from?"

"Are you hungry, Bastian Georg?" Gjertine asked. The baby looked for her breast. She cleaned him up before passing him to her sister, who nursed him.

Hans said, "Well, I'll be going then," but he said it with a big smile.

"Don't give your brother a name until it's been decided!" his father said.

"When are you coming back, Hans?" Gjertine asked.

"When I have another errand," Hans said.

"They're having a missionary meeting at the Sættem house

on Sunday," Gjertine said. "I was planning to go. They're going to talk about how things are in Africa. Children and adults are welcome."

"I'm neither a child nor an adult."

"Also young bucks," Gjertine said.

"We'll see on Sunday," Hans said.

He was about to be confirmed, and he didn't want advice on the subject. He didn't think anything new would be said, and memorizing psalms wasn't his thing. He put on his shoes to go.

"'Anything new?' Isn't he supposed to learn the Gospels?"

Nesje took out a book he borrowed from the Kvam library, but he didn't read for long before he nodded off.

"I'm young. I need a lot of sleep," Gjertine said, and climbed the stairs to the attic.

But they saw a light shining through the cracks between the floorboards, which told them that she was probably reading by candlelight.

"As long as she doesn't set fire to the bedclothes," Nesje said. Serianna didn't respond. She wasn't completely over her reticence.

"Bastian Georg," he said.

"That doesn't sound bad," Serianna said.

"No, that would pretty much do," Nesje said.

"Yes, that settles it then," she said.

"That settles it," he said.

"You're not going to be in the woods this winter, are you?" she said when they were finally in bed. She scooted up against him.

He put his arms around her.

She said, "No, not yet," and turned away.

"It won't be passable in the woods soon," he said.

"So you can take a breather for a few days?"

"I have to haul manure for Gørvell."

Nesje worked in the woods for another week. The days were long and the snow heavy. He trudged through snow up to his knees, and the snow was so wet, soaking him to the bone. It was hard for the horses make their way forward. In some places they slogged up to their bellies, and they exhausted themselves getting back on their feet, wandering to find solid ground.

It was Sunday, Gjertine was going to the meeting at the Sættem house, and lo and behold if Hans didn't turn up to go with her. It wasn't his thing. He fidgeted while they sang and prayed. The worst part was when Gjertine stood and explained who she was, how she had come to be here, and how difficult it was for her to find out what God wanted from her. After these winter weeks in Rekneslia she had realized that God wanted to test her patience.

"*All things work together for good to them that love God,*" Gjertine said, and the others sighed and agreed.

"How are you with God?" Gjertine asked Hans outside when the meeting was over.

"I am going out into the world," Hans said, "and we'll see if he helps me. I've heard that God helps those who help themselves."

"I wish I could go with you to Throndhjem!" Gjertine said. "We could be together there, me and you!"

"How would that look?" Hans said.

"Who cares what people say? Maybe you could go on ahead and I could follow you? But this summer I have to help Ola. I wish he would find himself a wife soon. Then I could come."

"You're certainly not going to come to me!"

"I want to go and see things. And when you're in Throndhjem I'll know someone there."

"So, what are we going to do then?"

"I don't know. Will you put your arms around me?"

"Is that what you want?"

"I'm not a child anymore. And neither are you."

"How do you know that?"

"I can tell when you look at me."

"I don't look at you, do I?"

"I see you keeping track of me even when you don't look."

He put his arms around her.

"That's very nice," she said, and rested her head against his chest.

"Should I let go of you now?"

"No, hold me tighter," Gjertine said.

"You're so thin."

"Tighter! You're very thin too. What will become of us?"

"What do you mean by that?"

"I don't want to be like my sister. Her life is so joyless."

"That will pass when summer comes," Hans said.

"And when will that be? It's still so cold."

"I feel warmer when I hold you."

"You think it's nice too?"

"Yes," Hans said.

"But now you have to let me go."

"A little longer, then I'll let you go."

The spring sky above them was beautiful and clear. He let her go, and they walked back up the hill.

"Will you stay here tonight?"

"I'm just walking you home."

"Couldn't you stay until tomorrow?"

"I do best when I stay where I actually live. Plus, I have to study the catechism. The pastor says that I don't know nearly enough. He says I need to pull myself together, since I'm illegitimate."

"What are you talking about?"

"My mother and father didn't get married before I was born."

"And you're to blame for that?"

"Well, that's why I'm going home."

"You do your best when you're where I am," Gjertine toyed.

"I promised to go back to Kringstadhagen tonight."

She went inside. He stood and watched her until she closed the door. It pained her to see him like that, as if he'd been driven from his own home.

But he has me now, she thought, and soon he'll be a grown man. No one could find out what was going on between them. She had to keep up appearances.

"God's peace and good evening," said Gjertine, taking off her kerchief. "What news in the house?"

"The boy will be named Bastian Georg," Nesje said, "and he'll be baptized in Bolsøy Church. Would you like to be his godmother, Gjertine?"

"Of course."

5

When May arrived Serianna, Gjertine, and Nesje's brother took Gørvell's rowboat for Bolsøy Church. A shadow hung over them. Hans wasn't coming. Nesje was deeply upset his eldest wouldn't be there for Bastian Georg's christening. But soon after the truth came out. The pastor who was to christen Bastian Georg had said that Hans would have to wait a year to be confirmed. He wasn't good enough with the book, and he was a bastard. If he didn't become better acquainted with the scripture, he was at risk of straying as badly as his parents had. Hans became a bastard when his name was entered into the church register, and even if his parents had since married, he remained illegitimate in the eyes of the Lord.

That was Gjertine's last day in Rekneslia. She knew nothing of Hans's misfortune, and she was angered that he didn't come to say goodbye. She was going home to help her mother. Her elderly father was ill. Old Erik Olsen at Bortegard was bedridden, and he had a fatty heart. They didn't know if he would make it through the summer. So Gjertine became the little boy's godmother and went home.

It seemed as though Serianna didn't care if Gjertine left. Far too often the conversation between Nesje and Gjertine made Serianna feel like an intruder in her own home. This couldn't continue. It was funny that Gjertine and Nesje, who were at odds about so many things, should have hit it off.

Nesje did as the custom dictates. The children were written into the church register by first name, then a patronymic from the father's name, and then a place name. The place was the farm where they lived. This was why on the rare occasions when someone like Nesje wrote their name, they wrote Knut Hansen Reknes, though everyone called him Nesje. So when he was baptized, the boy's name was written as Bastian Georg Knudsen.

Gjertine Grows Up

I

Summer and fall followed. When Nesje heard that Hans wouldn't be confirmed this year, he made the unfortunate mistake of remarking that his son was unwise in neglecting his catechism and failing to study his psalms. As a way to encourage Hans, because most of their family was bright, he made mention of his father, who in the military had received a certificate for being uncommonly fit for duty. From then on, to his father's great regret, Hans rarely came to visit.

Gjertine spent the summer at home at Bortegard. She should have found a domestic position, but Ola didn't want her to leave the farm, and her father needed help with the smallest things. Her mother wasn't good for much anymore, so Gjertine watched her father as he just lay there, silent, without any sign that he recognized anyone. He was sixty-two years old.

Gjertine's soul was in distress, but she tried to rise to her everyday tasks. When people asked if she was looking for a job she replied that she was waiting for a sign, but she was really waiting for her father to let go of life, because he was the living dead.

And yet she remained herself. If it was too hot out she unbuttoned the front of her dress for some air.

"I can't breathe," she told her mother.

"At least wear a shirt under there," her mother said. "Someone might stop by."

"I'll sweat to death!"

She was intractable.

2

It was the spring of 1876 when Lars Stavig, his wife, Maren, and their three sons knocked the dust of the old country from their feet. They boarded a steamship in Bud. From there they took a misdirection north to Kristiansund, where they boarded a steamer for England, which then took them south to Bergen and south again to Hull, where they traveled overland to Liverpool to board yet another new ship for the long journey to Halifax, Nova Scotia, and from there continued on the long, long journey to Minnesota.

3

Hans's godfather, Hans Hansen Kringstadhagen, arranged for Hans's confirmation and gave the boy money for a suit. Hans Knudtsen was confirmed in Molde Church on April 23, 1876. He stood last in a line of many poor boys and bastards. It was more than a year since Gjertine had seen him, but she hadn't forgotten him. From one of Serianna's letters she learned he had traveled to Throndhjem by steamer the day after his confirmation to intern at Trolla Brug, and that he was at the stove factory, with a tiny little room in Lade.

He wasn't planning on coming home any time soon, Serianna said. He had to work before he earned any time off.

Gjertine was worried. She wanted to go and be with him! She thought she might die before she got his address from Serianna, and when she did she wrote him a long letter. Gjertine had read enough books to know how people spoke when they wanted to get a boyfriend.

Lord, it took so long to receive his reply.

She went in and out of the cottage at Bortegard. With a shawl over her shoulders, she walked the hills around the village in her homemade shoes, then sat on the hill and listened to the cuckoo on the mountainside and the chaffinch in the woods.

There were people on the other farms whom she could talk to, but they weren't interested in her problems. She was searching for the meaning of life.

"The point of life?" they said. "Isn't the point of life to live it? And once we've lived as best we can, we die. Then new folks will come along and they'll live as best they can and they'll die too. That's how it has to be. Otherwise the earth would be filled with old corpses and people would be unable to feed themselves. What a world that would be!"

And then they went back to talking about how many calves they could breed, how many milk cows they could keep if they cultivated another field, and whether it would be a good summer since there was so much snow this winter, or if it was the other way around, that there had been so much snow because there had been so many rowanberries the previous year.

Every Sunday Gjertine went to the Readers, but it wasn't as good since she had attended the missionary meeting at the Sættem house.

"You've become a stranger to us," they told her. "Do you walk around with your buttons undone in Molde? What happened to you; who turned your thoughts upside down? It wasn't a man, was it?"

"We need to send missionaries to the heathen lands," Gjertine told them.

"The heathen lands!" the Readers replied. "When there are so many at home who haven't repented?"

"You mustn't stay here at home for my sake!" old Ingeborg said as midsummer approached. "I'll get a girl to help look after your father. You need to get out among some people. I have to live here with my pain and grief, and without a scrap of my youthful song that gave me so much comfort."

Gjertine was grateful. Not everyone could see how important it was for a young woman to get out.

"What happened to the song of your youth, Mother?" Gjertine asked. "I actually can't remember you ever singing."

"I was so old by the time you were born that it as already quiet," Ingeborg said. "The song of my youth remains across the fjord, in Stavika Cove, where I ran as a little girl. But I used to sing every bit as much as you do when you walk through the woods."

Gjertine said, "I heard that Lars Stavig found your youthful song in the rocks at low tide in Stavika Cove, and that he packed it up and took it to America with him. It wouldn't surprise me if the Norwegians there listen to your song when it's dark outside and the prairie winds blow."

"Lars Stavig's mother was my friend, and she often sang the songs she learned from me. So Lars Stavig didn't need to pack anything in his luggage—he has my song in his heart."

"Couldn't you sing it to me, Mother? Just once?"

"Oh no, my voice is so old and rough," Ingeborg said. "I don't want to ruin a song with it. But the song I liked to sing most was a Christmas song. *Et lite Barn, saa lystelig*, it was called—'Little Children, Sweetly Sing.'"

"Please, Mother?"

And Gjertine heard her mother sing softly, almost inaudibly:

> *Little children, sweetly sing,*
> *On this birthday of our King;*
> *Now a joyous anthem raise,*
> *In glad notes of grateful praise.*

"Please, sing more so that I can learn it too," Gjertine said.

"Aren't you going to the Readers today?" Ingeborg asked her daughter. "You could just make it."

"I don't think I'm in the mood to meet my Savior."

"Is there a man in your thoughts, my daughter?" Ingeborg asked. "Perhaps the one you wrote to, in Throndhjem?"

"That's the one, Mother," Gjertine said.

"Couldn't he come and see you this summer?"

"He wrote that he can't come this summer because he doesn't get any time off this first year. Next summer maybe, but God forgive me, I can't stand it."

Then her brother Ola walked in.

"How much does it cost to take the steamboat from Bud to Throndhjem?" Ingeborg asked. "It couldn't be more than a dalar, could it?"

"I think it's two and a half," Ola said. "Or four kroner and sixty-six øre, as they say nowadays. Who's going to Throndhjem?"

"Gjertine might go if we took care of the ticket," old Ingeborg said.

"Does she want to visit that Nesje boy?" Ola asked. "I couldn't help looking to see who sent you that letter when I picked it up at the post office."

"I didn't ask for money for a ticket," Gjertine protested.

"But it would do you good to go to Throndhjem," old Ingeborg told her daughter. "Then you could find some peace and come home again. I've never made it past Kristiansund."

"What did you do in Kristiansund, Mother?"

"My blessed husband's uncle was a fiddle maker there, and we went to see him."

"Many people have never been that far," Ola said. "I myself have never been farther than Setnesmoen. And I don't think I'll get any farther than that."

"Your destiny has not yet been revealed," Ingeborg said.

"If I go anywhere, it will be America," Gjertine mumbled.

"That's what I'm afraid of," her mother said, "that you'll harbor such thoughts. If you take a trip to Throndhjem then perhaps this young Nesje will stop you."

"Let's sleep on it," Ola said.

The next day Gjertine went to her brother and borrowed two kroner, got three more from her mother, added to that what she had saved, and found the money for a ticket.

She had to wait until it was warmer so she could travel without a cabin. She tended her father through the spring, but when a girl came to care for the ailing Erik, who no longer knew who his lips, Gjertine went to help Ola on the farm. The days grew longer, and lighter, and she grew increasingly enthusiastic about her letters, but the next one she received from Throndhjem made her cry.

"Why do you cry with a letter from your beau?" Ola asked.

"He's not my beau!" Gjertine said, sobbing.

"Is that why you're crying?"

"I'm crying because he doesn't want me to come see him!"

"Then you should go anyway," Ola declared.

4

By the time Ola took Gjertine to Bud so that she could catch the steamship to Throndhjem, she had received every imaginable bit of advice from her mother, who thought this trip might lead to one thing or another.

"Button up your bodice when you're in a big city," her mother advised.

"I'll try," Gjertine said.

"If that young man wants to put his arms around you, let him," old Ingeborg said.

"I don't know what he wants," Gjertine said.

"But if he puts his arms around you and you put your arms around him, don't let him unbutton your dress."

"Mother!"

"And no matter what, he mustn't be allowed to take your dress off."

"Mother, stop!"

"Because once boys get excited like that, they aren't able to stop," Ingeborg explained. "And it's up to us womenfolk to keep them at bay."

Gjertine was so excited that she couldn't sleep. The trip took over twelve hours. She sat in the lounge with the food that she brought, and when the big city rose up before her, she was so excited she could hardly breathe. It was the height of summer, and the harbor was quiet. When she disembarked, she was confused. Hans wasn't on the wharf as they had agreed. Perhaps he wasn't off work yet. The steamer was ahead of schedule, and he wasn't allowed to leave early.

It took her a while to figure out what to do. She had never seen a city like this, but she wasn't frightened. She asked for directions to Trolla Brug's stove sales office on Nordre Gate, but when she found it Hans Knudtsen wasn't there. The clerk who told her this was more curious than she liked.

"Are you really his cousin?" he asked.

"Yes, I am," Gjertine said.

It turned out they had passed each other in the street. Hans came back to the office, and how he had changed in a single year. He was big and strong, almost a full-grown man, and he took her hand but didn't hug her. He smelled strange, probably something in his hair, which looked like it was glued to his head. She was so happy that she trembled. Could they go somewhere to be alone? He said that he had to work and asked her to wait until six o'clock, when the store closed. Then he came to where she sat on a bench in the park by Our Lady's Church. He thought it was late, and he was worried, as though something might go wrong at any moment. He acted strangely, not like himself, even though it had only been a year. He was more grown up, in a way, and he spoke in a different style, like people did in this city, like he didn't want anyone to know he came from a small village in the south. He had decided to become one of them, she realized, and had no use for her. As he sat down, she knew she had made a mistake. She should have given him more time. Then, maybe, everything would have been different. She had hurried something that wasn't ripe.

"It was good of you to come," he said.

"That's not what you wrote," she said.

"I didn't want to encourage you," he said, "because I can't receive you."

But he did receive her. They walked to where he lived in Lade. She saw the little houses there. He had one room and shared a bathroom in the backyard. It didn't smell good, and there were flies. The flies would give up when the weather cooled and the rains set in, she thought.

And the room? It wasn't very nice. He had a bed and table with a crust of bread and a block of cheese in the drawer. She sat on his bed while they tried to talk to each other. There were flies buzzing, but it was otherwise quiet.

And it was hot.

"Shouldn't I take off my coat?" Gjertine asked.

Yes, she probably should. She took off her coat and set it beside her on the bed.

"Maybe you'd like to hold me?" she said.

"I want to, but I can't," he said.

"Why can't you?"

"I can't start something that I can't follow through with," he said.

"What can't you follow through with?"

"I can't be responsible for anyone other than myself. I have to work my way up. They need to have confidence in me. I can't become involved with women."

"Become involved? What's that supposed to mean?"

"My boss said that. I came here as an errand boy, and in two years I'll be a clerk. After that I can be in charge of a department—the crown stoves, for example."

"The crown stoves?"

"They have their own department."

He took her to a café and he paid for the cod they ate, but even then they weren't able to really talk. She said some things about her life since they were last together, but he wasn't very interested, and he knew most of it already from the letter he had received from Nesje. He didn't care about news from Molde.

"Nothing ever happens there," he said dismissively.

What was she to say to that?

She saw how lonely he was. And although the word didn't occur to her, she could tell that he was scared to death. It had been clear that her trip had been a waste. He wanted a Throndhjem girl, as they called them, so he could ease into the right connections, enter the proper social circles, become one of them, render his own background invisible. He did loosen up a little after he had a glass of beer. He didn't ask if she wanted one, so she drank water. He talked about his plans, which stretched at least ten years into the future. He was going to save his money so that one day he could own his own home. Until he was safely established, he couldn't make any commitments.

She thought he was thinking about things the right way, and he was grateful that she endorsed his plans. Maybe he didn't have many others to talk to about these matters? Oh no, of course he had friends. He often socialized with several of the guys at the stove foundry.

What did they do together? Well, they went for walks and promenades. Did they look at the ladies too? Yes, sometimes that did happen. But there wasn't anyone in particular he thought about? No, no, he needed to be careful. If he settled down with a wife and children now he would never get ahead. That being said, he pulled out a pocket watch and said it was time to go to bed.

"Come to think of it, where are you going to sleep?" he asked.

Couldn't she sleep at his place?

"We can lie with our backs to each other, or head to foot," she said.

He said that was a dangerous risk, but the idea no longer seemed completely alien. So they walked together. Her heart beat like mad. She didn't take off her skirt, nor her blouse. She lay down by the wall and made herself small so there would be room for the both of them. Then he lay down. He had taken off his outer garments. It didn't take long before she felt him stroking her back with his fingers, over her hips, reaching for her breasts. She lay stiff as a log, but when he tried to reach under her skirt she stopped him.

"Not the skirt," she said.

"Why not?" he asked.

"You mustn't risk a commitment," she said.

"No, you're right," he said, but he kept trying.

He pressed himself against her now, but she wasn't afraid. He rubbed himself against her, and then it was over. She could feel her back was wet. What difference did that make, one way or the other? A moment later he was asleep. But she was still awake when the sun rose, and she still wasn't asleep when he left at seven. As he hurried off, he asked her to stop by the shop and say goodbye.

"I'll keep you in my thoughts and my prayers," she said. "You must never think that you're alone."

"Thank you," he said unhappily, as if he were making a mistake, and he left.

Then she got up. She couldn't stay in that room.

The southbound steamer wouldn't leave for many hours. She wandered around the harbor and roamed the streets, watching people all morning. There were enormous differences between them, but to her it seemed as though all of them, poor and rich alike, were profoundly contented with their condition. Before the steamer arrived and she boarded, she made up her mind to never come here again. The city of Throndhjem was not for her. It was the city where her dreams died. She knew less than before about what God wanted for her. It wasn't until after she boarded that she second-guessed the decision to not say goodbye. Would he ever write to her, and did she even want him to write?

On instinct, she ran back down the gangway. She left her suitcase on board and someone called after her, but she ran as hard as she could to the shop where he worked, yelled from the doorway that she had come to say goodbye, and saw how surprised he was—perhaps even ashamed.

"Goodbye, Hans! I hope you have a good life! The Lord bless you and keep you!"

He took her hands as if to stop her, but she pulled free and ran back to the steamer. The bell rang for the second time, but she saw the clock tower on the church and knew she still had a couple of minutes. She sat down out on the deck in second class. As the *Ole Bull* began its trek south along the coast, four men sat nearby playing cards. They were laughing and making lots of noise.

"You're paying attention, we see," they said to her. "Which of us do you like best? We're playing for you, you see? We have cabins, each of us. You don't need to sit out here tonight."

She didn't care what they said or thought. It was sinking in that not every dream comes true.

5

The summer of 1876 was over for Nesje before it began. He put in his contractual days haymaking for Governor Leth before he started haymaking for Gørvell. When it got dark in the evening he mowed his steep meadow, dried his hay in the field, and brought the hay back to the barn.

Serianna was heavy again with child and didn't walk down the hill any more than she had to. Nesje found her unpredictable. One day she would smile easily, the next it seemed like she had seven winters and seven woes. He lived with that. She was a faithful wife. She had chosen to share his circumstances, make his bed, and serve his food. He was grateful for it.

"Can't this baby come already," she moaned. "I can't keep carrying him around anymore!"

She wasn't due until the frost at the earliest. She was anxious and scared.

"Could you do me a kindness?" she asked. "I want Gjertine to come and stay again."

So Nesje sent a message with the steamer, and four days later Gjertine was back in their house. She was changed. There was something hard in the way she set her mouth now.

"Do we really need a midwife?" Gjertine asked. "Isn't that expensive and unnecessary?"

Nesje was annoyed. His mother had railed against ignorant women who stole responsibility and income from the midwives. But he remained calm as he explained that he was the son of a midwife who had delivered a thousand babies.

And not just that. She had taken sham midwives to court for illegally delivering babies.

"It will be as you want it," Gjertine said.

Nesje sent for the midwife. The baby was big and lying the wrong way. The birth lasted an entire day and continued into the evening. Serianna was torn up and lost a lot of blood. The midwife washed and wrapped the baby in a blanket and gave it to Nesje. Gjertine ran back and forth with hot water.

Serianna said, "I'm bleeding to death."

They looked in each other's faces. The situation was perilous.

Gjertine looked at her brother-in-law and said, "You know I can staunch bleeding. Do you want me to?"

"It certainly can't make it any worse!" Nesje said.

"Then everyone has to get out."

"Get out?"

"Yes, just for a little while!"

The frightened young midwife did as Gjertine said.

But Nesje said, "I will not leave my wife in this state."

"Then you must never reveal what you will see," Gjertine said.

"I take God in heaven as my witness that I will not speak of it," Nesje said.

"And what you hear, you will never mention to anyone."

She never took her eyes off him as she put her hand on her sister's forehead and mumbled the same short string of words again and again. Nesje heard Gjertine from where he stood. He could just barely make out the words as she repeated them over and over.

"Jesus crossed the River Jordan. Staunch the bleeding, staunch the bleeding!"

Slowly, bit by bit, the blood began to trickle. The midwife came back and confirmed it: a miracle had occurred.

"We come from strong stock," Gjertine said, "and my sister is the strongest of all."

Then the midwife began to stitch, and once she had the big boy at her breast, Serianna slept. Nesje lit a lamp, Gjertine set out some food, and the midwife ate and thanked them. Nesje sat with Bastian Georg on his lap, but the boy was too upset by the birth and had to be carried, crying, up to the loft.

Nesje ate thoughtfully, clearing his throat a few times, and tried, wordlessly and in many ways, to show his gratitude. Gjertine saw in his facial expressions that he thought the credit was due to her, and she reminded him that it was God who stops the bleeding, not her.

He said nothing.

Serianna was bedridden for more than a week. Gjertine took care of the housework, she took care of Bastian Georg—a year and a half old and a lot of trouble—and she changed the hefty baby as if she were wrapping loaves of bread.

Nesje said, "What should I do?"

"It's the weekend," Gjertine said.

"And what of it?"

"You could go take communion."

He looked at her. "What's that supposed to mean?"

."That you might want to thank your creator for holding his hand over you."

"I don't know if I'm in the right frame of mind for that," Nesje said. "*I don't want to eat and drink unworthily, eat and drink damnation to myself.*"

"He gives and you receive," Gjertine said.

On Sunday, Nesje went to church and listened to a man named Laurentius Borchsenius Fredrik Fabritius. He seemed to be a human being, but to Nesje he might as well have been from another planet, standing there in his wig and chasuble and gazing wide-eyed upon the worshippers. Nesje sat in one of the pews in back with the other poor people. He had no pew of his own, of course—he wasn't even a member of the congregation. He sat there, staring at the big altarpiece with angels ascending and descending, and his eyes wandered over the pews. They rested on the families who had their own pews, the Dahls and the Leths and the Møllers and all of Claus Gørvell's siblings.

Nesje didn't know if Marie and Adam Gørvell noticed him. Maybe they didn't recognize him in his Sunday attire. Here he was nobody. When he walked around with the scythe, he was someone: the haymaker, the lead hay-maker, who everyone respected. He had to remember to be humble, even though he had such a prominent position in the field.

"Man, remember that to dust shall you return!" he told himself, with no idea where those words came from.

He bowed his head during the prayer and continued to pray for his family while the hymn was sung. What have I done for God in his mercy to care for me? He wondered. He knew he did his job well, but surely that wasn't enough? Had he thought of his creator during the busy years which lay behind him? No, he had to admit that sometimes three or four days had passed at a time. Had he at least said the Lord's Prayer every night when he went to bed? If he was honest, no. That was what he needed to do to get right before God: it was high time to admit that too often he fell asleep as soon as his head hit the pillow and more than once he had fallen asleep through his prayers! Maybe that was because prayers were difficult to pray?

Give us today our daily bread: that was an easy line, but *Forgive us our trespasses as we forgive those who trespass against us*? That was harder. Had anyone trespassed against him? Not in terms of money. But here, in God's presence, he had to admit that he thought that Claus Gørvell, who knew Governor Leth so well, could put in a good word for him so that he could take ownership of the four acres that he would soon have under cultivation. He wanted to tell God that he did not bear any ire toward Gørvell, that ultimately it was in God's hands.

When the usher signaled his pew, he stood to take communion; he walked forward in his Sunday best, leaving his hat in the pew. He knelt at the rail where Borchsenius administered the host. "This is the body of Christ given for you," Borchsenius said. "This is the blood of Christ given for you." Time after time, he said this in a gentle and soulful tone. Nesje's heart beat faster and faster as the pastor approached. Nesje received the host. It expanded in his mouth, but he swallowed it. One hand shook on his knee with the little wine cup in his other. Borchsenius poured the wine.

"This is the blood of Christ given for you."

Nesje coughed. Some of the wine went down the right way, but he sprayed the rest on his white shirt like a mighty hand had given him a shove. He grabbed the communion rail, got to his feet, and staggered back to his seat. Did someone laugh?

It was one of his drinking companions from his youth, one who still drank whatever he could guzzle down in his everyday clothes, but who sat and laughed at Nesje, who worked day and night on his farm for fifteen years!

Nesje cringed and looked away as the service concluded with nine chimes of the bell. He leapt up after the ninth and quickly left the church with his hat. He went home. Bastian Georg reached his hands out to him, and he picked the boy up into his arms, and Serianna went "out" for a walk to get some fresh air, the first time after the birth, and Gjertine immediately asked Nesje: "Was it to your liking?"

"Yes," he said, "it has never been so much to my liking as now. But I don't understand..."

"What don't you understand?"

"I had a coughing fit," he said. "Most of the wine went down on my shirt."

"That could happen to anyone!" Gjertine said.

"Spilling the blood of Jesus is not the path to happiness."

"You should think of him who spilled his blood for you," Gjertine said.

"Sure."

"You're not the main character in the story," Gjertine pointed out.

That hadn't occurred to him.

"He is, the one who died."

"Yes."

"And who rose from the dead, as you will on the day of resurrection!" Gjertine said, as if there weren't anything simpler than that.

"There's something I need to ask of you," he said.

"What?"

"It's not worth your mentioning to Serianna that I took communion today."

"It can wait until the day you're ready to profess Jesus's name," Gjertine agreed, and he was profoundly grateful. He wasn't ready to face the questions.

Gjertine stayed for three more weeks. Serianna thought she was underfoot now that she herself could handle things;

Bastian Georg was sleeping through the nights, and so was the new baby. Gjertine thought Serianna should sleep until the children woke up, and that it was important for Nesje to be well looked after since he had to get up early and had such a long day. Serianna said that Nesje had managed on his own before she came, and Nesje agreed. He thought it was pointless, that Gjertine didn't need to get up until dawn—but she still got up while it was dark out to set out food.

She did him good. Gjertine heated milk so he could dip his crust of bread if it was dry. He didn't have great teeth. And Gjertine threw together a dough in a flash, the scent of freshly baked bread filling the house, and then she sliced it up for supper, even if he thought they should finish the old bread first.

"No. Old bread is old bread," Gjertine said. "And you support us all."

She respected him. Serianna knew who the master of the house was, but Nesje appreciated Gjertine's consideration, which was so bold that he almost felt a little ashamed. If he sat browsing through a book about one thing or another, Gjertine would come over and lean against his back to ask what he was reading. Other times she might sit and watch him, as if deep in thought. He had expected her to turn his thoughts toward the spiritual every day, but he was wrong.

It was strange, what happened. He had figured that her presence would be difficult, but she got him to change his thinking through her presence alone. She went to town with milk for their customers so he didn't have to do the rounds when he came home dead tired. One would presume that she would eye other young people, the young men hanging around—there wouldn't have been anything odd about that. But maybe she wasn't interested in boys? Of course she was, but she didn't want to ruin her reputation, she replied when he asked. It might happen, but she would wait.

Then a letter came from Hans saying that Gjertine had come to visit. Hans knew from his father's letter that Gjertine was in Rekneslia. But Gjertine hadn't said a word of her trip to Throndhjem nor had anyone in the family heard about it.

Nesje sat and looked at her as she cleaned the stove. Serianna lay in bed with the baby, and Bastian Georg tugged and pulled at his father to play some game or other. Nesje thought: She could be holding any secret at all. He, too, had a secret: He knew how to staunch blood.

6

Gjertine left in November for a wedding in Bud. Her sister Ane-Martha was getting married to the widower Andreas Vestad, fifteen years her elder. But neither of Ane-Martha's parents attended because old Erik Olsen was near death, and he in fact passed away in December 1876. Before he was called home, Gjertine sat vigil, night after night, and when his soul departed it was Gjertine who closed his eyelids. She woke her mother, who stopped the pendulum in the clock, and they lit candles so that Gjertine could write a letter to Serianna.

Because all the roads were buried in snow, the folks in Rekneslia did not come to the funeral. The snowfall over the fjord was so thick that even the steamer to Throndhjem couldn't run.

Old Erik Olsen shriveled like a flower in the autumn wind, Nesje said when he shared the news. When she received the letter, Serianna only said, "That's how it is." But she went and stopped the clock in the west living room.

It was winter and it snowed. It snowed on the mountains and on the grave of Erik Olsen that Erik and Ola dug out of the ground, and which the neighbors filled frozen. But there wasn't so much grief aside from his wife, Ingeborg, who could not understand how to be alone.

7

Nesje was in the woods for Gørvell when word came of a public probate at Bortegard that he had to attend. He had another errand: the new woodstove that he ordered for Ola was at the steamship office in Molde.

It wasn't so easy to get away. Serianna was alone with the livestock and two children. But Olaus Sætten agreed to take care of the stable, and what needed to be done needed to be done.

Nesje carried the crates of stove parts one at a time onto the steamboat, and then he boarded to second class. Ola picked him up with the horse and cart at the dock about a mile and a half from Bortegard. When they arrived, the stove boxes were dropped in the barn because they had to head straight to the probate.

Ola would increase his mortgage loan from Norges Hypotekbank to a thousand kroner, as the new coin was called. That was two hundred and fifty *spesidalar*. With that money, he would buy out his siblings. The two brothers would each run his own half of the farm, so they couldn't spare any of the equipment or tools. The three sisters, who by law would inherit half of the inheritance the brothers received, would receive their shares in cash.

The brothers had worked all this out between themselves before the probate began, and the county governor, Hans Stabo Hagerup, who attended in his own powerful personage, approved.

Bortegard was assessed at a value of six hundred *spesidalar*, in addition to the retirement provision that the widow Ingeborg would receive. That was over twice the amount of Ola's loan, which meant the bank effectively owned half the farm. Ola received the farm, the farmland, and the rights associated with it: seven cows, two bulls, twenty-four sheep, a pot in the stable, a copper kettle, a grindstone, a two-year-old horse, two mares, a cart, a coarse sieve for separating the grain from the straw debris, seven sleds, a hay sled, two dozen tables, a work bench, and a pickling barrel, all set at a certain price. Then there were two wooden tubs to store grain in, a hat and a southwester, various articles of clothing, twelve herring nets, three suitcases, seventeen wooden milk dishes, two waffle irons, one keg, four butter tubs, pastry boards, a grater, frying pans, a fireplace trivet, four iron pots, a neck hook, nine scythes, a sieve, a dip net, two field plows, eight cowband-stakes, and a large *faering* with a sail, worth five *spesidalar*. There was also a rowboat, a one-quarter stake in a *faering* with boathouse and tackle, two benches, two spinning wheels, two sleeping spots up in the loft, a dagger worth three *skilling*, three teacups (whatever that meant), a loom, three pastry rollers or rolling pins, four ornamental swords, some springs, a grandfather clock, an end table, a folding table, three benches, a mirror, a tea cart, two chairs, two stools, a bread basket, a churn, a drinking mug, shoemaking tools, part of a thresher, a feed device, a half stake in a cast net and a one-eighth stake in a herring net with equipment, worth sixty *spesidalar*. The sisters would receive fifty *spesidalar* each, and that was more than old tables and benches, Ola thought.

The other siblings sat there. They could not say no.

Gjertine burst into tears, even though she was seventeen years old and was considered an adult. The others controlled their emotions, but there was no doubt as to why Gjertine cried. The old life at Bortegard was gone. A new era would begin.

But before the new era was proclaimed, the new wood-stove needed to be installed. Truth be told, the stove had cost Ola more than he could afford. He had borrowed five hundred kroner more to pay his sisters and paid for the woodstove out of that five hundred kroner. Gjertine sat with the stove's instructions because she was the best reader. They assembled the plates so the grooves lined up, screwed it together, and hung the door to the oven. Hallelujah! What a life.

"Who would believe that those two would become such good friends?" said Ola.

"We share a secret," Gjertine said.

Ola fired up the woodstove with birch logs, and the stove glowed red. The sisters baked white bread and sang. They put the bread into the baking oven, and then the family ate the best meal since Serianna and Nesje's wedding.

The brother-in-law from Rekneslia was addressed with kind words, and when the evening was over, there was a dram. Even Gjertine let Nesje enjoy his drink. He needed to fortify himself before his trip.

Trouble under
the Stars

I

It was well into March, and it was almost three years since Nesje and Serianna met. Nesje trudged laboriously where the path turned along the fence to Humlehaven. The garden was closed, the herbs lay hidden, and all the trees bore snow-laden branches. As soon as they have leaves, Nesje thought, the herbs will blossom. One could easily call it a miracle, because it was, and the farmer lived close by with it. People strove all their livelong days, those who had no inheritance, or those who established their own place with their own steam via struggle or swindle.

He noticed an old man was removing snow from the roof of the little summer cottage in the garden. Couldn't he wait a few days? Warmer weather and rain were near, and the snow would melt! But, Nesje knew: the old man had to make himself useful, so he performed this useless task and received a crust of bread.

The spring passed as quickly as all the springs since Nesje had started at Rekneslia. Then the powerful mistress of Gørvell farm, Anne Margrete Gørvell, died, and a strange mood came over the household. Who would run Claus Gørvell's household for him now?

Nesje was a little stiff and under the weather. His sleep was often disrupted with little children in the house and he couldn't always tell one day from the next. As they approached the busy season on the farm, he staggered away in the morning light. Once he got going, he would find his mood, and he had to keep it up for many years to come. But why didn't Claus Gørvell come and let him know when the work would begin?

Nesje started to worry. Actually, now that he thought about it, he had not seen Claus for a full fourteen days.

A week before the haymaking he lost his patience. He put on his good shirt, his best shirt, and carried his work shirt with his lunch. When he came down to the Gørvell farm, he cautiously approached the door and knocked. The house girl, Sina, came and opened the door with a serious face.

No, he could not speak with Claus Gørvell.

"Master Gørvell isn't feeling so well," Sina said. He had been in bed for days, but of course he would be back on his feet again soon. "The Gørvell farm without Claus Gørvell would be an empty shell," Sina said.

What was she babbling about? Was he that sick? Should they prepare? Was he, the lead haymaker, to make the decisions about the haymaking now? But Sina would not let him in.

Worry took hold of Nesje. And then Claus Gørvell's two siblings came into the yard, Adam and Marie Gørvell. They walked right past Nesje and into the house, and they let the door close behind them.

Nesje walked over to the toolshed and looked over the scythes. But then someone called. Sina stood on the stoop waving to him and said that Master Gørvell had asked for his lead haymaker.

He stepped into the front hall, hesitating there, wondering if he should take off his shoes or not.

In a whisper Sina urged, "Come on, come on!"

She led the way, gesturing, showing him to the bed where Gørvell lay.

Adam and Marie Gørvell stood by the window and did not seem to notice that Nesje had come in.

Claus Gørvell was unrecognizable. His face was contorted, tugged sideways, and he made a gurgling sound when he breathed. He was pale as a corpse, and the hand that he stuck out from under the covers to wave Nesje closer was just as pale. Nesje felt sorry for the man. For all his misgivings, Claus Gørvell deserved to prosper. But what could Nesje do? It was clear that he maintain order during Gørvell's illness. He just needed to know when the haymaking should begin. He could handle everything once he learned the day.

Claus Gørvell could barely speak. He did not answer Nesje's question, or the question about his health.

It dawned on Nesje that this, this here, was serious. Fear cut to his heart, so it slammed and stuttered.

Again, Clause Gørvell waved Nesje closer. He said that Nesje had been a good man for the Gørvell farm, and he thanked him. He hoped that Nesje would continue to make his mark as before, if he himself was too sick to run things.

"I will keep it going, we all will, until you're well again," Nesje said. "We'll bring in the hay. Have no fear."

But Claus Gørvell was done talking. Nesje, moved, said the years at the Gørvell farm had been good years. Then he was standing outside in the deepest despair. When he told Serianna, she wouldn't at first believe it was as bad as he described.

But two weeks later, Claus Gørvell left behind his earthly shell—a figure of speech in a book Nesje had once read—and was buried. The haymaking was in full swing, but Adam Gørvell allowed the servants and farmhands to take time off to attend Claus's burial. On a hot July day, Nesje felt an icy wind. Never before had he felt so precarious. Never had he had so many mouths to feed. Should he just ask what Adam Gørvell planned to do? No, the time was not right. He had to wait for Adam to speak to him.

It occurred to him that, maybe, he would be asked to take over as manager. If so, what should he say? Would that leave him time to look after his own little place? That wasn't certain. The hardest thing was that he didn't dare discuss the issue with Serianna. He was afraid she would insist that he should announce his interest in the manager position, but sticking his nose out like that—that wasn't Nesje's style. The thought of it embarrassed him. Keep going and get the work done: that was his method. Bring the hay in, so the cattle had something to eat.

When the hay was in, the grain harvest loomed. Everything was early this year.

But there was no change in the work once Adam Fredrik Gørvell took over. Adam Gørvell wasn't going to run the whole operation the way Claus Gørvell had. He needed a manager, and Nesje could have become that manager, but he was not asked. Another was taken on once the potatoes had been harvested, a man called Lars-at-Gørvell, because whoever was the manager at the Gørvell farm didn't need any other name—he belonged there through and through. The mood between the haymaker and Adam Gørvell, not to mention the new manager, was not like it had been. But Nesje would remain at the Gørvell farm for twenty-five years.

2

And such is life among the people: while one is laid to rest under six feet of dirt, another stands in the summer sunshine to taste the noblest fruits that the earth offers its citizens, the fruits of love, those fruits known for the sweetness of the first bite.

This is what Nesje was thinking the following winter when Serianna said that she had received important news from Bortegard. The letter was written by Gjertine, so one could appreciate the events that must truly have been amusing. For the first time since Claus Gørvell passed Nesje treated himself to a quiet laugh.

Well, Ola had noticed three sisters living on a farm in Malmedalen. They were pretty girls, all three, so Ola got it into his head that he would take whichever one he could get, be it one or another, likely the eldest since the girls' father would want to be rid of the eldest first.

One Saturday night, Ola heated a kettle of water in the cookhouse. But before he poured the hot water into a tub, he instructed Gjertine to clean him with a bundle of fresh birch twigs that he had picked expressly for this purpose. So the letter said.

Gjertine wrote that she slapped her brother all over—when she was finished he looked like a freshly scalded pig, she wrote. He held his hands over his genitals and stood in the tub and rubbed himself with scented oils he bought at the market when he went to Setnesmoen for military training, where it was said that he nearly killed a man who had tried to take his lunch box. Ola used this oil only once or twice a year, usually at Christmas and Midsummer. But this was May, so it was serious.

A scalded pig, Ola put on his undergarments and his confirmation suit, and it wasn't too small because Ola was fully grown already when he stood before the pastor. Ola had a slender waist and a broad chest, just like the men in the ballads.

He climbed into the shay, hitched up to one of his military horses, and drove to Malmedalen.

At the farm where the three sisters lived he didn't even knock. He walked right in. They were all astonished, the farmer and his wife and their three daughters, but what else could they do when Ola said good evening but reply, good evening? They were just sitting down to dinner, so there was nothing to be done but offer the guest a seat as well. Ola sat at the table and ate so much that the three sisters laughed in amazement. Their mother had to go to the pantry for another loaf of bread, because the one she had sliced was gone halfway through the meal.

But once they had finished eating, the time came to learn what business had brought this man out here. The farmer waited for a long time for Ola to state his business unprompted, but he finally asked straight out why the Bortegard owner had come. Ola looked at the man in amazement and said that he figured the farmer would have understood, given that he was a man with three daughters. Such clear words did not require any further explanation, but the farmer still didn't know which Ola wanted.

"The prettiest," Ola said.

Yes, of course, but which was the prettiest?

Now the smiles were gone from the daughters' faces. They had never encountered such a self-confident man before. He came from Bortegard, they knew that, and they had heard it had once been a good farm, but was there much of it left since Ola had to share it with his brother?

The father chided his daughters for being arrogant and said if they continued to be silly, he would ask them to leave the room while he finished discussing the matter with their guest because he had fed them long enough. The eldest was in her late twenties.

But they didn't want to leave, because they wanted to have a say in this matter themselves, and they were curious to learn which one of them Ola thought was prettiest. Then Ola said that in his opinion the youngest one was the prettiest but that he could not be sure of that because they were sitting there so stiffly. He said, no one had moved since he had come into the house and they had taken their seats at the table. Ola wanted to see if their figures appeared to an advantage when they danced, he said.

"Appeared to an advantage! He looks like someone trying to appear to an advantage!"

But the father did not think this was a bad suggestion, because it happened that married couples grew tired of each other, he said, and usually this happened because they had not seen how they appeared in all situations. For example, when they danced.

"If you learn that your old lady looks like a scarecrow in the moonlight as you dance your wedding dance," said the wise Malmedal farmer, "it's too late to back out!"

The man went and got his fiddle and his daughters had to dance whether they wanted to or not, thank you very much, and then something remarkable happened. Because none of them wanted to be taken for the worst dancer, Ola was permitted to take them each for a turn, one after the other, for as long as he pleased. And he made the most of it, then also danced with their mother, who was so thrilled and enthusiastic that she said he could not leave the house until he took at least one of her daughters with him, if he didn't want two or three. Such a man.

The youngest caught Ola's eye. She began a strange, solitary dance, all the while keeping her eyes fixed on Ola. Ola could not help but notice that she smiled so happily and sweetly, and she did so while seeming to be swept away by someone other than herself. She danced right over to the door, and there she stood, waving goodbye, before she came dancing back over and sat down in Ola's lap. Then the two sisters yelled that there were limits! She couldn't behave like that! She was an embarrassment to the family, they said, the way she was offering herself!

But their father shushed them, and they were instructed to fetch a dram by their mother, who wanted to see how Ola handled himself when he was drunk. That was a daring experiment. It was known that Ola had almost killed a man over a lunch box when he was sober. Ola drank, and the man of the house played his fiddle, and the daughters danced like there was no tomorrow. But suddenly Ola set down his dram glass and said that he wanted a decision now. Who dared to go with him?

The older ones laughed and said that it shouldn't happen so fast. They thought there were still more details to be worked out.

"I will not leave until I'm carried out!" said the youngest, Sara. It could not be stated any more clearly.

"Then I will carry you!"

So he hoisted her up onto his shoulders and walked toward the door, and they laughed with their bellies. They didn't believe he would take off with her. But he held the girl as if in a vise as he untied his horse, and Sara started pretending she was at a loss, pinching and squirming, but that did not bother Ola. She squawked and complained a couple of times as he drove away. But they were scarcely out of sight when she started running her fingers through his curly hair, and then it wasn't long before she was hanging around his neck, and thank God it wasn't one of her sisters he had carried off.

That was how Ola had relayed the story to Gjertine, and Gjertine believed everything; Serianna did not; Nesje believed, by and large, it happened the way Ola said.

3

When Ola and Sara arrived at Bortegard, the story crashed to the ground, because then Gjertine saw how it was. She burned a fire in the stove so the kitchen was hot and delicious dishes were served before Ola showed Sara to the bed in the storehouse loft, where she would sleep on her own—if not until the wedding, then until they had the desire! Because Ola was not one to pounce on a woman as soon as they were alone. He wanted to live as a Christian man and to respect and honor Sara before and after she became his wife.

And so the fall passed, there was a wedding, and two months later Sara was with child.

It hit Erik suddenly that Ola was a married man, and Erik felt the need to find his own wife. Erik married one Anne Jørgensdotter Mittet in 1878, and in same year old Ingeborg died and the siblings were orphaned. They were free to do as they wanted, and to go where they pleased.

It was too cramped for two women to share the one house at Bortegard. Anne Jørgensdotter expressed quietly, then loudly, a demand for a home of her own. Her husband was a carpenter. Her village was near a good forest and lumber was plentiful. So Erik and Anne planned their own house and farm buildings on the portion of the farm that was theirs, some distance from the old farmhouse. That left Ola with the mortgage of one thousand kroner from Norges Hypotekbank; he struggled to make the payments, and the people knew about it. Sara sent letters to Serianna that explained how tough things had become. It was important that fall fishing not fail. Ola went out every day with Erik in his large *faering*. If that didn't go well either, he would have to fish over the winter off the coast from Bud.

One October evening that year, Nesje stood outside his house looking at the fjord. A vast, starry sky stretched above him, and it roused his thoughts and longings. He liked to stand out under the starry sky. From this point, he had an unimpeded view of the world that was his. You saw the fjord and the beautiful chain of mountains on the far side. Molde was no metropolis, but the town was a world in miniature. Light shone from the windows, and he saw the stream of light from Reknes Hospital, hidden behind a hill. He could also see the municipal hospital, the light from Simonsen's hotel, and the glow of lamps from Moldegaard Manor.

Nesje stood and contemplated the point of it all, people toiling away, living and dying in an unending chain, generation after generation and kin after kin. When you were in the middle of it, you forgot to ask questions. When you lived with a single-minded focus on the way to eat the following day, rarely did a man like Nesje have free time. When he did, he could have remarkable thoughts about the Lord's purpose, indiscernible to him, the mysterious ways of natural creatures.

Serianna came out and joined him. This meant that the boys were asleep, but she had other news. She moved her hands to her belly, and he understood.

4

That same summer, Gjertine learned that a young saddle and harness maker named Ole had come to the Slutås farm across the fjord in Frænen. He was from Ottadalen in what is now Oppland. Ane, his sister, was a serving girl at Ola's house, where Gjertine currently lived. Gjertine had seen this saddlemaker, Ole, one time in Vågøy Church, so she knew he was a handsome man.

The saddler, who went by Ole Ås, was twenty years old. But what she heard about the young saddler made Gjertine unhappy. He went from farm to farm up and down the fjord, showing off his leather skills making harnesses and saddles. To wealthy farmers, he demonstrated mastery in the art of upholstering because that was the latest fashion, for those who could afford it. Saddler Ole could make gilt leather out of calfskin for chairs and wallpaper, and he had the necessary equipment: edge bevellers, awls, creasers, stamps and embossers, and brushes to paint with. But gilt leather was expensive to produce, so Ane thought only the county governor or maybe the pastor could afford to hire him.

Gjertine had a comment to add to this as well. Gjertine snorted and scolded, saying that he ought to stick to saddlery and not fool around with fripperies.

But Ane would have more to say about her brother. Since it was a long way back home to Slutåsen, Ole often had to spend the night where he was working, and the serving girls and the farm girls, because he was such a fine-looking lad, often asked if he would stay until Saturday.

Gjertine scolded and scoffed. But Ane said her brother had told her that in the villages on the other side of the fjord young people were doing something called *bundling*. The girls there had Saturday nights off, and they were allowed to have male callers.

"What in the world is that supposed to accomplish?" Gjertine said, agitated.

Ane said that Ole was making a harness at a wealthy farm. Jenny had been left in charge while her father was away on an errand. Jenny didn't want to have any male visitors, Ane said, but apparently that was to fool the other boys, because as soon as the other boys gave up, Jenny went to Ole, sleeping in the storehouse loft, and explained how he should behave.

"And just what did she explain?" Gjertine said angrily.

How she wanted things!

"Things, what things?!"

"How she wanted things when they were together."

"Together? But they're not even engaged yet!" Gjertine yelled.

"I don't know more than that!" Ane yelled back.

"But then what happened?"

"Do you want to know or not?" Ane yelled.

Gjertine did not want innuendos.

Ole had to promise Jenny that he would never visit her empty-handed. He was to bring a sip of liquor. It wasn't that the girls drank—they maybe took a little swig to get in the mood—but the custom was that the boys would bring a little splash in a bottle, which they would deliver to the girls as soon as they had come up the ladder and through the window. And it was the girls who were in charge of the party, so that the boys didn't become drunk and worthless, as Ane put it, worthless both in conversation and the art of love.

"This sickens me," Gjertine said.

Ane didn't think Jenny minded being up in the loft with Ole, and he visited her almost every Saturday while her father was away. But by the third weekend Jenny's father had returned. Saddler Ole had been to Bud to buy liquor.

When Jenny's father heard the ladder against the wall of the house—Ole had grown confident and therefore careless, Ane said—he pulled on his pants as he cursed and swore, flew out the door, grabbed his blunderbuss, and out in the farmyard saw Ole up there on the ladder. He shot into the air. Ole jumped off the ladder to the ground, and hid himself in the hay in the barn.

"I wish he'd taken a load of buckshot to the backside!"
Gjertine said.

Gjertine already knew the rest of the story. In the winter
the county governor's son came to pay Jenny a proper court-
ing visit, and by summer Jenny was the wife of the county
governor's son, who had not only built his own house but
would eventually take the post of governor from his father.
Now Jenny called the shots at the governor's manor, where
they lit lamps in the garden whenever they had company and
kept a monkey that romped around in a ringmaster's coat and
offered people cigars.

Ole the saddler was unable to end the art that he had
mastered. In the ink and murk of night he paid visits to serving girls and farm girls, and the girls competed to let him
in, since he was agile and pleasant. It didn't do him any dis-
service that Jenny had mastered him in the arts of love. Ole
moved on to a farm where the woman who let him in was
none other than the young lady set to inherit the farm, and
who gave birth to a girl given the name Olava.

"At least the poor child doesn't know anything of her
parents' indecency," Gjertine said.

Gjertine had been very young when Ole's little daughter, Olava, was baptized in Vågøy Church, and she noticed
how handsome Ole was. He should be above breeding bastards, she thought. The saddler was mature enough to stand
up in church when the pastor asked the parents and godpar-
ents to stand. Nevertheless, she was upset when Ane asked
if Gjertine wouldn't like to go there with her sometime. Had
Ane lost her mind?

5

Nesje and Serianna's only daughter came into the world in the summer of 1879. She was named Ingeborg Kristine after their two mothers.

Ingeborg Kristine cried until midnight and slept until noon. Nesje walked around dazed. Birds began singing at three o'clock in the morning at Rekneslia, and at five he was up to tend to the day's work. At six, he walked down to the farm to sharpen scythes. The pay was two kroner per day, which was the same as he had received before, but times were tight, so he had to provide his own food. He peeked in to look at his sleeping children before he tiptoed out. How was he going to feed them all? After a long day of haymaking he came back up the hill practically on his hands and knees.

One day Nesje arrived home in time to catch Bastian Georg teasing a bull that had broken in from one of the mountain pastures. The boy could have been trampled to death if Nesje hadn't arrived when he did, but Nesje snatched the boy by the waistband of his pants and tossed him up onto his shoulder as he ran to safety. The bull charged until he crashed into the stone wall below the house.

When Serianna rushed out of the house and saw the bull staggering away half-stunned, she realized what had happened.

"I'm their mother," she said, "but you're their guardian angel!"

Nesje was too tired to respond. He sat down, pulled off his boots, and waited for his food.

6

Ola, the farmer at Bortegard, wanted a saddle on which to ride to church. After all, he owned a farm.. And as usual Sara did not contradict him. Ola asked Ane, the serving girl, to take a message to her brother Ole that he should make a magnificent saddle, because, while the other farmers were driving shays and carriages and carts, Ola liked to ride. Ane was afraid of what would happen when Gjertine saw her brother, and she thought she might ask Ola, but she was afraid that such nonsense might make him chase her off the farm.

So the saddlemaker Ola Ås came to Bortegard, and it was none other than Gjertine herself who opened the door. At first she didn't realize who was standing there, but it didn't take that many seconds before she recognized who he was. And if she hadn't realized before, it became clear when the saddlemaker made a rather straightforward comment about Gjertine's appearance. She stiffened, and he realized that he had gone too far, so he put a hand on her shoulder to excuse himself, but she slapped him and yelled to keep his fingers out of the serving dish. She hadn't meant anything other than a smack, but he turned his head a bit suddenly and ended up with a bloody nose.

Saddlemaker Ole had never met a woman like Gjertine. Gjertine was also alarmed and yelped so loudly that Ola came to see what the matter was. The saddlemaker said he had been unlucky; he had whacked himself in the face with his oar as he went to pull his boat up onto the beach.

Ola did not believe that. He could see that the injury wasn't from an oar. Gjertine was usually a person who wanted the truth, but this time she understood that it was best to keep quiet.

Ola directed his sister to help the stranger and tend to his nose with a boric-acid solution and clean cloth so it wouldn't get infected, because there would be no fancy new saddle for the Bortegard farmer if the saddler kicked the bucket, said Ola, who had started referring to himself as the "Bortegard farmer."

A man's chances of dying from a slap have probably never been smaller, but the sting was gone from Gjertine's lips. She opened the door for the stranger to enter with his cases, tool-box, and stand.

Gjertine brought the saddler to the kitchen and sat him on the bench while she built a fire under the kettle and got out the acid solution. Then she washed and tended his nose so deftly that an angel flew through the room. She and the saddler shared the room in silence. Ane rushed in and threw her arms around her brother's neck, but when she sensed the mood in the room she murmured a cautious "Welcome, dear brother!" Then he was shown the way to the storehouse loft, where he would sleep until he was done with the new saddle. Ola said Gjertine should show him the way while Ane prepared his meal.

Saddler Ole followed her up to the storehouse loft with his things as Gjertine carried up the bedding. She pulled out to its full width the extendable bed that was kept there. The saddler sat on a chair nearby and watched as she prepared everything. Since the bed was pushed in against the wall on three sides, the storehouse loft not being very big, Gjertine had to lie down across the bed to tuck the far edges of the sheet around the straw mattress. There lay Gjertine on her stomach, tucking. She could barely reach to the far edge of the bed, and her rear end bobbed up and down.

The saddler could not help himself. He reached over and took a handful. He thought it was worth risking another bloody nose. But nothing happened. Gjertine kept making the bed, and said in a quiet voice that he should desist. But he did not withdraw. When she stood up again, she was the one who said that she believed it was God's will that they should have each other.

Now it was the saddler's turn to ask: Shouldn't one heed the Lord's will?

Gjertine could not conceal that she liked him well, but if her slap had been harsh, that was because she couldn't bear the thought that as soon as he was done with Ola's saddle he would crawl into another woman's bed. The thought made her stomach turn.

The saddler sat down on the edge of the bed, and they talked together for the first time, the way people should talk when large, long-lasting consequences are about to coalesce, without those facing them having any control whatsoever. Ole was willing to make whatever sacrifice necessary, if they could only come to some sort of understanding with each other, but she shook her head and looked down. Some vast sadness had come over her. She was unable to believe he was capable of improvement.

"I'm done with all that," said Ole the saddler. "I am twenty-three years old, and I had my first child five years ago. It is time for me to settle down and make a home. What do you require, Gjertine?" he asked in his lilting dialect. "You can't think of anything I won't be able to provide!"

She slowly explained that he needed to acquire a new outlook, that he needed to repent and give up his old desires, and that she was making it a condition that he would abstain from all women for at least two years so she could have confidence in his ability to be a faithful husband. And if he made it for these two years, then he could come back and ask for her hand. And if he was able to put these habits of his on hold for that long, then he could count on her saying yes.

Saddler Ole said that it would be easy for him to meet these conditions if he knew what kind of joy would await his firm resolve. But given that the old Adam in him still had not fully expired, he might need to come to her every now and then, since he was forsaking all other women and it was the Lord's will that they should have each other.

But Gjertine would not go to bed with a man before the pastor had blessed their marriage. Two years was a suitable period. Gjertine, who was a strong reader, had picked up somewhere that after two years all the fibers in the human body are replaced so that the body is new. Ole the saddler's old body, which all those feckless women had caressed, would no longer exist.

Ole said that he accepted her terms, and that the two years would pass quickly.

In the kitchen, Ane had long since finished setting out the meal of oatmeal and sliced cured ham. There sat Ola, who was fresh in his marital bliss with Sara. They all wondered why Gjertine and the saddler were still up in the storehouse loft. Sara, who was young, had heard this and that about Ane's brother. Surely he wasn't so cheeky as to make a move on Gjertine in the middle of dinner?

Ola began to chuckle.

"No, no, that's out of the question!" Ola said. His sister wasn't that type of girl. But if he was wrong, and she had yielded, that would make one less mouth to feed here, because then the saddler would take Gjertine with him when he finished with the saddle.

They went out onto the front steps to listen and see if they could hear anything from the storehouse loft. The two turtledoves emerged, both unusually quiet. They came in and sat at the table. Gjertine said a whispered grace.

What transpired? They couldn't take their eyes off each other, but they couldn't seem to say anything to each other either. A curious mood prevailed for the duration of the meal as Ola tried to describe for the saddler what kind of saddle he was envisioning. The saddler was in another world. In the end, Ola stood up and made it clear that he wasn't going to waste his time sharing his vision when people weren't paying attention.

To everyone's great amazement, particularly Ane's, Gjertine explained that they were going to wait two years, and if the saddler managed to live a clean life, he would win her hand and her heart in gratitude.

"Good thing I decided to buy this fancy saddle," Ola said. "Because otherwise this wouldn't have come to pass."

Ola added that he didn't understand why a person would wait to begin a life that was already settled and decided on. And Sara agreed with her husband, pointing out that there were many enjoyable aspects of being a couple. But to avoid seeming indecent, she explained that on the rare occasions when you drank coffee there would be two of you, and that it was lovely to have someone to hold your hand when you went for a walk in the hills. Her remarks set her husband to laughing so hard he nearly sobbed.

At this point, Gjertine could have shared the secret born when Ole had stroked her bottom: this was a man she could travel to America with. But she, so often bold, just smiled as the saddler said that he would spend the next two years renovating buildings at Slutåsen.

While the women cleared the table, Ola made another meditative attempt to explain what he envisioned for this magnificent saddle, his saddle for church use and formal business, which he had been contemplating for many years. It had long since fallen out of fashion in these parts to ride to church. People walked or rowed, and they did so even if the distance was greater than it was from Bortegard, where the road to the church ran just around the corner of the house and you could see the church from the kitchen window. In the winter when the ground was frozen he could take a sleigh. But regardless of what other people did, Ola wanted to ride.

He had cleaned the hide from a big bull that he slaughtered the year before. He had washed this hide a hundred times in cold water and after that thirty times in hot water, until the hairs started to loosen, to clean the leather on both sides. Bark tanning took time. He had traveled far to find oak bark. Most people had to make do with birch or willow bark. For Ola's saddle, only the best was good enough. At the end of Romsdalen Valley was a farmer who supplied Ola with oak bark for a price. So Ola sailed in and paid the price, which no one else knew, not even Sara. To bark tan a hide, whether for shoe or sole leather, or in this case for a church saddle, the hide was soaked in a river until the hairs could be removed with a wooden knife or spade. The bark was crushed with a club and placed in a vat with water to extract the tannins, and Ola and his brother agreed that this was fun work, although the smell made you hold your nose.

The hide lay there for weeks until a thin middle layer remained unbarked because leather like that, with what's called a raw stripe, was totally stiff and impervious to wind and water, which was important for a saddle that would sit on the horse's back during the service. There was enough time for a downpour before the pastor got the body and blood of Christ distributed. It was easier for raw-stripe leather to crack, though, so it had to be oiled frequently, but Ola figured that he could handle that. Ola loved horses. Sure, he only had the two, but they glistened.

So thoughtfully, so very thoughtfully, Ola sat there on the day leading up to Christmas. He scraped and skudded the bull's hide until it was clean of flesh before he removed the tissue beneath the skin with a broad knife that he had forged himself. Finally he had gotten far enough to oil the leather and roll it up, but he unrolled it many times over the winter to look at it and oil it even more, until early summer came.

Many things could be said about how Ola presented the materials he had procured for his church saddle. He had bought a piece of gilded leather as decoration. The saddler thought this was hopeless. The gilded leather would be exposed to moisture, and it was goat leather tanned white. Ola thought it should be used along the edges of the bull leather so that Sara could also ride on this saddle without being miserable. The saddler wondered how long Ola expected the goat leather to hold up.

The saddler also wondered if Sara should maybe have her own saddle, maybe a side saddle, but she dismissed that idea. She wasn't a fancy woman, and on horseback she was happiest on Ola's pommel.

Best to follow local custom, the saddler thought. In two weeks he made an incredible saddle. He did not contradict his landlord. He tried to finesse the situation so that the result would be something that would be talked about for years to come. So he started stitching. But why squabble about something that has been decided? He made a channel for the stitching by pulling the groover along the leather's edge, then poked holes with the awl and stitched together the two pieces of leather that he had cut for the bottom of this showpiece. He wrapped a piece of leather around the oak that made the frame and pinched the edges together with an edge marker. Then he burnished the raw edges and finish the cantle, which would be Ola's seat when he rode to church.

Gjertine and the saddler had plenty of time to talk and get to know each other, but they kept their distance and tried not to get too close. When the saddle was finished down to the lambskin, Ola had to admit it that this was a saddle he would be proud of. And the gilded leather? The saddler had stitched that on with a couple of buckles and straps so that on highly formal occasions, when the weather was fair, it could be secured over the top of the saddle like a cap.

"As far as I'm concerned, the wedding can take place any time," Ola said. "Because I have a saddle I can ride to church."

"But the bride will walk," Gjertine replied.

The Saddler and His Bride

I

The winter that followed, saddler Ole went after what was left of the pine on the farm that his parents had bought. He felled the trees dozen after dozen, and when spring came he hauled the logs to the Tornes sawmill. He neglected his profession, the times were bad, and no one wanted new saddles or harnesses. People were mending their old ones.

Ole cut lumber for framing, joists, rafters, and siding, and then he started on a retirement cottage where his parents could live, because he knew that Gjertine would need her own space. His parents crossed themselves and couldn't understand why so many buildings were necessary. Couldn't they just have a room in the house that was already there? But the saddler said he wanted to have at least eight children.

When he finished the retirement cottage, it was summer in the year of our Lord 1880, and an unexpected message arrived: Ole's brother, Hans, one year younger than him, had earned good money in the town of Aalesund. There they needed men who were good with their hands, who could assemble freestanding stone walls and build buildings, and Hans could do that. But Hans developed an itch in his soul that couldn't be alleviated by smoking tobacco or fiddle music or singing or reading scripture. So, Hans Ås, who had accompanied his parents from Ottadalen to the Romsdal coast by foot when he was just a boy, shook the dust off the fatherland and took a steamer to Hull, and another to Liverpool, before boarding the boat bound for Quebec. His destination was a little town in Minnesota called Hancock, where he knew someone. He didn't even come home to say goodbye, which upset his parents greatly.

Ole the saddler didn't understand the point of such an outrageous journey. But two years had passed since he and Gjertine had made the promise, and the saddler needed to focus on his own horizon.

How often during these two years had he walked alone in his home in Slutåsen, burning and aching on Saturday nights! He didn't dare leave the farm, because he was afraid that his old ways would get the best of him. He didn't drink a dram. He just paced back and forth, up and down, and looked at all he built. He was a man in his prime. Why didn't Gjertine come to him? She could comfort him and see how nicely he had readied things. But this was the great trial, and they mustn't ruin it. Everyone knew it would be difficult for even Gjertine to remain chaste.

2

In the fall of 1880, Erik the cabinetmaker began building the foundation for a house on his section of the Bortegard estate, named in probate documents Ytrehoemsbakken, "Outer Hoem Hill." It was no castle: just a living room with a half-loft bedroom.

The lumber was shipped by the waves and the wind from Anne's hometown of Mittet, tucked deeply in the long Romsdal Fjord. Ola transported the lumber in his faering.

There were, of course, cargo ships that could have taken the load, but it would have been expensive. The expedition cost him one week of his time. As usual, he made use of the offshore breeze to travel out the long fjord in the morning and waited for the onshore breeze to pick up in the afternoon. The passage took them north through Julsundet, "Christmas Strait," and around Aukra Island before struggling into Frænfjorden with the logs and finally bringing them ashore at Ytre Hoem. This was in the fall. After the snows came they hauled the lumber by sled up to the site where cabinetmaker Erik built his home. It was two years before the walls were notched and the roof was on.

The cabinetmaker spared no effort. He worked early and he worked late. The walls of his parlor were tongue-and-groove–pieced panels that he planed himself with a decorative trim, and the window moldings had profiles. Likewise, Erik turned the posts for his stair railing on a lathe that he rigged under a little roof out front and operated by his own man power with a treadle. He pushed the treadle as he worked so that the wood, secured to the spindle, would spin around as he held a chisel to it. It was the home of a cabinetmaker.

As Erik worked day and night a suspicion darkened his mind. Could it be that Anne couldn't have children? They had been together for two years now, and Erik had not neglected his marital duties, but there weren't any babies in the spring. When Anne's face lit up with a smile, he thought she might have a secret to share. Each time he was disappointed, and when he discussed it with her she cried. She took all the blame. He knew that you can't force nature and said aloud that a good life could be lived without children. He even went so far as to generously suggest that maybe it was the Lord's will that Bortegard, which had been cleft apart, might be reunited by one of Ola's sons.

But Ola had only one son, Anne said, and it wasn't clear that he was a suitable candidate. She found his behavior a bit off, even if he was only two.

Erik building his home did not strengthen the friendship between the brothers. Ola was left with the expenses from adding on to Bortegard, and Sara having more space didn't change that. Not everything worked out for Ola. One could sooner say that misfortune followed him wherever he went. Their eldest son, Bastian Elisæus, had some sort of intellectual disability. Sara was the first to notice that he wasn't like other children, and she dreaded saying anything about it to Ola for a long time. But then one day, when Ola wanted to discipline the boy because he had spilled a pail of milk, Sara said it like it was: "Don't be hard on him—he's not like the others."

Ola stood there for a bit, looking at his little son, who didn't understand why he deserved a spanking and was busy chasing the cat, and Ola realized it was true.

"Do you think he'll learn to read and write?" Ola asked.

"I don't know, Ola."

"Do you think he'll be able to support himself?"

"I don't know."

"It's probably unreasonable to assume that he'll be able to take on the burden of running the farm from us one day when we're not able to do it anymore," Ola said.

"I don't know, I don't know," Sara said.

"It may be that we have to support him for as long as our lives spin within us," Ola said. Then he walked down to the field to hoe and weed. But the wind went out of his sail. He watched his brother's new house rise and he was unhappy.

3

Nesje and Serianna's fourth child at Rekneslia was born on his father's forty-third birthday: June 17, 1881. As Anton Edvard lay in his mother's arms, Serianna told Nesje, "There is a time for everything, and my time for bearing children is over."

He knew what she meant, and thought he was too young to give up what women and men enjoyed when they were young, but if that was how it was, that was how it was. Serianna watched him with calm eyes.

He cleared his throat and said, "You have given me four children. That is more than I deserve."

She smiled.

Nesje's sister, Karen, looked after things while Serianna recovered. It wasn't unpleasantly hot, but the crocheted curtains were drawn so the sunlight wouldn't be too bright. Nesje didn't start any real work. He had to keep asking if there was anything he could do.

Eventually Nesje realized the women would manage. It was almost Midsummer, and he was awaiting word from Adam Gørvell about when to begin the haymaking. He decided to make up some excuse to visit Adam Gørvell to have a word with him. His sister sent him with little Kristine, the new baby who was getting more attention than she liked.

He sat the little girl on his shoulders as he walked down toward town. He passed Humlehaven, where the gazebo that had stood by the path had been moved to the top of the hill, and where carpenters were midway through building a Swiss-style chalet in the garden. The exterior walls were going up, and the slate roof stood stacked nearby. This would be a sight: a Swiss-style chalet with a big flower garden, surrounded by big trees with whispering crowns.

Peter Dahl, who owned the place, did not appear to lack money, though there was nothing left of the fleet of clipper ships his father had owned in his day. Peter Dahl was a charming man, but had he achieved anything? He had the brewery, which he ran with his brother-in-law, Herlof, and people who brew beer can surely always count on finding buyers?

One would think that a plague had ravaged the Gørvell farm, so quiet it was. But Nesje felt at home and stepped into the yard. Rows of long-handled scythes hung on one wall under the storehouse. He walked over and felt their edges to see whether they were rusty. He needed to plan well ahead. It was his responsibility.

There weren't any people around; everyone appeared to be off farm. He realized it was Saturday morning and that Adam Gørvell had presumably left to go socialize with his clan. Nesje wandered around, strutting about like any Sunday farmer. He wasn't jealous of the gentry; he was content with who he was. It was the twentieth summer he would be making hay for the Gørvells, a bit of an anniversary, and although he knew that he tired more quickly now, he looked forward to getting going. He was lead haymaker, and a grown man couldn't run away from responsibility.

His little girl tottered along ahead of him, and it occurred to him that he liked taking care of his own child for once. There was no denying that he was fond of his two young boys, but if he were to be honest, there was something extra that came with having a daughter. Maybe men were more attached to their daughters, and especially when they only had the one, as he did. What would things be like with this daughter once she was grown? Would she settle down in the Molde area some-where, or would she travel far away? He was reminded of the proverb that children are ours on loan. Wasn't he lucky to stroll around with his little girl! Serianna had just blessed him with another son, and postpartum, both he and the kids were in the way. But Karen had taken the boys to the woods with her on some errand, real or imagined. Personally, Nesje didn't seek his peace in the forest. When he didn't have anything particu-lar in the offing, he felt drawn to the farm.

Then he heard some movement in the stable, and the manager, Lars, came out with the brown stallion in the fancy harness, and led him over to the shay which stood freshly painted and gleaming on the barn ramp. Then Adam Gørvell emerged from the house and stood impatiently while Lars hooked the horse to the shay so that his patron could drive away. Only then did Adam Gørvell notice that his lead hay-maker was standing a short distance away. He called to the lead haymaker, and Nesje picked up his daughter so she wouldn't get her shoes dirty or dart in front of the horse. He noticed that Adam Gørvell also had a little girl, who had turned two in January. She was quite precocious. She could tell you what her name was, and when Adam Gørvell asked, she wasn't shy.

Adam Gørvell was in a hurry and wanted to get going, but not until he found a piece of candy in his pocket for Kristine, and as the father made sure the little girl said thank you, Adam Gørvell climbed up into the shay. With the reins in his hand he seemed impatient as he asked his lead haymaker, Was there something that Nesje wanted on this Saturday afternoon?

He just wondered when the haymaking would begin, Nesje said.

Adam Gørvell responded that they would start in two weeks.

Yes, that was what he had been thinking himself, Nesje said.

"You've been with us for many years now, Nesje," Adam Gørvell said. "How many has it been, actually?"

Well, this was his twentieth summer, Nesje said. Otherwise he was just out for a walk with his daughter since his wife had given birth this morning, and the mother and the newborn needed some quiet.

What was this? He was a father again? Now Adam Gørvell had to offer his heartfelt congratulations! And wouldn't you know, the man leapt out of the shay, came over and shook Nesje's hand, and gave his servant a krone! Not all the gentry would have cared, Nesje thought. Adam Gørvell wanted to know if he had more children, how many children all together—as if this were the first time it had occurred to him that Nesje had a life outside of his work. Nesje explained that the little boy who had arrived today was his fifth child, if he included Hans from his first marriage.

That was a whole herd! But this wasn't what made the day memorable. It was the words that Adam Gørvell spoke next. Nesje would carry them with him as long as he lived.

"*To think that you've been making hay with us for twenty years!*" Adam Gørvell said.

"The years pass quickly," he replied.

He was forty-three now. His best years were behind him. No employer would care if he should get it into his head to offer up his services. If he were thirty-six, that would be something else. It was all downhill from here. There was no getting around that.

Adam Gørvell leapt back up onto the shay. It was hard to tell that the man was over fifty. Adam Gørvell put on his black driving gloves and drove off, kicking up a cloud of gritty dust as he flew past the gateway.

Nesje walked back up the hill and entered his house with his girl asleep on his shoulders. His sister, Karen, had gone home, and the boys were in bed. He fixed his own supper and, since both mother and baby were asleep, Nesje sat to write a letter to Hans. When he received letters from Hans, he always read them to Serianna, whose facial expression would usually show if she agreed or disagreed. She often thought that Hans had rather valiant plans. Hans hope to be installed as a store manager in a year or two, but if he was to accomplish that, he would not be able to visit his father back home. He had three new siblings he had not seen. He didn't ask about them much either.

It pained Nesje that Hans was so indifferent about his nearest kin. He knew that relatives aren't something you choose. It's not like with your friends, not even like taking a wife. Your kin are your own flesh and blood, you are one of them, and you belong with them no matter how far you go. But Hans just wanted to know if his father was doing well or if he felt his age. It was as if the boy felt guilty for leaving. It was strange that the boy phrased it as if the father were an old man. So Nesje wrote a few lines about each of the children, about Bastian Georg now six, Eilert who was almost five, and about the sister and baby brother. He would have sent a portrait, but it cost money to be photographed, so that would have to wait until the following spring, when Anton Edvard was old enough that his facial features could be made out.

4

There was to be a wedding at Bortegard. Serianna and Nesje would not attend. You cannot travel to a wedding with a newborn. But Serianna was on her feet when the trial period for Gjertine and the saddler was over.

Ola didn't spare any expense this time either, because this was the last of his sisters to be leaving home now. He slaughtered the fatted calf, as they say, so that it would be a well regarded wedding. Perhaps he should have set aside some kroner for the mortgage lender. Then for music he called in the sons and daughters of the quack doctor to play mandolins and Guri the fiddler at a farm that had once been a manor.

The guests came by boat from far and away: the Slutås folk, who were a fairly small group of newcomers, and those who came from Stavika, also a small contingent after Lars Stavig took his children with him to America. Neighbors from Hoem had to be fetched to fill out the numbers for the bridal procession.

The day arrived. The groom came across from the other side of the fjord with his parents. In the box his mother had was a valuable document: a letter from America, from his brother, Hans, which had arrived the day before.

Gjertine was a woman who wanted to have everything right, and because the saddler never contradicted her, she could live with him. Gjertine was lucky, because there weren't many men in that day who would have tolerated life with a woman calling the shots, but it was all right with Ole.

Others thought that it was the saddlemaker who was lucky, and that he knew it himself. He needed a wife who would tolerate his having a bastard from a previous tryst, and Gjertine more than tolerated that: she adopted Olava as her own.

It was a joyful summer wedding arranged at that time *when nights are light as days*, as the Ivar Aasen poem says, and Gjertine was a fair and beautiful bride. It was a sunny Sunday, with both sun and rain, so that there were a few drops on the bridal crown to signal a happy marriage.

They walked, the bridal couple, because Gjertine wanted to walk on her own feet away from Bortegard to the altar in Vågøy Church. They walked down the old cart track behind Bortegard, where there were still skid marks across the road from back when sleds were driven before the farms got wheeled carts. Then they walked down the old church road to the beach. There Gjertine took off her shoes and her stockings, too, and then she walked barefoot over the muddy ground, where the water, which was at high tide, reached up to the middle of her calf, before she climbed up on the beach on the other side.

There was a new pastor, and face to face with this pastor and before God, Gjertine and the saddler exchanged their assents. Gjertine, who had been so serious in her youth, had come to see that authentic joy was not an abomination to God. She flung herself into the wedding dance as the mandolin players started the music. Little Bastian Elisæus, Ola and Sara's son, walked around in his new fancy clothes, and although he didn't make a peep, he danced to the music.

America was a topic of conversation that night. And the party was over well before Gjertine stood up on a chair, with her wedding veil reaching right down to the floor, and read the letter that her brother-in-law had sent from Hancock,

Minnesota. It said he had found work as soon as he arrived and that he wanted to look around and see where he should claim land. He thought that anyone who had faith in the future and longed for a better life should do the same thing he had done, and he even suggested that his parents, who were only in their fifties, should come so that he could take care of them in the evening of their lives.

His parents, Sivert and Ingeborg, looked at each other and felt quite proud of their son's intrepidness. And they knew they had to travel to where he was if they were to see their son again, because he wasn't going to return.

This story could certainly end there, and everything would head in the right direction. But there is one more thing to mention. After the commotion died down and the wedding couple retired for the night, Ola could not sleep. Many thoughts came to him now that he had fulfilled his obligations to his siblings and married his youngest sister off so well. Now he had only himself and his family to think about. He toppled out of bed, still drunk, to go and drink milk until his thirst was gone, and to relieve himself too. Surely everyone else was asleep by now, the groom's parents in the cottage and the bridal couple in the storehouse loft?

Ola stepped out onto the front stoop and gazed out at the fjord. It was so light at this time of year that he could have read a book if he had wanted to. Then he heard such shouts of delight from the storehouse loft. They shuddered through him, marrow and bone. It was unmistakably Gjertine, wild with joy and elation.

Ola thought, sadly, that this was what happened when women were too strict on themselves: Once the dam breaks, then comes the deluge. He went back inside to Sara, who had woken up in an empty bed. Ola said the newlyweds needed to leave first thing come morning. If people didn't want to exercise their bliss with modesty, they could go home to their own mountain, where they could scream as much as they wanted.

5

Haymaking began two days after the wedding.

Nesje felt worn out after the first day of scything. He sat outside the house and Serianna brought the food out. Herring and potatoes and cold milk, food for a workman. He looked at his life's work—almost three acres of land he cleared and the house and barn he built. He had built in the middle of the parcel. He had to carry the grass that grew below the house uphill with a hayfork, and the land above the house was even less accessible. He had to carry cow dung up there in a vat he carried on his back. His farm was too small for him to feed a draft animal. But people everywhere had draft animals and machines now. It wasn't easy to get help when you did things the old way and used yourself as a horse. Maybe his place would be too small for those who came after? Would his children reject the land he had cultivated as too poor and meager?

He thought of the little boy in the cradle, so like himself and yet so unfamiliar. Maybe this was the boy who would take over the place. Maybe he would get his hands on more land and expand it into a real farm. The other two sons were too close to himself in age. He and Serianna must work this land as long as they had the strength, because this land couldn't feed two families. Bastian Georg and Eilert would have to go out into the world to feed themselves, and probably little Kristine as well. But the youngest, Anton Edvard—maybe he could provide Serianna and himself with a dignified old age.

He went inside and looked again at the baby boy, who seemed just as distant. But the thought came that this boy might also not stay in Rekneslia. What if all the children went on their way and he remained with Serianna when they were old?

He was being pessimistic because he was worn out! One day he would buy this land, and if it was too small, he would buy an additional parcel. It made sense for his descendants to follow after him, on the same steep footpaths, under the pine trees that had grown to a towering height.

Yet another summer he carried the hay up the steep hills to the barn and tossed it in, load by load. This summer he didn't receive much help from Serianna. She had enough to do. Three children were running around her now, and the fourth lay in the cradle.

Nesje cut his grain with a sickle. It was a good crop. He got four barrels of barley and ten barrels of oats. He got the potatoes up, sixteen bushels, and he dug up the root vegetables, turnips and kohlrabi, eight bushels. After the crops were in he put his youngest son on his back on Sunday and walked down to the dock with Serianna and the other three children. Hans and his wife rowed over there from Kringstadhagen, and they all made the journey to Bolsøy Church, where the pastor christened Anton Edvard Knudsen Nesje on Sunday, October 16, 1881.

6

The marital delight that Gjertine felt after she married Ole did not fade when they returned to his farm. Gjertine ran her hands over the freshly painted walls and took the sheets and the coverlet out of the big travel bags she had brought.

But everything had been expensive, and there were times when the saddler was away early and late. Often he didn't come home at night, too far away, or the work he was doingrequired him to stay for at least a week when he came to a place. He had to keep at it to pay for everything he bought for his bride and he owed the merchant in Tornes for linseed oil and ochers. He hadn't yet paid for the sawing he did at the Tornes lumber mill either. The saddler had not budgeted well. He had been so focused on making things nice for Gjertine's arrival that he was gone when she finally came.

During the first years, that didn't bother her. In the second year, she had a son they named after Ole's father, Sivert. When Gjertine was awake, she couldn't take her eyes off of him. The boy's grandmother, who had thought that she would have grandchildren to relish in the evening of her life, found herself without access to the child. Her daughter-in-law reigned supreme.

Then a letter came from Hans Ås, who yet again wrote that his aging parents must come over to him, and he would look after them better than anyone could in poor Norway.

What should they do? This summer, Markus Hustad left Hustad, and Ole, Sivert, and Hans Løset from Frænen left for South Dakota. Lars Stavig had written to his brother describing all the land available in Day County, where he was going to settle down with his family after six years in Minnesota: a little stream of emigration from Romsdal.

One day when Ole wasn't home, his parents asked Gjertine what she thought. Gjertine could not pretend. She said it was best for them to go, because Slutåsen could hardly feed more than one family. While that was true, of course, it was not welcome to Ole's parents. They took this to mean that their daughter-in-law wanted them gone. But though they thought it was wrong to be driven from a farm they had bought and tended, Sivert Ås and Ingeborg left that summer, just after little Sivert came into the world, to travel to Hancock, Minnesota, and from there the following spring they would travel into the Dakota prairie. Things felt empty in their absence. The fall evenings were long and dark.

"What are you thinking about, Gjertine?" the saddler asked when he finally came home to stay for the weekend. "You're like a stranger in your own home!"

Then Gjertine turned to her husband, and tears came to her eyes.

"You'll have to put up with me, Ole," she said. "I'm so grateful and happy for everything you've built here, but is this really where I was meant to come ashore?"

"Give it time. You'll settle in eventually," the saddler said, but he wasn't particularly happy either.

After a long time away, Gjertine sought out other Readers in the village. It was a long walk to where they held their meetings, but that didn't matter to her. There was something else that was worse: they had started discussing whether it was right according to God's word to baptize babies. Such a thing would never happen among Paul and the other apostles, they said. The fall when Gjertine came to Slutåsen, they decided everyone needed to be baptized again. It was deep into the winter when a flock of women and men put on the white robes they had sewn out of sheets to be dunked in the Tornes River by their leader. Then Gjertine did not attend anymore. Two years later, she had her second child, who was given the name Sanna, the same name that Ola and Sara at Bortegard gave their fourth child, also born that year.

That spring a letter came from the town of Starbuck, Minnesota. It said that Ole's father had died on the journey from Minnesota to South Dakota. Hans and Ingeborg had found a grave for him in Starbuck.

7

Before the ground froze and the snow settled, Nesje needed to add new land to what he had plowed. He got up at five thirty and walked to the Gørvell cowshed. He was home again by ten thirty, at which point he ate his first meal. Then he marked out the gravel and dirt with his tools. His spade scraped a rock at the bottom of the ditch. He banged with the pickax until he got the rock loose at one corner, then got in there with the crowbar to pry it free and into the daylight. He wiped his sweat with the back of his hand before kneeling down and grasping the rock with both hands, hoisting it up onto the edge of the ditch in one single lift. Once there, he threw a rope around it and pulled it through the sand and dirt and onto the rock wall by the edge of the field. Then he returned to the ditch and noticed water where the stone had been. In the running water was something white. There was an old pine stump there he hadn't seen before. He spent the rest of the morning digging around the stump. As the wind picked up, the cold air bit his fingers. He chopped through thick roots that extended from the sides, then threw a rope around the stump and fed this rope through a pulley secured to a boulder. But he could not budge it.

He went to his porch and poured water in a basin, washed his face, and cleaned his hands. Then he walked down to the Sættem house, where twenty-year-old Olaf Sættem lived, and he talked to Olaf's mother, Julia. If Olaf could come up after he came home and give Nesje a hand, he could move a stump that he couldn't manage on his own.

He thanked her and went home to rest for half an hour. When he woke up and looked out the window, he saw that it wasn't just Olaf who had come, but a whole gang coming to his ditch at dusk. He hurried to greet them. They were much too nicely dressed, he said, and they brushed it aside. It wasn't going to stop them from pulling a rope! They stood all in a line and pulled on the rope that he had fed through the pulley. His two little sons got to join in, and they all hollered yo, ho, and there came the stump with a heave ho, up the ditch and onto solid ground. Nesje was overjoyed. He thanked them all, shaking all their hands, and the men walked back to the Sættem house smiling.

He needed to head inside now; it was late. He looked at the stump, which gleamed at the edge of the ditch in the fall darkness, and the sight gave him such encouragement. As he had gathered up his tools and removed the rope from the root and was going to call it a night, he heard singing from the Sættem house. There was a crowd, and their song rang over all of Rekneslia. That's why there had been so many men there: It was a mission meeting.

Nesje knew that he would have been welcome if he had washed up and put on a clean shirt. But that wasn't for him. He wasn't one of them. Sometimes he felt like it would be nice to belong to a larger community, but Nesje was a family man, and that didn't leave much time, not with a workday like his.

Bastian Georg and Eilert, who should have been in bed, came running outside, and to his surprise he heard Eilert humming along. He had to show them how happy he was that the stump was out. So he picked up the boy and said, you're not going to become a missionary and travel to China, are you? And when Serianna came to bring them inside, he told her the whole story, which made her laugh. They sat by the open window for a while even though it was chilly as the full moon rose over the fjord. The moon lit up the Sættem house in Rekneslia, and they listened to the song down below.

8

In 1884 the house was assessed for fire insurance. For years the assessed value had been twelve hundred kroner, but it was lowered to eight hundred. With that big flock of children and all his work, Nesje had not been able to keep it up so well. The roof leaked a bit, and the unpainted paneling on the west wall was rotting. Maybe, Nesje thought, the assessor noticed that the local farmer was struggling and granted him a more affordable premium? If so, this was a handout from someone who took pity on a fellow human being, Nesje wrote to his son, but his son never replied on the subject. It was as if it weren't important.

Throughout the winter, Nesje wrote letter after letter on a common theme: *I want to see you, new things are happening here in Molde all the time!* He could hardly stop reporting the local news. The ink in one letter wouldn't be dry, and sometimes he left even [?], before he needed to write a new one.

In midspring the town council in Molde decided to demolish the old church and build a new one on the lot. Two days later, on Norway's national holiday of the 17th of May, the flag was standing out straight, dust swirling to the west. The official celebration was a parade with banners that ended with a cheer and the national anthem. The Circus Oriental was in town and its trick riders had made the parade festive by riding in front with little flags.

After the parade, some attended the circus and others went to the party hosted in city hall by the temperance movement's Good Templars. As evening approached, someone noticed smoke coming from the church and yelled, "Fire in the church!"

There was a strong northeasterly wind. There were various parties in town, many people were the worse for drink, and many were watching the circus, which was perilously close. The flames engulfed the spire and rooftop instantly; the church was doomed. They managed to rescue the altar silver, most things in the nave, and a large wooden cross.

The wind sent thick smoke over the town. Everyone concentrated on preventing the fire from spreading to other buildings. Verger Johansen's home was damaged but didn't burn. One man was smothering a small fire at the carpenter's house with a hat and sweater when he saw the merchant Samuel Pettersson's house burning along with four other farmhouses. Almost simultaneously a barn and a wharf's decking caught fire. People sat on roofs watching over the town until late in the night. In the morning bits of hemp from the cannon salute on the hill above the church were found throughout the cemetery. The fire likely started in the wadding used in the cannons, but no one could say for certain.

Despite the losses, there was a sense of optimism in town, as if it had been the finger of God telling them to start on the new church!

Things were happening in Molde, more so than in most places, Nesje wrote Hans. The increase in tourism gave people hope for better days.

The Grand Hotel opened on Midsummer in 1885, a month after the fire. Dressed up, Nesje and Serianna stood with people of their class outside the fence of the Grand while high-society folks celebrated inside. The garden wasn't finished, but a fence had been built so that onlookers wouldn't push their way into the building. A pianoforte was on the patio and an orchestra with both wind and string instruments wore festive uniforms. One by one, residents stood and spoke, all representatives of the liberal Venstre party. But the proprietor of Moldegaard Manor, Ulf Møller, came out to greet "the masses," as he called them, with a white handkerchief that he waved back and forth in the wind.

As they walked home, Nesje and Serianna, with their four children ahead of them, had plenty to talk about. That's when they saw him by the pier: the famous author, Henrik Ibsen.

He had not attended the party at the Grand Hotel. He was a short, striking gentleman wearing a strange, tight-fitting coat that seemed unnecessary in the mild weather. He wore a wide-brimmed hat, which he was holding on to his head, as if he were afraid a wind would pick him up. Nesje carried his worn coat over his arm. Nesje could see the great Ibsen was a short man when it came down to it, nor did he have much of a good name for himself. You could read about anything in the newspapers. Here stood the great Ibsen on Alexandra's Pier staring into the water. They wrote about him in the big Swedish newspapers, Mr. Ibsen, who was the topic of the day. Ibsen had recently released a new play, *The Wild Duck*, that was going to be performed everywhere: Berlin, Paris. Nesje had never seen a play with his own eyes, but he paid attention. Nesje imagined Ibsen was a radical. Nesje himself was not an adherent of the conservative Høyre party. The conservatives were opposed to suffrage for people like him, and he had no right to vote, but he was afraid of freethinking, and unfortunately Norway's greatest poet, Bjørnstjerne Bjørnson, was dangerously close to it. Nesje had read in the local newspaper that Bjørnson said he didn't approve of anything in the name of Christianity other than the personal relationship between the individual and God's son, Jesus Christ, and that people should try to live up to Jesus's good example.

Nesje was no churchgoer, although he had been there more often after Gjertine shared her healing spell. He clung to what he had learned in his childhood home, what one might call his childhood faith. Bjørnson was one thing, and Ibsen another. Who knew if the one was better than the other? Ibsen had global renown, but here in town he wasn't especially well regarded. He had no relationships with the people here at all, while Bjørnson drove from house to house and from social occasion to social occasion every time he visited the town of his youth. Bjørnson wrote *Synnøve Solbakken*, and both Nesje and Serianna had read that book before they were together. What Ibsen imagined he didn't know much about. But the word was that he wrote some trash about married life in a play called *Ghosts*, and that was why he wasn't invited to visit Humlehaven.

It wasn't easy to guess why Ibsen had come to Molde. There he stood on the pier staring down into the sea. People said he had dropped a krone and hoped to spot it.

"Do you think Ibsen dropped a krone coin today?" Nesje asked his wife, but he received an unexpected response.

"You know full well he was searching his own heart and mind!" Serianna said. "He just looks down into the water to keep any other impressions from impeding him in that." And then she said something that Nesje had never heard in all their ten years together: *"Heavy hammer, burst as bidden, to the heart-crack of the hidden!"*

"What was that?" Nesje asked.

"What was what?" said Serianna, playing coy.

"What you just said there!"

"Something Ibsen wrote," Serianna said. "I read it at the Frænen library! It was probably actually one of Jervell's books that he gave away."

So Jervell, the provost in Aalesund, had once bought a book by Ibsen? So strange.

Heavy hammer, burst as bidden? Serianna was the biggest mystery. Was she going to say more about the poem? The boys ran on ahead: Bastian Georg was ten, Eilert eight, Anton Edvard only four, but he had a mind of his own when it came to making his way. Kristine, who was six, stuck with her parents. She was careful with everything that was hers, and she was probably thinking that she mustn't get her shoes dirty.

Much had happened over the past summer in the area they were walking. After a fire had been set by children in the woods in Reknesskogen, Gørvell turned part of the woods into a park. At the site of the fire he planted all kinds of plants, and the Town of Molde's Residents' Association built paths through the terrain. Nearby, on the other side of the path that Nesje walked every morning, was Humlehaven, which had never been in fuller bloom. Margarete Dahl, sister of the Consul, was in charge of the practical details. An old gazebo shaped like a small Greek temple with four columns in the front, which was built before Nesje began his daily walks down the path down the left side of Humlehaven, was moved to a corner of the garden. It was covered with ivy, woodbine, morning glory, climbing roses, honeysuckle, and clematis.

They were building a hilltop pavilion as an attraction for the tourists who came to town in summer. This was not a good time for those who worked in farming or fishing, but Molde had become a destination. People with shops did well in the summer. Ships anchored in the fjord because there wasn't yet a way to dock at the shore, so ferrymen brought the travelers from the ships to the docks. Most of them brought so much clothing with them that they needed help getting to the Holms Sisters' hotel. Those who were going to assist Germans and Englishmen needed to learn foreign languages, and Nesje wondered aloud if his sons would need to learn them, but when he told Serianna this she just looked at him.

Serianna and Nesje said to each other: the town was no longer recognizable. In the winter, the town was the way it had always been, a dark hole. But in spring and early summer, steamboats came and went several times a day, the newspapers were full of advertised departures, and the ship clerks had to announce departures in advance to get the goods loaded aboard. The steamer *Henrik Wergeland* traveled to Christiania and Throndhjem. The ship named after a recently deceased violinist, *Ole Bull*, set its course for northern Norway, and the DS *Throndhjem* made its way to Hammerfest. Flocks of visitors were rowed ashore, and every week the newspapers printed the names of the most distinguished ones.

There was high society in the town, too, people living a different life, but Nesje and Serianna no longer ignored what was happening around them with their heads down and focused on their own affairs. They sometimes discussed what "society" was up to and what the newspaper had to say about politics. The *Romsdals Budstikke* had made its way into their home. They had a subscription shared with the Sættems, who received the paper first. Nesje had a wife who could not only read the paper but also wanted to discuss politics with him. She had gotten it into her head that women should have the right to vote, and Serianna had started smoking a pipe again. She had a clay pipe, and when evening came she lit the pipe and smoked while she read *Romsdals Budstikke* under a paraffin lamp or by the natural light of the summer evening. Like Gjertine, Serianna had been a reader all her life, from their early days at the Frænen public library.

The oldest boys were encouraged to read everything in *Romsdals Budstikke*. What they grasped was another matter. Bastian Georg asked too many needless questions, and his father didn't like it. And Bastian Georg found it strange that some people lived without working, while others toiled for their whole lives to stave off hunger. Bastian Georg mustn't forget that he stemmed from good people who had just been a little *unfortunate*. But what about Serianna? Why did she stand by nodding as the son wracked his brains over questions there weren't any answers to? Serianna couldn't vote, but the liberal Venstre party had her full and complete sympathy.

Nesje walked up over Rekneshaugen Hill with his family on this Sunday afternoon, and he saw himself, saw himself as he lifted Anton Edvard onto his shoulders and as the two oldest children clung to their parents' pant legs because Bastian Georg wanted to discuss politics. What an alert ten-year-old! Nesje strolled along in deep happiness: four children, and a son from before, to boot, who was a clerk in Throndhjem and might even come home for Christmas! He felt a pang: how long could this kind of happiness last? He knew that happiness isn't something that likes to stick around. But on this August evening there wasn't a cloud in Nesje's sky.

Bastian Georg dwelled on every injustice he could find. Some people lived in houses, some in palaces, some didn't get to live at all. Many were distressed and dejected, even in Molde. Sometimes they even came to the door at Rekneslia and begged for a glass of milk or a piece of bread.

There were many people at Reknes Leprosy Hospital living in the most extreme poverty, with open sores, and weren't people struck down in the their prime of youth by leprosy, and didn't these people often come from families that labored more than was necessary?

Nesje couldn't deny any of this; that was the way of the world, but he still felt uneasy talking about it.

"Why cast a shadow over this beautiful Sunday?" he asked. "Not another word!"

They should set this aside, as they walked over the bog hole past the Sættem house, so that they could see the blessings God had given them as they reached their own home.

It was a summer moment Nesje didn't know he would see again. He stood there with his four children and his intelligent wife. They stood outside the house and the barn, and everything was in peak condition. The barley was yellow on the western slope. The grass had grown back in the meadow since the first cutting. What more could a person expect from life?

Gjertine's Plan

I

Ole the saddler's parents gave up the old country and traveled to Hancock, Minnesota. The retirement cottage at Slutåsen stood empty for a while before a lodger couple came. They had lost everything when their house and barn burned to the ground in a storm. They worked at Slutåsen for food and clothes and a tenth of the crop, which they sold to bring in money for the rebuilding.

The arrangement meant Ole could once again travel and make harnesses, and Gjertine didn't need to milk every night. She could be with her children, including the saddler's daughter, Olava, who lived with her father and Gjertine during the summers.

But when Gjertine was alone there, thoughts came to her that she couldn't find a way to share. Wasn't there more to life than this? They were making a living, but what kind of a future could they offer their children?

Times were not good standstill and declined; wages went down in the country and in town. They were at too high an elevation for the grain to ripen every year.

Ole was now constantly on the road. He made harnesses, but few who needed harnesses could afford to buy them. Mostly he mended old things: patching and oiling and replacing cinch straps and bridles. That wasn't what he preferred, but what are you going to do?

When there was mail service, Gjertine walked about three miles to the post office, though a letter rarely came. She had a worry inside, and this walk was her break from the children and the lodgers, who watched the children while she was away for two to three hours.

One day in June 1885, there was a letter written and postmarked in Roslyn, South Dakota, where Ole's brother and mother had settled. Gjertine stood and held it in the sunshine, weighed it in her hand, studied the foreign stamps, turned it over, looked at the writing on the back. Ingeborg had added in her own maiden name, Svarre, in the middle: *Ingeborg Svarre Ås*. Of course the letter wasn't addressed to Gjertine. It was to *Saddler Ole S. Ås*.

The postmaster was more curious than Gjertine thought, and wanted to know what the emigrants wrote. He hinted desperately that Gjertine should open it so that all could benefit from the good news, as he put it. They knew so many people over there now, the Hustad family and the folks from Løseth.

Gjertine made it clear to the postmaster what his business was. Gjertine was dying to read it, but could she open a letter addressed to her husband?

She walked along the edge of the road on a day too hot for town, almost seventy degrees. Naked legs stuck out under her cotton dress. She maybe had a couple of mosquito bites, but she didn't mind. Whosoever goes without stockings will find that the mosquitoes bite. She had her hair up in a bun.

Once she was out of eyesight of the post office, she sat down by the roadside on a rest stone, where she debated with herself what her husband would say. Maybe he wouldn't notice? If she said that a letter arrived for him from America, wouldn't he just ask her to read it?

Gjertine tried to open the letter in such a way that she could glue it shut again later, but that didn't go well, and perhaps she thought of what it said in the Bible about how man and wife shall become one flesh? Then she lost her patience and tore it open.

Her brother-in-law, Hans, whom Gjertine had never met, and his mother, Ingeborg, had built a large house on the Dakota prairie on 320 acres of land. That was almost 1,300 *mål*! The only thing the Norwegians in Roslyn lacked, it said, was a good saddler.

Gjertine looked around. No one could deny the incredible beauty of such a summer's day by the Frænfjorden. But the quiet and the hum of insects, the scents of flowers, and the birdsong that surrounded her couldn't guarantee a good life.

Gjertine grew afraid of what would happen to her now. A tremendous anxiety grew, and she couldn't sit still. She had to get up and walk—yes, she ran up the hill, because she was young and fast, but it was three miles and she was gasping for breath by the time she was finally inside her own kitchen and could sit down at the table to rest. Her mind raced. The sound of the wind on the Dakota prairie filled her, mixed with something else.

Since she had been of confirmation age, Gjertine read the Bible almost every single day, and the stories of departures and how people left lived inside her. She thought of how Abraham traveled from Ur of the Chaldees and came to Canaan's land. She pictured the people of Israel in the thousands fleeing from Egypt to find their way to the land of milk and honey, and though Gjertine was not an Israelite, she was the same as the hundreds of thousands of people who left poverty and a lack of freedom in Europe to find a new life across the ocean.

That morning, so quiet at Slutåsen that you almost couldn't believe there were the children and the lodgers nearby, Gjertine made a decision. She couldn't sit any longer, she had to get up, she needed to find out where everyone else was. There came Olava running up from the retirement cottage with Sanna in her arms and Sivert at her heels. Olava said that she wanted to go visit her mother. Olava thought she was old enough to go by herself. She was eight years old! But Gjertine couldn't let her go. No one had seen a bear or a wolf in these parts for a long time, and the young girl was reliable, but what would it be like when evening arrived, and they had no idea if she was safe or not?

Gjertine decided to take her, and maybe she could walk off her nerves. The lodger woman would have to watch Sivert and Sanna again. Gjertine and Olava packed a change of clothes, nothing more, and walked hand in hand down the long road to Løset. Gjertine stopped before they entered the yard. She didn't have any desire to talk to Olava's mother. They didn't get along so well, and it was best if they didn't see each other.

She stood a stone's throw away, listened as the young girl calls to her mother, saw the mother come out on the step. Olava waved and went into the house with her mother, and Gjertine headed for home.

When she reached home, the yard and the house were unfamiliar to her. They had turned themselves against her. Then she started cleaning up her things and thinking through what she would take. As she put the two little ones to bed, her thoughts were on roadways. How soon could they leave, and what if the saddler didn't want to? In the other families, men were those who brought up the idea of emigrating. It was the women who were tied to the place, to the earth, to relatives and the life that was built. But what did Gjertine care about dead things? You could just get new things, settle in as your income permitted, and build up from the ground in a place where the future was open.

Gjertine had no clear picture of what the Dakota prairie would look like. She imagined the prairie and the ocean as looking similar, the journey across the ocean as an induction into life on the endless plains.

2

It was now or never. The shortage of saddlers in Dakota was her most dependable trump card.

Thus she didn't mention the letter when the saddler came home late, long after the children had gone to bed. He went in and looked at the two little ones briefly, then sat down at the table, and she could see he was tired. She let him eat without troubling him. She let him read through the worn copy of *Romsdals Budstikke* he had brought with him, and then she made love with him in the summer night.

Only when he was running his hand over her hair and settling down to go to sleep did she seem to recall the letter, and then, naked as the day she was born, she walked across the floor in the light of the Scandinavian summer evening. She took the letter out of the top drawer, sat on the end of the bed, read it to him in her youthful voice, and said that they needed to make a decision now or never: if they were going to go, it had to be next summer. Because the Lord never holds the door open for us forever. At some point, the grace ends. We need to make a decision: sell our things, tear ourselves away, and walk the path that he has made ready. And when God's finger comes into view as clearly as it has, making known the glaring lack of saddlers in the Midwest, surely there was nothing to be done but obey? Was Ole going to repair old harnesses for the rest of his life, or was he going to make new ones?

Ole no longer had many objections to Gjertine's dreams. He was tired of patching and repairing. There was no profit in it. He did not consent with cheers of joy. He remained silent. When she finally asked him with anguish in her voice whether they were going or staying, he responded with a single word: *Going.*

His statement was so decisive that Gjertine felt a tingle run through her, a kind of fear, and she snuggled up against him.

"We're going?" Gjertine asked, as if she weren't sure she heard correctly.

"Yes, we're going," he said quietly. There was no hesitation in his voice.

"Think of the kind of leather you'll get to work with there!" Gjertine said. The strong hides of bison, wouldn't that be something for a man like him!

"Cowhide is probably the strongest," the saddler said.

3

The saddler woke up at the cock's crow and wondered: Would the authorities allow him to leave?

A man who could in principle be called up to serve as a soldier and who was between the ages of twenty-two and twenty-six but wanted to emigrate needed a license to leave from County Governor Hagerup in Tornes, the young governor who married the legendary Jenny.

It didn't take many days before Ole reported to the county governor's office, curious to see what Jenny had revealed to her husband about her youthful transgressions. He said the reason he wanted to emigrate was that he was seeking a better financial situation for himself and his family.

The governor said, "You're the one who once knew my wife, Jenny, so well way back when, aren't you?"

Yes, he couldn't deny that.

"She mentions you sometimes," the governor said.

Oh, said Ole.

"You shouldn't be granted permission, but I'll grant you it as long as you never come back!"

Ole took his license and quickly left.

Ole the saddler typically proceeded in a pragmatic, sober-minded manner that frequently made Gjertine feel impatient. He now picked up his pace. The only thing that worried him was whether he would be able to bring Olava. He picked her up from her mother's house the next day and he explained that he was going to emigrate. The girl's mother, who struggled to feed herself, asked him to take Olava to a better life. Olava herself wasn't hard to convince, even though she was unlikely to see her mother again, but no one talked about that. She was going to join her grandmother and her uncle, Hans.

Gjertine put on her best clothes and borrowed a boat from one of the cotters by the fjord. She rowed with strong strokes, holding the oars lightly around the handles so that they danced in her hands, to Vågøy Church, where she met her sister Ane-Martha.

Ane-Martha sat on the stones along the shore, waiting for her. Gjertine thought her sister looked small and sickly. Ane-Martha had married a man fifteen years older, and it was too late for her to start over.

The sisters walked to Ola and Sara's house with important news to share. Ane-Martha was dreading it.

4

Ola sat in front of his big stove on a windy, rainy evening in summer. He wasn't afraid to get his hands dirty, tolerated the fickle weather, didn't care if his back got wet or his clothes stuck to his body—but once he came indoors, he wanted it warm! He peeled off his clothes and washed himself here and there in icy cold water and fired up his woodstove so that it hummed. And when strangers weren't coming over, he wasn't careful about wearing clothes. He sat in his underwear by the stove, contemplating.

But he had to find a pair of pants because here came his two sisters and Sara was preparing tea. Ola was a man who would treat himself to a cup of tea, and if he came across something like that, he bought it.

Ola was speechless, and Sara, who was usually so warm, snapped at her sister-in-law. It was reckless when you thought of the work Ole the saddler had put into making Slutåsen nice, Sara said.

The two sisters exchanged looks and said that they had to get going. Where were they going? To walk over the mountains back to Molde! Surely they were going to spend the night and stay at least until the next morning? Ola said, looking at Sara, whose lips were pinched tight and who gave no indication that her sisters-in-law were welcome.

And so they left, even though Ola had at least a dozen questions, because Sara couldn't get rid of them quickly enough. Ola followed his sisters out, and walked with them for the first bit, even though Sara came out and yelled after him, wanting to know where he thought he was going.

"To the summer barn to fetch a rope," Ola said.

"You have plenty of rope here at home!" Sara said.

But this was his nicest one, Ola yelled, and he wanted this one to hang himself with. He had a reckless mouth at times.

When it was time to say goodbye, he said, "Don't be surprised if I follow you."

Gjertine asked, "Are you really thinking of coming over?"

"Yes! If the fishing isn't good this fall."

Back in Molde, Gjertine was nervous. She knew how Nesje felt about people's America dreams. How would he respond now that it was reality? Might as well get it over with.

"Well, it turns out we're emigrating!" Gjertine said.

Serianna froze and everything grew quiet. The children were quiet, too, or three of them—not little Kristine, who asked the question: "Where are you going?"

Eilert shushed her.

Serianna walked over to Gjertine and hugged her sister as tears rolled down her cheeks. They stood holding each other, and Ane-Martha began to cry. No one had ever seen her do that, and now little Kristine was scared, so she started crying. Ane-Martha walked over to the cluster of hugging sisters as Kristine clung to her mother's skirt. She wanted to go too. They stood there, a knot of women, then stepped apart, cleared their throats, and went to sit down on chairs or the windowsill.

Nesje knew that the time for argument was past. Now they needed to make sure they parted amicably. Serianna wiped her eyes and rose to set out supper. But then she stopped.

"I think you're expecting," she said, studying her sister.

"Yes," Gjertine said, "I believe I am." Her own words seemed to take her by surprise.

"Gjertine!" Ane-Martha said. "You didn't tell me this!"

"No," Gjertine said. "I wasn't planning to mention it until I was positive, but now that Serianna's brought it up, it's not easy to deny either!"

If you hadn't felt the seriousness every time the conversation quieted, one could have said it was a cheerful evening.

"I think it happened the night we decided to emigrate," Gjertine said, "because that time we tried twice!"

The sisters looked at each other in fear, because a person just could not say such things, and burst into laughter. Nesje got up as if he were taking his leave before he veered off into the west living room. If it hadn't been his own sister-in-law, he would have said something. And now she was asking if they wanted to join her? He didn't know anyone who got involved in other people's lives like that.

It was quiet. The two boys were listening, and Kristine stood with one finger in the corner of her mouth. The only sound was the ticking of the pendulum in the living room clock.

"No," Serianna said, without even looking at her husband. "We're staying here. Nesje is too old, and I'm infirm," she said, with a little extra limp between the food cupboard and the kitchen table.

"Like everyone these days," Nesje said, "we've thought it over and talked about it, but we're going to stay here."

5

Monday morning was dark. Nesje walked down to the barn, the horse stalls, and the cowshed. Inside it was so dark he could hardly see his hands. He went to the four horses, that stood stamping in their stalls, to give each their hay. He greeted the two fjord horses, Mons and Markus, that stood beside the two Danish work horses Nesje liked to use in the forest. Adam Gørvell had fifteen cows, and Nesje fed them. He mucked out their manure since it was the middle of the week and the barn boy was at school. The light came in through the cracks in the cowshed, but the window panes were so dirty he still couldn't see well when the milkmaid arrived with a pail in each hand. The milk at the Gørvell farm was made into cheese or churned. Some of the cheese and butter wound up in what was now Adam Gørvell's store, but just as much, or more, went to the household's own use, because Adam Gørvell had a lot of employees, and, especially before Christmas, they went through a lot of milk.

The powerful milkmaid was so heavy that she once snapped the leg of a milking stool. She sat down beside a beast and tugged on the teats. Nesje cleaned and fed the animals and went to get them water with the bucket from the well, which was frozen, so he took a stick and broke a hole in the ice. He made fifteen trips between the well, which was outside the cowshed door, and he emptied the water into the big trough.

It was eleven by the time he finished. It was winter and he still didn't know if he would be told to go join Gørvell in the woods with the boys. Yes, they had to take one more load before it got dark because that's what the manager wanted. So he went home to rest and eat. The two servant boys had the harness on when he returned. They left quickly. It was getting dark as they reached the cold deck in the Årø woods. You couldn't say it was heartwood lumber—what they were supposed to bring back—but it was wet and heavy. They loaded up six or seven logs, threw a chain around them, and headed back to town. One of the boys sat on the load with the reins. Nesje and the other boys walked in the snow.

6

It was a memorable spring in 1886. Hans Knudtsen wrote to his father with the news that he was moving to Kristiansund. Trolla Brug was going to build up a new stove business, and Hans would be the store manager! He would start the position on May 10, and he and his wife, Berntine, whom he had quietly married without any reception, had just been in Kristiansund to look for accommodations, and they had found a nice, big apartment.

Hans probably had to take the position that was offered, but the suggestion that Kristiansund was somehow better than Molde, this Nesje couldn't understand.

He wrote back to his son: *God's blessings on your work in Kristiansund!*

But he never strayed from his fundamental position: Molde was where it was happening. There was always something happening in Molde!

When the foundation stone for the new Molde Church was laid on the morning of May 17th, was that not something happening?

The population of their small town had now passed sixteen hundred souls. Many of them were present when the foundation stone for the new church was laid. Nesje was one of those who stood in the background there. He didn't make any attempt to push his way forward, so he didn't see much of the solemn ceremony, but he could certainly say that he had been there.

There was a party that evening at the Grand Hotel to celebrate the national holiday. It was open to all social classes and political views. Could a man like Nesje have enjoyed a place at such an event? The thought was by no means impossible. He didn't dread conversing with folks, because he knew how to conduct himself. He had manners from his mother, who had walked to Kristiania by foot to attend midwifery school. He could afford the entrance ticket. It cost forty øre for a man to enter, a twentieth of his daily wage from Gørvell. Women only cost twenty øre. And they owned the clothes. He had the black wedding suit worn only for Hans's confirmation and the other children's baptisms.

There was a rich program at the Grand detailed in the advertisement in the *Romsdals Budstikke*. There would be singing and speeches and opportunity later in the evening for a turn around the dance floor.

Nesje was no rich man, but he could have managed it. You didn't need to attend the actual dinner; you could eat at home beforehand. But Serianna said no. She couldn't imagine anything more ridiculous than humble people partying with fine society folks at the Grand Hotel. So Nesje did not go to Johnsen's barbershop, he did not go to Bækkelund's mercantile to purchase a ticket, nor was he among the stragglers who secured an entrance ticket when the doors to the Grand Hotel opened at 7 p.m. sharp in the evening. He was at home, and once the children were in bed, Serianna brought the bottle and poured a thimbleful of the purest dram. He had to rejoice in everything that was his.

Kristine was seven now. She sewed clothes for her rag doll and sang in a high, sweet voice. He recognized in her his own refined features. But unlike most farm laborers, he took off work on May 17 because he wanted to honor the Norwegian constitution, completed and signed at Eidsvoll on this day in the year of our Lord 1814. He observed the day the way the wealthy observed it, and read the various publications.

He found the descriptions of modern agriculture in them interesting. His window was open. It was delightfully green everywhere, and the air was wild with a hint of summer. He read about nitrate, which should be used on marshy soil. He himself had steep hillsides, but he figured it wouldn't hurt to know how to care for marshy soil. He wondered if he could afford to write to Throndhjem and have a grindstone sent that he could set up by the wall of the farm? He used a mower's whetstone daily. When he noted that the edge wasn't biting, he took his scythes down to the farm to sharpen them. But a grindstone of his own, that would be nice.

While he sat pondering all he had to do, people were dancing at the Grand Hotel, and you could hear the music all the way up in Rekneslia. Could Serianna hear the music? Now she smiled. Nesje wasn't a bad dancer in his younger days, and when his allotted dram kicked in, he asked Serianna to dance. Oh, she demurred. It was silliness and nonsense, but he was so gallant that she had to laugh. And in the end she danced with him in the kitchen. Kristine and Anton Edvard were already in bed, but Bastian Georg and Eilert watched, wide-eyed. Serianna was no longer light on her feet, and her limp did not make things any smoother, but the act of dancing turned everything pleasurable, beautiful, and cheerful. The dance was theirs, and what they shared between them didn't concern anyone else. They danced with the doors open to hear the music, and they smelled fresh new leaves and spring soil. They danced while the dancing went on below at the Grand Hotel. There in town the liberal-minded, politically left folks, the Møller people, danced to their Liberal anthem, while the Dahl contingent steered clear and the other tycoons did the same in silent protest.

But they stopped dancing abruptly when they heard voices, and saw it wasn't just anyone: it was Gjertine and Ole the saddler with their children, Olava, Sivert, Sanna, and little Edvard Ås, whom Gjertine had been pregnant with on the night Ole agreed to emigrate. This was the third Edvard in the family: the first was their own Anton Edvard, then Edvard at

Bortegard, and finally this one, who had been born in March and slept for most of the day. But right now he lay wide-eyed and alert in Gjertine's arms, and seemed so thoughtful that they had to laugh.

Gjertine and Ole had spent all their money on the tickets to America, but everything was arranged. The tickets were in their strongbox. Why should they worry about spring planting? They would be gone. The lodgers would take over.

At the end of June, Ole the saddler and his household boarded the English Wilson Line steamship SS *Hero* in Kristiansund. The boat sailed a route from Throndhjem to Kristiansund and from there on to Hull, where they took the train to Liverpool and continued on a new ship from Liverpool to Quebec City.

Gjertine and Ole had to pay 150 kroner each. The three older children cost 50 kroner apiece, but they didn't need to pay for little Edvard. His free passage was the rebate, one might say, since the whole family was going. They spent two hundred kroner buying clothing and gear for the trip. They would receive one thousand kroner for their farm. Then they had five hundred to exchange when they arrived in the foreign country, and it would be seven hundred total once they sold the horse and vehicles.

Gjertine was going to bring the chest that their mother, Ingeborg Gjertine, had brought with her from Stavig to Bortegard. Serianna did not like that. So, people were taking heirlooms out of the country? What would be left if people were going to start carting things away? Serianna wanted the chest for herself, but she didn't say anything since Gjertine had also been baptized Ingeborg, which was the name on the chest.

Their brother Ola had said that he might follow them to America, and the sisters laughed. They didn't think he would do it because Ola was forty-two, with four underage children, and Sara absolutely did not want to emigrate. He probably wasn't the one who most needed to leave, Serianna said. Bortegard was his. But Gjertine knew it was the other way around, that Ola struggled to make his mortgage payments. She knew that the bank showed no mercy to anyone.

Gjertine had a hard time saying goodbye to her family. The sisters cried as they clung to each other. Gjertine and her husband and children were going to stay at Miss Halvorsen's boarding house. Why had they rented a room? They didn't want to sleep on the floor the last time they were in Molde. Serianna found this arrogant, but again said nothing.

Nesje shook Ole's hand, and he told Gjertine that if they had ever disagreed about anything, they should forget about it so that they could look each other in the eye if they met again. Then Nesje hugged Gjertine—he couldn't help it—and his tears broke loose, a whole flood. No one had ever seen that before, not even Serianna. He could not control his emotions. He held Gjertine, and she held him, and this went on for so long that Serianna started looking a bit tight around the lips and Kristine asked, "Are you mad, Mama?"

The saddler was embarrassed and turned his hat around. The children stared. Then they left, and it was empty and quiet behind them.

7

As they drove from their farm at Slutåsen toward the pier with their horse Hadrian, Gjertine wondered what was going on with her husband. He hadn't uttered a word in nearly three hours.

Sivert, Sanna, baby Edvard, and even ten-year-old Olava fell asleep in the back of the carriage, and there wasn't anything left to do before they shook the dust of the fatherland off their feet but to hand over their horse and cart to the buyer they had arranged to meet at the steamship dock in Eide.

Maybe the saddler was sad for some other reason. Maybe because he had to say goodbye to his horse? Everything was happening at the same time now. Gjertine knew that wasn't easy for this good man. He loved horses, particularly this one. He had made Hadrian the most beautiful harness and named him after an emperor. Or was it a pope? There had to be a limit to his love for an animal!

Ole said goodbye to his sister, Ane, and she cried so heartbreakingly they all felt the pain. The saddler controlled his emotions the way one would expect of a man. He smiled and comforted his sister and said he didn't think the next time they saw each other would be in heaven; it would be in America. And couldn't Hans send her a ticket, too, as he had done for his parents?

But it turned out, and maybe this was the reason for the heartbreaking sobs, that Ane had written to their brother, Hans, a long time ago and asked for just that, but he had replied that he was no longer able to help. Ane was left, without Ole and Gjertine, alone in the world. Maybe they could have taken her with them, but they hadn't thought of that. Was there no other way out for Ane? As a serving girl at Ola's house she earned her food and clothing and a few paltry kroner. It wasn't anywhere near enough for a ticket to America. She was cast aside by her own people, and now she learned that even Ola at Bortegard, who had been a head of household and a guardian to her, was also thinking about leaving. All that was left for her in this life was misfortune. She might as well drag herself out into the cold water of Frænfjorden one day, she who couldn't swim.

Gjertine didn't want Ole to suffer in silence. She wanted to share them with him and bear her portion.

"You haven't spoken a word to me since we drove past the Moen farm," Gjertine said. "And you don't respond to anything I say, either, even though I love the sound of your beautiful voice!"

The saddler looked at her but didn't respond, didn't smile.

"Have I done something wrong," Gjertine asked, "since you are being so unkind toward me?"

"I'm not being unkind," the saddler said. "I'm just quiet. I'm going with you to where you want to go, and I won't contradict you. And if we should experience a change of fortune, I won't remind you how little of our doing this was because of me. But you can't demand that I pretend to be convinced at the bottom of my heart, or cheer and thank the Lord for the journey."

"I appreciate your candor and honesty," Gjertine said. "You will feel convinced of how right this is in the *fullness of time*, as it says in the scriptures."

He smiled at her, and their marital peace was restored, in a way.

8

They arrived at the steamship pier in Eide. The steamship was at the dock, spewing acrid, black smoke, and the man who was to buy Hadrian and the harness was there. He was a little milksop, Gjertine thought.

But that milksop had written them a letter and made an offer on the horse. The agreement had been that he would pay two hundred kroner for the horse, harness, and cart, but now he said that he couldn't do more than a hundred and fifty kroner. He would have to send the rest on later, he said, once they had an address over there. After all, surely it couldn't be harder to send money in the one direction than the other, could it? Many who had emigrated to America sent money back home to their relatives, so they in turn could afford to buy a ticket.

Gjertine noticed her husband's face changing color and she hurried to get all the children aboard. That was what they had agreed between them: she would see the children safely aboard, and then the saddler would find someone to help with their luggage. The saddler had not counted on the horse buyer reneging on the deal and conning him out of fifty kroner.

The saddler looked like he was losing his temper. His voice trembling, he asked the man to carry their food case on board while he tied the horse to a post. The man was slow and reluctant. He knew that the saddler didn't have a choice. He couldn't take the horse with him onto the ship, or the cart either. They had another chest, which contained the saddler's tools, because though saddler Ole knew such things could be acquired in America, he wanted to bring what was his: his plough gauge, round knife, edge shave, embossing roller, creaser, pricking wheel, awls, and the various punches including his crew punch. Though the chest weighed over a hundred pounds, the saddler carried it on board and set it in a safe place below deck. That left their bedclothes in a big seabag, their clothes in another, and some smaller chests, including a chest with the things Olava brought and the chest Gjertine inherited from her mother.

Olava came ashore again to make sure everything made it on, fully aware that her father was in a smoldering mood.

"You just carry the ship bags aboard," she heard her father instructing the man, his voice trembling. "And the chests and the suitcase, too, since you can't pay what you promised. I never have any respect for people who don't keep their word."

The man apparently thought he had the upper hand now, because he said, "It could certainly happen that you had promised them to someone else as well, saddler Ole, particularly to women, since you were so eager to win them over."

"Hurry up, old man, the ship is leaving," the saddler ordered, his face white. "Since you haven't paid more than seventy-five percent of what you were supposed to, I suppose it's only reasonable that I get a chance to say my goodbyes to Hadrian? Hurry up now, I'm sure you'll hear it if they ring the bell a second time!"

He flung the ship bags at the man. The man gave in, picked one bag up over each shoulder, and walked on board.

"Set them here!" said Olava, who was following him, keeping an eye on their things. She was ten years old and furious on her father's behalf.

"Why are you lugging so much stuff with you when everything is better on the other side?" asked the man, dropping the bags.

"Get back ashore, otherwise you're coming with us!" one of the crew yelled, and the man hurried off.

Too late he realized that the saddler, who had hopped on board after the hawsers had been cast loose, carried a little chest in each hand, and that beautiful harness over his shoulder.

"You're absconding with the harness, you hornswoggler!" the man yelled. "Stop that man, he's taking my harness!"

"You haven't paid for it," the saddler replied, "so it can't be yours, can it?"

The man tried to get back on board, but the crew stopped him, and the steamer *Nicolai H. Knudtzon* pulled away. Gjertine came over with the children and they stood, the whole family, as Olava laughed until she cried.

"Papa can do anything!" the girl shouted. "Papa can do anything!"

"Are you planning to take that harness with you to America?" Gjertine asked, without a trace of mockery. She thought he was an extraordinary man.

"Yes, if I don't find a buyer before we board the America boat, then I'll take it with me," said Ole the saddler. "But maybe someone or other in Kristiansund might need a harness."

"We can take that up with Hans Knudtsen," Gjertine said, because Nesje had written to Hans and asked his son to arrange lodgings.

9

The steamer to Kristiansund didn't take long, and at the wharf in Kirklandet stood Hans, waiting for them.

Hans was only twenty-six, but what had happened to him? He had put on weight and wore a watch chain across his belly as if to emphasize how well he was doing. Gjertine and Ole had been told by Nesje's children to call him Uncle Hans in Kristiansund, because that's what Bastian Georg and Eilert always called him, even though he was their half-brother, and though he wasn't uncle to any children and had no children of his own.

Gjertine was curious. Would he offer any sign that he remembered their last meeting? Would he pretend that they hadn't met?

He stood and, as he greeted them, took Gjertine's hand as if she were a person he had only met in passing. Then he greeted saddler Ole and leaned over to exchange a few words with Olava.

Gjertine saw the thick, gold ring Hans wore on his right hand as if it could not be said loudly enough that he was a married man. He could have expressed amazement at their long journey, could have asked why they decided to leave the fatherland, but he didn't. He didn't ask if their trip had gone well or if they were hungry. From the saddler's point of view this stranger may have been welcoming enough, but to Gjertine the meeting was painful. Before they saw him, she hadn't noticed the other things going on, but now she saw the crowds on the wharves, all the people there for no reason other than to see who was coming and going. She saw cargo lowered ashore by block and tackle: suitcases and bags, wooden chests and bundles. Their luggage was unloaded with all the rest. The saddler recovered each item and collected them in one place. A few drops fell. Gjertine glanced up at the sky. A dark cloud hung over Kirklandet. Was it going to rain? It didn't matter so much—the summer day was warm, and they wouldn't be harmed by a few drops. But a shower hit, and they sheltered under an overhanging roof to wait it out. Gjertine and Hans had no choice but to talk to each other there, so they chatted about how sudden the cloudburst was.

As they stood there, a young Kristiansund resident who was the agent for the Allan Line came by and brought them to the police station, where they were entered into the Emigration Protocol. The agent accompanied them to the shipping office with their baggage on a hand truck and made sure the chests and suitcases were labeled, in big letters, *The Allan Line*. They would be loaded onto the SS *Hero* that same evening. But the saddler wouldn't hand over his harness. He wanted to try to sell it before they left the town. And they kept one small case with them, the one with food.

Hans had found them a place to stay in town. They thought they would be going to his home, but there wasn't much room, he explained. His wife, Bertine, needed to rest and recover. He didn't say what was ailing her or what she needed to recuperate from.

A room was an expense they hadn't anticipated.

Oh, the room was paid in advance, Hans said. It was on him!

Well, they couldn't accept that! They wouldn't have any opportunity to pay him back!

They mustn't think of it that way, Hans said. After all, they were family.

On their way to the boarding house, Ole was quieter than ever. Gjertine realized they were no longer of the same social status, she and Hans. Hans Knudtsen, as he called himself, was a different sort. He had a different smell, and they would learn later that he struggled with his finances. How could they have guessed when he had grown a mustache and wore a silver chain across his belly?

They arrived at a little boarding house with *Mrs. Larsen: Lodgings for Travelers* in ornate letters over the door. A no-nonsense woman showed them a room without speaking a word. They had the food and the harness. It seemed the woman thought that was more than enough; at any rate, she rolled her eyes. They went inside with all their things and Hans Knudtsen was in a hurry. There was nothing else but to say goodbye. Did they have everything they needed? There was a little café just down the street, he said. He would be happy to buy them dinner.

Gjertine and the saddler assured him they had food with them, and plenty of it, food that Gjertine had packed for the day's rations in a little case, bread and butter, cured ham, boiled potatoes, all ready to be eaten. Food was included in their tickets both on the ship to England and on the America boat from Liverpool, but it could be a long time between meals, so they kept a few things in reserve, and they had prepared specially for their layover in Kristiansund.

Hans Knudtsen seemed sorry that they didn't take him up on his offer. He turned around several times, as if he realized he missed something.

"Why didn't you sell the harness?" he asked Ole. "That's going to be awkward to carry!"

Gjertine explained about the horse buyer who had shorted them and said that Ole wanted to sell the harness for forty kroner.

"Then I'll buy it, of course!" Hans Knudtsen said, and pulled out his wallet and took out seventy kroner. "I can see that it's a beautiful harness," he said. "And everything is so expensive here in town. Seventy kroner isn't too much."

He wouldn't back down, and in the end the saddler accepted. Gjertine couldn't stand it anymore when she realized he was apologizing. Hans Knudtsen had become Hans from Rekneslia, there he stood, and suddenly she saw that the watch chain and the mustache were just outward appearances. He wasn't a different person. It was as if no time had passed. Everything that had happened between them happened just moments ago.

She threw her arms around the neck of the young businessman, who seemed like he wanted to free himself. The saddler looked at them in surprise but didn't say anything. Then Hans Knudtsen grabbed the horse harness and left them without a farewell.

10

The next morning it was so light that they were blinded when they opened their eyes. There were no curtains in the room. A flock of seagulls shrieked somewhere, and while they lay there cuddled up in bed, all six of them, the day's sounds and smells came in. Through the floor they caught the aroma of baking bread. Olava was hungry, and Gjertine fetched a pitcher so they could do a basic washup. They got dressed. The weather was nice out, and they didn't want to stay in any longer than necessary. Then the hostess came to the doorway and asked how long they planned to lie around.

They said they needed to eat.

The docks teemed with people preparing to travel, and there was a lot of luggage to be loaded. Crates and chests and suitcases going to America and goods headed for England: casks of aquavit from Lysholm's distillery and big barrels of dry, salted cod. Olava was in charge of minding Sivert so he didn't fall overboard. She did a great job.

The Wilson Line had started a regular route from Throndhjem to Hull in 1871, and over the years built almost a monopoly on emigrants to England. Norwegian shipping lines had tried to take over the lucrative supply traffic for the big transatlantic shipping lines, but the Wilson Line didn't appreciate the competition, and were threatening to shut down all passenger service out of the country. Transatlantic companies like the Allan Line couldn't live with that. So they agreed that all their passengers from Norway to England had to travel with the Wilson Line.

Some of these Wilson Line ships were legendary and known in every port, such as the SS *Hero*, the third ship of that name under the flag of the Wilson Line, and the one on which the saddler's family would sail.

But there were other kinds of travelers here, people taking trips to England and back home again. Most of them traveled in first class and stood along the railing watching the activity on the wharf below.

"It's almost strange not to see anyone we know," Gjertine said.

The saddler looked around.

"There's a man over there I think I've seen before," said the saddler, who had traveled so much. "Well, I'll be—if that isn't Peder from Kjørsvika and his wife. Her name's Anna, if I'm remembering correctly."

"You usually do remember the ladies, don't you," Gjertine needled him.

The saddler walked over to say hello. Gjertine stayed where she was, standing with the children and following him with her eyes. It seemed like he had recovered his ability to speak. He laughed so loudly they could hear him, and then he returned with the Kjørsvika folks. The wife was a few years older than Gjertine, but still young. They didn't seem to have any children? Ah, yes, there came a boy who was Olava's age!

The Kjørsvika family was going to Roberts County, South Dakota, the county neighboring Day, where Hans Ås had settled, and they were on the same boats, the SS *Hero* to Hull and the SS *Parisian* from Liverpool. It was beyond mysterious that no word had reached Slutåsen that this other family was also going over. But the Kjørsvika family knew that Gjertine and Ole were going. The same agent had sold the tickets to both families, and they had even chosen their destination via Lars Stavig, who lived in that same area.

Gjertine knew that the voyage would be different now. Obviously it would be nice to have familiar folk to chat with on a long journey. It could be helpful if something unexpected happened, if someone got sick or suffered some mishap. This Anna Kjørsvika looked reliable and her husband was jovial. When Ole went through a quiet spell, Gjertine would have someone to talk to.

But it was also as though something had been lost. She had pictured Ole and herself discovering the new country together with their children. Now they would share it.

The agent who was to see them aboard approached. He was the son of a local shopkeeper. He was so friendly and helpful that the two women exchanged smiles over him. And he called them "ladies," both of them.

"Here, my ladies. You'd prefer to sleep together, right?" he said. They mustn't take that literally, hahaha. "Birds of a feather flock together," the shopkeeper's son said, and tried to walk arm in arm with the two of them as he guided them to the gangway. Anna acquiesced, but Gjertine freed herself. She had a baby in her arms. Olava came up with Sanna and Sivert. Why couldn't their father mind them for once, she thought? But then she saw the Kjørsvika people's boy, whose name was Anders, take hold of little Sivert's hand. The men followed, preoccupied with the ship. The SS *Hero* had been traveling the Norwegian coast for years, with room for four hundred passengers. But hadn't there been multiple boats with the same name? This one certainly didn't look new. They would ask the agent.

The ship was twenty years old, but refurbished, he said. It featured iron construction, that was the thing. Ships like this can withstand a hard blow, more than a thousand gross, the agent said.

"That's good, because I can't swim," the Kjørsvika man admitted. Gjertine was the only one of them who could, it turned out. But what could she do if they encountered rough weather?

"Oh, stop," the saddler said. "It's almost Midsummer."

The air smelled of coal smoke, engine oil, and turpentine. People pushed forward, looking for their berths. The sky was so bright, they had to squint to see each other.

At the gangway, they needed their tickets out. No one was permitted aboard without one. The agent showed them to their room under the poop deck, or the "afterdeck." All the berths down here were occupied. There were capes and coats strewn about, but most people were up on deck. The berths lined up in double bunks on either side, four by four high, and ran the whole central walkway without any delineation where one bunk ended and a new one began. The bottom bunks were secured to iron beams that ran lengthwise just a few inches above the floor, also made of iron. There was a glorious confusion of personal possessions. People had tossed down this and that.

The agent swept aside handbags and coats so the new passengers would have space.

"Would you look at how people spread out!" he said.

You had to accept that you were going to be in cramped conditions here. The bunks were two feet wide, separated by thick boards. The top bunk was right under the poop deck. You'd have to be a good climber to sleep up there. There was no partition or curtain between the bunks and walkway, and they realized they'd have to sleep with their clothes on. No room here for morning ablutions! But there were big tanks of water on deck to clean themselves up before they ate.

Then the engine started. They had a spot right over the engine room. It wasn't going to be easy to sleep here! The saddler said, "Oh, I'm sure we'll sleep once we're tired." He was in a good mood now that he had some male company, someone to discuss ship construction with.

But now they had to leave their food case, which they pushed under the bunk. They hung their coats on the hooks on poles along either side of the walkway. Luckily there was a vent nearby so they wouldn't want for fresh air. The children would share a bunk below them. Anders Kjørsvika would also sleep there—in the same bunk as Sivert, they found out. Olava didn't want to lie in a berth with a boy she didn't know right next to her, but the grownups didn't care about that. She was still a child.

The ship stopped out by Hustadvika. They climbed up onto the deck, where it was cold and windy, and they were on their way. The SS *Hero*'s coal smoke belched into the sky. They looked at each other. Despite her reluctance, Gjertine felt a deep sense of relief. What she had with Ole was unstable, she thought. Sometimes they were of one mind, while other times there was a vast distance between them. She stroked his cheek, and Anna Kjørsvika looked at her in surprise. It wasn't common for people in the villages to display their affection when other people could watch.

A half hour later, the dinner bell rang. The dining room was on the foredeck in first class. They brought their tickets and what money they had and went up the hatchway. They would be served supper, the last meal for this day. There was bread with butter, the coffee wasn't bad, and there was milk and sugar. Those who wanted a salted herring got one. There was salt on the table in abundance, and they could help themselves to as much water as they wanted.

At the table they talked about how much their farms had been worth, what a cow was worth in Norway, and how they would build up their herds when they arrived. There mustn't be too much inbreeding, they heard. Were there still wild bison in South Dakota? They had heard of such things, but the white man had gotten there a while ago now and helped himself.

They sat at the table for a couple of hours, because they

were the last passengers to be served. It was intensely bright on the top deck and not so appealing to climb back down to bed. Gjertine talked about Hans Ås and Ingeborg, his mother, who had 320 acres. And Hans Ås had planted potatoes on all of it!

To her surprise, the saddler said that he didn't know if it was wise to gamble on just one crop. He would think it best to have a little grain, some potatoes and rutabagas, and hay to feed some animals. Chickens were good to have, and turkeys, and geese, maybe.

"You look like a turkey to me!" Gjertine teased her husband, and Anna was again as amazed as she had been when she witnessed the previous display of affection.

How did he know all this?

Well, they would see! How could you even picture a 320-acre potato field?

"He's probably going to need some help harvesting all those potatoes," Peder Kjørsvika said.

At around nine, they went to find their bunks. Ole's bunk was too short for him, so he had to lie curled up. The children fell asleep quickly, but the noise of the engine kept Gjertine awake. At midnight she realized she'd drunk too much water. She found the stench of the toilet unbearable. She hurried back to her bunk. The trip would take less than three days, and she would simply endure.

The next morning they left Aalesund for Hull. With the new passengers, there wasn't much room, but most people understood there was nothing to do about it. Gjertine realized she loved traveling, and that maybe the journey was as much an experience as the arrival, but the other woman didn't seem to understand what she meant.

II

The crossing to Hull took two days. It was Sunday afternoon. A filthy city opened up before them when they came up on deck to see. The train to Liverpool wouldn't leave until the next day, but they didn't have anywhere to stay other than the ship, and the women remained aboard with the children while several of the men, including Ole and Peder, went to see the city. Their wives exchanged glances. They thought that the men should stick close to the tent, as they say, but what were you going to do: men were men and did as they pleased.

"You don't need to bring money," Gjertine said. "Leave your wallet. I'll keep an eye on it."

The conversation between Gjertine and Anna didn't flow any more smoothly with the men gone. Did they have anything to discuss? Anna pulled out a book, Bjørnstjerne Bjørnson's *The Fisher Girls*. As if Gjertine hadn't read *The Fisher Girls*! She had a long time ago, back when she was a girl helping out her sister at Rekneslia. Why hadn't she brought a book or two? Gjertine knew that she had read more books than most passengers aboard the *Hero*, but now she just sat here like a fool. She had to take out her Bible, given at her confirmation when she stood ninth in line. Anna from Kjørsvika looked at her with the same look of astonishment. But Gjertine didn't care what people thought.

Ole and Peder went ashore and returned at midnight. They were jolly. They had been to a pub! All Englishmen went to the pub on Sunday night. Gjertine was glad the children weren't awake. How had Ole paid for his drinks? Gjertine didn't want to know! But Ole claimed someone had bought them. Who? An Englishman!

Wasn't he ashamed to stand there like some poor tramp and accept a handout? Well now, shouldn't they have some peace and quiet for the night? But Peder and Ole lay in bed quietly discussing what they seen and heard. There was a lot of poverty to be seen, and such squalor, and the coal dust. They didn't want to live in a big city, the men agreed on that.

"Farmers we are and farmers we will remain," Peder Kjørsvika said.

"I'm a saddler," said the saddler.

People around them were acting annoyed by their racket when suddenly there stood the captain, in uniform, doing his inspection rounds. He never showed up this late. "I pray you, silence! Good night," he said, and there was silence, in which Gjertine felt ashamed.

Monday morning was gray. The Ås family and the Kjørsvika family, with a herd of emigrants, were led down the wharf by Allan Line agents who wanted them to inspect their luggage as it was loaded. The men made sure everything got on board and the women were left standing among longshoremen and young boys with handcarts and pushy street peddlers. It took a long time before Peder and Ole returned. They had seen their chests, clearly marked *The Allan Line*, loaded onto carts and driven to the train station. The agents, who spoke Norwegian, said things would be placed in different train cars depending on which ship they would be boarding, so there was no risk they'd end up in the wrong place.

Meanwhile, the emigrants would have their breakfast in guesthouses the Allan Line arranged, first to the café and then to the dorms. Those who were departing that day were mostly people traveling the other direction, who'd had to wait for permission to travel to the Scandinavian countries or Germany. The hosts at these guesthouses were Germans who also spoke English. What the emigrants didn't understand they could guess, and they understood that they weren't going to dawdle at the guesthouse. The food was nothing to speak of, and the dining experience was worse. The hosts received one English shilling per traveler from the company, and they wanted to get them on their way as soon as possible. The bathrooms were foul.

And then they were on their way. Their baggage was stowed in the first cars. The passengers sat farther back on wooden benches grimy with coal dust. The train rattled off to Liverpool, a bigger and dirtier city, of which they only caught a glimpse. Something else captured their interest, the SS *Parisian*! If anyone had concerns about the ocean crossing, they could lay those fears to rest now. This vessel was a dream.

"Steel hull!" Peder exclaimed softly, and Ole could only nod and repeat, "Steel hull!"

We are taking a carriage to the gates of heaven, the saddler said, and Anna freely showed her admiration for the man from Oppland. But Gjertine just grumbled that she found the ship too cramped to be Ole's carriage. He was full of it sometimes.

Still, she couldn't help it. The sight of the SS *Parisian* made her happy. In addition to the steam engine, pumping smoke through two midship funnels, the ship had four tall masts with glimmering white sails. The SS *Parisian* was five years old, the agent said. This vessel could carry a thousand passengers, but there were only 646 people on the manifest. Eighty-five more passengers would board in Ireland.

After an examination at the gangway by two English doctors who felt their foreheads and looked into their throats, they boarded the SS *Parisian* for Quebec City.

The third-class lower deck was divided into twelve compartments with room for forty passengers in each. The berths were separated by a low board. The Ås family had three berths and the Kjørsvika family two. Peder and Ole lay on the very outside and the very inside, with their wives in the middle and the children between them. The berths were stacked four high. Anyone with children was on the bottom. They half sat, half lay down when they were in the berths. They were there most of each day. The meals were good, but they had to wait because the dining saloon didn't have room for more than a hundred passengers. Englishmen went first, then the Germans, and then the Scandinavians and the Slavs. There was tea, coffee, chocolate, sugar, crackers, bread, and butter. That was the time for people in different compartments to mingle, and single men and women had an hour to socialize. But when they returned to their compartments, they were separated in a way for the young women to have peace. The shipping company had learned a thing or two.

For dinner, served at one in the afternoon, there was soup and pork or beef with gravy and potatoes. On their Sunday there was dessert, a type of English pudding. For supper at six there was bread and butter again, or crackers, with coffee and tea. The crackers were hard and the bread tasted dry, but there was plenty of water.

Gjertine and Ole would describe their voyage on the SS *Parisian* as an adventure. They dared to undertake something together, and this had built their confidence. With each passing day, the saddler grew certain that they'd made the right choice. Gjertine was given the credit for knowing what was best for them, and she accepted it gracefully.

The days blurred into each other. They traveled in the most beautiful time of year, high summer on the Atlantic, and the people on board were friendly and courteous, even if they couldn't understand each other. They had known it would be colder on the ocean than on land, but they hadn't imagined that it could be *so* cold. They had to wear everything they had brought whenever they went up on deck for fresh air.

When the ship put in at Londonderry, the Catholics came aboard. They knelt in lines, evening and morning. This drew Gjertine's thoughts to her own faith. It was night, a northern night in June. A dim twilight enveloped them at midnight, and the ocean turned black for a few hours before the next day began.

They washed their hands and faces. They changed clothes when they began to smell poorly, and they rinsed a garment or two when the sun was shining. There were young women on board who said they had beaux ahead of them and older folks who were going to find their children. Some young women dressed as if they were going to a Norwegian dance on a warm summer's evening. The vainest of them coughed the marrows out of their bones in the berths.

But there were also enigmatic men with mustaches bigger than Bismarck's, as Gjertine put it. She had seen his likeness in a newspaper. Others daily shaved every last bit of stubble. Ole let his beard grow and his hair curled over his collar. But one day Gjertine took a pair of scissors and cut off his curls. He shouldn't get any ideas. He removed his beard as well, giving himself a clean shave. Sivert shrieked. He hadn't seen his father's chin for many years. It took a long time for him to get over it.

12

The SS *Parisian* was nearing the Canadian coast. The ship didn't pitch or roll, but Gjertine couldn't sleep.

Ole rolled over. The children were asleep. They were together, lying side by side, and everyone was breathing deeply. Some snored. Further down the compartment was packed, and because so many were squeezed together you smelled odors. But now, in the early morning hours, it could be like this, with everyone asleep and a fresh draft cleaning the air. Then Gjertine found herself filled with gratitude. What riches had not been granted her? God in heaven carried them away, and he would not fail! And so she turned to her husband and whispered into his ear, "Show me a kindness, Ole."

"What, now?" he asked, incredulous.

"Yes."

And so he showed her a kindness. It transpired without a sound. During the crossing, Gjertine learned what she hadn't understood or cared to understand while she was in the old country: that a delight voiced by quiet sighs can be just as great as that which proclaims itself to all the world.

They approached Newfoundland, and the temperature dropped so low they stayed in their quarters. When they went out on deck for fresh air they felt in their bones the mighty icebergs they saw to the west. Then came the fog. The waves were large, and those who were seasick lay on the deck, faces pressed against the planking. The stench of the vomit was unmistakable. Every morning the ship's crew scattered sawdust, then they swept the sawdust overboard and washed with salt and ammonia, but the smell clung to the deck like barnacles.

What Gjertine was proud of later was her knitting, socks and mittens for all her children. And the men?

A little way from their quarters a group sat playing cards, and soon Peder was one of them.

"Oh, why don't you go join them!" Gjertine told the saddler happily. "It can't be sinful to kill time. But Lord forgive you if you play for money."

"You used to hate cards," Ole said.

Yes, in Norway, where people wasted time instead of being useful. On board that wasn't easy.

So Ole went to join in cards, and soon she heard him shouting, "The ace! The ace!" She noticed his word for "ace" was masculine instead of neutral, and thought again about where they were going.

"He who's lucky at cards is unlucky in love," Gjertine said when he returned. They had been playing for matches, and Ole had a full box.

The days flowed together, but one day would be etched in their memory: the day Sivert went missing.

It wasn't supposed to be possible. The railings were shoulder height against a grown man. They ran all over the ship looking for him. Gjertine was consumed with fear. In her bunk, face down, she bit on her handkerchief, but her wailing cut through everyone anyway. The saddler didn't know what to do, and he went to get her a little aquavit so she wouldn't destroy herself.

When he opened the chest to get the dram, he discovered Sivert, lying asleep inside. Hungry, the boy had opened the chest in search of some food and then fallen asleep.

The terror sat with them a long time.

It sometimes happened that Gjertine would lie awake, hour after hour. One night she swung her feet out from under the big blanket and pulled on her skirt and jacket to go out on deck. It was almost as bright as day, but when she stood alone, she could see the stars, and she was filled with peace. They were the same stars she had watched and dreamt beneath, on the hillside at Bortegard. They stood there like a promise. During these moments, Gjertine was proud of her courage to leave and her ability to convince her husband to go.

As she returned inside, she saw that she wasn't the only one awake. There were others on deck, but none of them talked or bothered each other with happy dreams or fears of the future. They left each other in peace. They were introverts, loners, who didn't like snoring and who preferred to stand alone under the night sky in the presence of God.

The sun was coloring the sky red. She went to find her way back to the berth. Maybe she could sleep in a little, once the baby had what he needed. But when she snuck in, little Edvard woke up hungry.

The two weeks of their journey were like this. She began to sleep through the nights because the winds died down, and each day the SS *Parisian* brought them closer to their destination. The mood lightened. She didn't invite him in earnest, but she wasn't unavailable for his secret caresses and kisses.

The Promised Land

I

On June 17, 1886, three weeks after they last saw their home, Ole and Gjertine and their children made landfall, in Canada. Before them rose naked cliffs and wide green plains with small shrubs, and then they saw Halifax: without a single tree, rows of buildings, warehouses at the shipyard, and their port.

"Well begun is half done," the saddler said, but the Kjørsviks folks thought the most difficult part of the journey still lay ahead.

The ship remained in Halifax that night, but the emigrants weren't allowed ashore. Then the ship sailed up the long St. Lawrence River to Quebec City.

Agents from the Allan Line were waiting on the dock, and the Norwegians stood there as their baggage was unloaded and placed on carts pulled by horses. Canadian horses, they were called, descendants of French horses that had crossed the Atlantic at the end of the seventeenth century and mixed with the horses of New England: beautiful, muscular, dark animals, sleek and lithe, stepping proudly like young men.

"Maybe this is where I should have settled," Ole said. He was examining the harnesses of first one horse and then another. It appeared harnesses were harnesses regardless of where you came.

And the language! The French tongue prevailed here, and it was unfamiliar. But Gjertine thought it sounded beautiful. And the way they dressed! These were a colorful people! And the women, all of them, wore high heels and swiveled when they walked.

"There's a lot to learn here," the saddler told Gjertine.

"I don't have time," Gjertine said, "I have to keep an eye on the children. Their father is too busy ogling the women of Quebec."

The saddler put Sivert up on his shoulders, and the boy stared every which way, pointing at people who walked by. They were a friendly people, these French Canadians. They smiled at him and tweaked his nose or blew him a kiss when they walked by. A young man in yellow leather pants said something to Gjertine that she didn't understand, but she blushed just the same.

Edvard was hungry, so she put him to her breast. People stared at her, though of course she didn't care—or did she? Did people not nurse their babies here?

The steamship that would take them to Toronto was at a different dock. The agent accompanied them and delivered their tickets. The ship was no luxury boat, but they had berths to sleep in and they could go up on deck for fresh air when they wanted.

They didn't talk to each other much. They mostly sat and took it in. It wasn't as crowded here as on the transatlantic route because quite a few of the other passengers were taking a train to Toronto. They had chosen the steamship, which was a little cheaper and took a little longer.

They greeted and exchanged a few words with Norwegians who were going the same way, but there wasn't much more to say. Everyone had enough to do keeping up with their own thoughts.

Gjertine realized that it was *sankthansaften*, St. John's Eve, in Norway. So had they left that behind as well? Maybe they would celebrate it when they arrived? Would they create a new Norway in America, or would they step into Americanness? Gjertine had read about American customs and holidays: Thanksgiving, which was apparently in the fall, and Christmas, which they celebrated not on Christmas Eve but on the day of, December 25th.

But it turned out the French Canadian celebration of St. John's Eve was no less impressive than the Norwegian version—it was just that they celebrated not on the evening before, but on the day itself, June 24, and they called it Fête de la Saint-Jean-Baptiste. On the fourth and final day of their steamer trip bonfires blazed on the beaches around the lake under the darkening evening sky, and they heard music. Gjertine stood by the railing and could not get her fill. The children were in bed, their father with them. Ole understood that he needed to help mind his offspring when there was a risk that they could fall overboard.

There were people of a different sort on the top deck of this ship too. This evening there was music and the sound of dancing.

In Toronto they were escorted to the train they would take to Collingwood, a couple of hours away. They whizzed through a birch forest, and when the train slowed down before pulling into small stations on the route, they saw the flowers on the forest floor and in little meadows between new houses. There were big trees with leafy crowns, willow and oak and species they didn't know the names of. This was the province of Ontario. The houses that homesteaders had put up were still far from each other, and the prairie sat largely unused.

In Collingwood they boarded a ship that took them west across Lake Huron and on to Lake Michigan. In one week they'd reach the biggest city, Chicago, where there were many Norwegians, but they weren't stopping. They went to the immigration office and registered, then went to the exchange bureau, accompanied by another agent, and traded their kroner for dollars.

2

Every time they switched to a new mode of transportation there was an agent in a suit wishing them welcome. The suit wasn't always nice or the collar clean, but it was a suit. For the Allan Line, the journey to American was an industry. The trip had been so simplified that even the biggest lily-livered mountain rabbit could safely venture out.

On the first day of the train from Chicago they sat apart, the two families traveling together. The night was almost as light as in Norway and it was hard to sleep. Gjertine started talking with a young Norwegian woman she had seen during the crossing from England, and had noticed because the girl was so dressed up you'd have thought she was going to a wedding. Now she had an excuse to say hello. The girl had seen the saddler set his watch by a clock in Chicago and asked what time it was. Her name was Karina and she was on the way to her fiancé. She would find him in the new town of Webster. That was where he had mailed his last letter.

Karina joined them. She played with the children as if it were the most natural thing in the world. For the first time on the trip, Gjertine had a couple of hours to herself, and she opened her Bible. But she didn't like the text she read. How was this verse to be understood? "Whosoever hath not, from him shall be taken away even that he hath"?

Sometimes the Bible was so inaccessible that she felt downright discouraged. And sometimes she was overcome by doubt. Was everything just a beautiful dream? Some said that Jesus Christ had definitely lived but that he couldn't be the son of God—that he was a teacher of wisdom, but human. Hadn't he called himself the son of man?

She watched Karina, who lay on a hard wooden bench with a towel under her head. She felt such a profound goodwill toward this girl. How would she fare? Would she find her man?

All the travelers around her settled down.

And as they fell asleep, there were prayers in many languages. Gjertine prayed morning and night, but her prayers had taken on another form. She didn't pray for God to forgive her sins, because she no longer felt sinful. She lived in grace and it was grace that interested her.

Was it something other than the gift she had received? Her mother-in-law had written to them and said that they should come to the Dakota prairie, and Ole had said one word: *Going*.

Gjertine prayed for her children, one by one, every single night, and she prayed for her good husband with his noble face, and she had prayed for her siblings, and often prayed for Nesje. Strangely enough she prayed more for Nesje, of all people, than she prayed on her own behalf.

On this train, Gjertine started praying for the promised land, for the people who had come, and those who were on their way. She prayed for its leaders and the president in Washington. And she prayed for the Dakhóta.

Gjertine no longer had milk for Edvard. They had to buy and mix it with oatmeal into thin porridge. Edvard did not like this food, but when he was hungry enough, he ate it. Sivert and Sanna sat straight as rays of light, eating their hard ship biscuits. The train rattled over the rocks and swayed through grasslands, and when the hours grew long, they slept.

This was Minnesota, America's breadbasket, where soon there wouldn't be any more land available. Here wheat fields billowed, here corn stood fresh and green forever. Here there was no room; the Dakota Territory was the goal. They crossed Minnesota and saw vast fields. It looked like farming had been there for ages. Virgin land: that is they would find in Dakota. They were emigrants who were now immigrants, even pioneers!

3

The train approached the town of Starbuck, Minnesota, which sat on the western shore of Lake Minnewaska. That was where Sivert Ås, the saddler's father, was buried. The place was crawling with Norwegians. Ole wanted them to stop here for a day so he could find his father's grave. Gjertine thought it was reckless to leave the train that would take them to Browns Valley, sixty miles west.

"Shouldn't we find our way to the living instead?" Gjertine asked, but she regretted the question as soon as it left her mouth.

But the train would have a one-hour layover in Starbuck. And since she was terrified they wouldn't make it back in time, Ole was ready to jump as soon as the train slowed to a roll. He took Olava with him in search of the Norwegian cemetery.

Gjertine, with the youngest three, paced back and forth on the platform. People asked, in Norwegian, if she had come to stay. No, they were continuing on, but Gjertine didn't say where. She was furious with Ole for terrifying her like this.

She got back on the train, determined to travel on alone if they did not come back in time. The train personnel came down the platform, encouraging people to close the doors. Why was Ole subjecting her to this? Only after the station master had blown his whistle did Olava and Ole come running. And the train had begun to pull away when the saddler tossed his daughter in and leapt up like a tiger.

Gjertine said no more about it. Ole said after a while they had found a grave, marked with a wooden board, bearing the name Sivert O. Ås.

They were on their way, west across the prairie. The train came to the cluster of homes that bore the name of Melrose. It wasn't so much different than she had imagined as it was prettier. She had seen a fair number of drawings in newspapers and books of emigrants' hard lives out here. But it was summer, and there were colors and scents and slow clouds in a sky infinitely blue, blue as the lakes. The little locomotive with cattle cars full of people climbed up the hill into Glenwood, where they passed yet another big lake, and continued all the way to Morris. Then the last leg, to Browns Valley, where they disembarked late in the afternoon, and where the travel company put them in a hotel.

4

The two families shared one big room, but that was nothing after sharing a compartment with more than forty people. There stood Karina. What would happen to her? Was she really going to sleep in a room with ten men? She could stay with them. They would put the children in their one big bed and sleep on the floor with a blanket under them.

"I'm still young," Gjertine said when the saddler wanted her to sleep in the bed. "The children will have it. This wasn't their idea."

They fed the children and put them to bed, and Karina wanted to be with them.

"You go on," Karina said. "Just bring a little back for me; I'm not that hungry."

They went to the dining room, where people spoke Norwegian at every table. There were emigrants from the Helgeland coast who had lived in Minnesota for years, and who said the best land was taken. Where were they planning to go? To Marshall County. Some of the men had been there the previous summer and put in their boundary stakes. Now they were going to Britton to register their claims.

One man asked if it might make sense for them to travel together, since they were going the same way. Gjertine and Ole looked at each other.

"It's easy to tire of seeing the same faces," another man explained. "It would do a world of good to have a little fresh Romsdal blood in our flock!"

"We'd like that," Gjertine said.

"And we probably ought to take Karina with us," the saddler said.

Back in the room, Karina took off her fancy clothes and pulled on a pair of men's pants before wrapping herself in a blanket. The others fell asleep right away, but Gjertine couldn't sleep. Karina was surely dreaming, because she was whimpering and mumbling. What would the men think?

5

Word got around in Browns Valley that two new immigrant families had arrived in town on the train, and in the afternoon a man turned up with a team of oxen and a homesteading wagon. He had bought the oxen on his way west; now he had returned to buy horses.

Ole and Peder bought his wagon and oxen for twenty dollars. It included the yoke; there was no use for harnesses. They had seen plenty of oxen, but these were different, with big shaggy heads and legs. Would they get them to obey? Ole removed their yoke, as if he were an old hand, so they could graze.

"I'll call them Abraham and Isaac," the saddler said. "Good day, my patriarchs!"

But Abraham didn't respond, and Isaac merely defecated.

"Do you guys understand Norwegian?" the saddler asked them. "Or do I need to speak English to you? *How are you?*" That was his first thing in English. People said it all the time here.

The seller gave Ole an iron rod with barbed wire twined around it for backup. But the oxen were good natured, he said, and when it was time to yoke them up, they stepped into place between the shafts of the double yoke.

The wagon was the same type they saw others with, the so-called prairie schooner, a four-wheeled cart with a piece of canvas pulled over bows. The canvas would protect them both against the rain and sun. The Ås and Kjørsvika families loaded their chests and boxes and suitcases and bags, but it was so late in the evening that they tied up the oxen to graze. They would leave the next day.

Then the six families, plus one young girl from Helgeland, set out together for Nutley and Roslyn. They didn't know exactly, but it was supposed to be about twenty miles. With oxen, that would take three days through a landscape of lakes and hardwood forests. Everything was fresh and lush. Birds crossed a blue sky.

When evening came they settled down, arranged to put the children to bed, and sat by a campfire they built in between the wagons, arranged in a circle.

They were quite a little flock on the move, but they didn't talk about life's big questions. They made their plans one day at a time and went to bed early. After the second day they began to cross the Sisseton-Wahpeton Reservation, a beautiful landscape of lakes and rivers. The summer heat made the air quiver and the trees took on fairytale colors. They didn't see any Dakhóta, but there was smoke rising in a couple of places. After two days they climbed the Coteau des Prairies plateau.

What a sight! There were hardly any trees as far as the eye could see. Prairie grass, mile after mile, all the way to the horizon. It almost shone the way they had heard about and pictured, as tall as a man and higher, with all sorts of flowers in bloom. Geese flew overhead. Pelicans swooped over the fish in lake waters. One man with a dip net filled it with fish as soon as he plunged it in. How they laughed when he emptied the net onto the ground and the fish started bouncing!

That night they built a campfire and grilled the fish. One of the Norwegians had a harmonica. They listened to the music and delighted in it, but no one danced. Why didn't these people want to dance? Oh no, they didn't dance. They were Haugeans, you see. But hadn't they left home to find a new country and freedom? Yes—freedom from civil servants, government officials, merchants, and other bloodsuckers, but also freedom from their own desire.

Karina muttered to Gjertine, "I would have liked to dance."

The horizon was a line, with not a house to be seen.

From what she had read, Gjertine knew many people felt a chill in their hearts when they saw the vast magnificence of the prairie without any humanity, but she was different. She was filled with a joy for which she had no words. It was like her prayer was answered. This was the country she had longed for, in all its glory. A country without government, where thousands of animals roamed. They would inhabit this world as if on its first day.

That night she couldn't sleep. It was warm, but not unbearably. The starry sky twinkled above. Beyond the little grove of cottonwoods—which they called prairie aspens, even though they weren't aspens—she heard voices. Karina. Gjertine recognized the voice. But who were the others?

She stood there for a second before she composed herself and walked back. As she was fumbling around in the dark, she realized that Ole had gone out. For a brief instant she thought she would die. Then she heard his footsteps as he came walking back.

"Where have you been?" she asked breathlessly.

"Been? I peed!"

He was asleep a minute later.

Gjertine went to the creek to fetch water in the morning, and Karina came up behind her.

"You saw someone was after me last night," she said.

"Yes, but I didn't see who."

"Do you want to know?"

Gjertine thought about it and she said she didn't.

"I don't have a fiancé waiting in Webster," Karina admitted. "That was something I said to be left alone. The truth is that I haven't heard from the man who was my sweetheart for three years. He was one of the people who went to Webster, South Dakota, when it was still just a train station. Then there weren't any more letters. What am I going to do?"

"Go to Webster," Gjertine said. "And see if you can find him. If he has committed himself to someone else, you must demand money because he betrayed you and fooled you into taking this long journey. And if he's a free man, you shouldn't settle down with him, because he failed you once and will do it again. Stay in Webster and find work on a farm, or at a hotel. After a few months you can marry, but not the first man who's interested, or the second. Choose the man who comes night after night and sits by the window while he eats his supper without talking to anyone else, the one who always says thank you and good night."

"You're a psychic. You can see what's going to happen to me?"

"If you don't see the quiet man who eats his supper and says thank you before he leaves, then go to my brother-in-law, Hans Ås, in Grenville, and find us. He's a young guy. If I've understood everything correctly, he might even have an opportunity for someone like you."

"Is he nice? Is he handsome?"

"He's my Ole's brother. You'd better believe he's handsome! Although I've never seen him . . . he lived in Aalesund."

"What kind of woman are you, who can see the future?" said Karina. "What else do you know?

"I can staunch the flow of blood," Gjertine said.

Arrival

I

The last night they slept by the lake named Enemy Swim Lake. There wasn't any road, just a cattle trail into which the oxen's hooves sank deeply. Some rain had just passed, and the creeks flowed swiftly.

"Well, at least we won't die of dehydration," Gjertine said.

But they got dirty, and tired, and there was still a day left before they reached Sisseton.

Nothing challenges travelers like rain. Wet clothes become cold and uncomfortable, and shoes are miserable. But soon the sun returned, the trail dried, and little by little their clothes dried too. Then, another rain.

Three young men stood in the middle of the cluster of homes that was Sisseton with a mule and a load of furs, motionless. It was the Stavigs—Hans, Andrew, and Magnus—who came from the Nutley township, where their father, Lars Stavig, built a house and barn the past three years.

Gjertine had seen these boys once before when visiting relatives in Stavika. Back then the Stavig brothers had been little boys. Now they were strong men who carried huge buffalo pelts as if they were nothing. The eldest, Andrew, spoke English quite well as he negotiated with the fur trader.

The Stavig brothers were able to tell them where Hans Ås and his mother had settled, and that there was land available between the farms and homesteads of Norwegians already there, with names like Hustad and Nerland and Løseth.

There was a cheap guesthouse in Sisseton, run by a Norwegian. There weren't that many buildings yet in what would become the heart of town. Most farms were located far afield, but farmers came in on Saturdays to sell their goods and buy what they needed.

Gjertine, Ole Ås, and their children left Sisseton early in the morning, headed to a place called Roslyn, the others still asleep in their wagons. They had divided the team of oxen to each keep one the night before. The saddler took Isaac.

With the vast prairie sky above, they drove Isaac on a cattle trail toward Roslyn, near Lynn Lake.

Two miles from Roslyn stood a one-story house with something that resembled a tower. That was the house that the Stavig brothers had described as Hans Ås's house. Hans had come across a log building in Webster that was to be torn down. It was the town's first hotel, but after four years the hotel owner decided he ought to build something new, and Hans got the old one.

Gjertine had never seen a house like this. It had six or seven rooms on the back, but in the front was one big room, which, as she understood, used to be a saloon or dining room.

She had also never seen a potato field. And they didn't see a human being anywhere. Ole the saddler didn't want to barge in. He took the yoke off the ox and let him graze and called out so that people would know they had arrived.

There was no response. Gjertine walked around the house. Her brother-in-law had managed to do all right. But where was he? After a while they heard a cart, and Hans Ås emerged from a distant grove of trees with his horse and shay, walking alongside with old Ingeborg in the shay.

Olava ran to her grandmother but stopped short. Her grandmother looked so old, so toothless. She had changed so much in three years. The brothers did not embrace; they exchanged a vigorous handshake, and Ole hugged his mother.

They stood there until they were invited in. Hans and Ingeborg had arranged things the way people did in Norway. They did not have running water, so things weren't finished, Hans said. A bucket of drinking water sat on a bench with a dipper beside it. Plates sat on a shelf. It was meager, but they weren't deprived. They kept their food in a large cabinet, and the little rooms were furnished with beds, boards with straw mattresses Hans also acquired from the hotel owner to use before he built new ones.

Old Ingeborg set out the food, and Gjertine came over to help. The sun was out and it was hot. Gjertine unbuttoned the top buttons on her dress. The old woman glared at her. Gjertine asked if they couldn't eat out under the open sky, since the weather was so nice, but Ingeborg replied that they were people, not animals.

What did she mean by that? Animals (at least domestic ones) ate inside and outside, and so did our Savior, Gjertine thought. He fed a multitude with five loaves of bread and two fish by the Sea of Galilee! Gjertine hadn't come all this way for a lecture. She knew that it would feel good to retort but restrained herself. She would grin and make nice and see how things went.

"So why haven't you found yourself a wife yet, Hans?" Gjertine asked. "With such large fields and what with everything looking so well, you must be highly sought-after."

"Maybe I should decide when I get married?" Hans said.

Gjertine realized that she had hit the wrong note, but she couldn't stop herself.

"We traveled with a girl from Nordland," she said. "Karina was her name, a beautiful young thing. She was headed to Webster to look for a beau who hadn't been in touch with her for three years. I don't think she's going to find him. So I told her that I have a brother-in-law in Roslyn I thought was still single."

"A girl from Nordland!" Hans said. "Do you imagine me wanting a Nordland girl?"

"What's wrong with Nordland girls?" Gjertine said. "She was attractive and kind and had a nice figure. Don't think you should judge before you've seen her."

"They dabble in witchcraft, those Nordland girls," Hans said. "And I don't want any of that in my house."

"Witchcraft? Really?"

"They cast spells on men and take control. I saw it myself in Aalesund. One guy I knew jumped into the ocean at night because a Nordland girl he had been with laid down with another man."

"You can't believe that they're all one way because they're from the same place," Gjertine said. "Surely there are untrustworthy women everywhere?"

No, Nordland women were more wanton and irresponsible, Hans Ås was sure. They came south to Aalesund to work with the klipfish, and trouble always followed them. They had bastards, and then the workhouse had to feed them.

"Whoever ends up with Karina will have the most loyal wife imaginable," Gjertine said. "I'm convinced of that."

Hans had turned away, but when they sat down on the benches around the table, his eyes settled on her, and suddenly Gjertine realized that he was carrying a rage inside of him that would frighten anyone. What was he so angry about? With his dark bangs and that harsh glint in his eye, he didn't look much like his brother.

Pea soup was cooking and Gjertine moved again to help, but the old woman didn't want help.

"Sit down and stay out of my way," she said.

The soup was boiling hot. They had to blow on their spoons. Hans turned to his brother and explained that things were hard because prices were rising. More settlers arrived every year. There were several hundred farmers in the area just around Webster. Lumber prices were the worst because so many people wanted to build houses. They would need to earn before they could build. But Ole and Gjertine didn't need to build right away, Hans said. That could wait until later. He had two small rooms in his house that were empty. What would happen when he reached the point of marrying was another matter, he said abruptly, with a sharp look at Gjertine. The two rooms he could let to them were northernmost, so there wasn't much sun, and only one little window in each, but that should do to start.

Why did they look so confused? This wouldn't cost them anything! He had thought it through. If they could help him harvest the potatoes, they could have both potatoes and space to get them through their first winter.

2

Ole sat there and said nothing. Hans noticed. My husband, Gjertine thought, is not one to do another's bidding.

"But there's still a month to go before we can harvest the potatoes," Hans said. "Maybe you could make me a new harness? I was planning to buy another horse before the harvest."

He had a share in a plow team, an eight-bottom plow pulled by a four-horse hitch. Maybe Ole could repair the old harness that Hans had?

Ingeborg slurped as she ate. They heard the slurping and the spoons scraping the clay bowls. A grandfather clock sat in the back of the room, every tick like a hammer striking, and when it struck the hour, it was so loud that little Edvard started to cry.

Ole took a deep breath and cleared his throat and said he was done repairing old harnesses. He had done that for ten years in Norway and that was enough. He had come here to get away from the repair work, he said.

It grew quiet again.

Then Hans started laughing, and it was not a good kind of laughter. Oh, brother Ole had decided there was work that was beneath him! He advised his brother not to be too picky. In this country work was work, none better or worse: that's how the people who coped thought about it. Newcomers had to work for someone else before they found a way for themselves. A day's wage might be less than they had dreamt. Around here a day's wage was no more than a half-dollar now; farmers couldn't afford more. And crop prices were bad since everyone was growing grain and potatoes. Which was why everyone had to take what work that was available. A person couldn't be too good for it, Hans said.

"Ole knows what he's worth," said Gjertine, who walked back and forth with the baby in her arms. "He'll have a name for himself as soon as he shows his first harness. He brought his tools and it won't take him long to get going. It's good that there's a steady stream of new farmers coming. There's probably demand for harnesses too?"

"I'm familiar with my brother's ability to throw together a harness," Hans said, smiling. "You don't need to chew up the food for the pig, Gjertine!"

"Oh, I thought you were a man," Gjertine retorted.

His smile disappeared.

It was fine that Ole had brought his tools, Hans said. But it was going to take more than that to make harnesses. Where was Ole going to work? He was going to need a roof over his head, wasn't he? And a workbench and a chair?

Hans needed to know if they wanted to work for him, he said. Otherwise he needed to line up someone else. He figured that, together, Sivert and Olava could handle as much as an adult. The question, Gjertine said, was whether Olava shouldn't go to school. Hans asked, How were they going to manage that? There was a Miss Russell who held school in Roslyn, but that was a long way to walk. Maybe Olava could live with another family so she could go to school, Hans said. There might be a family in Roslyn that needed help.

In terror Olava looked first at Gjertine and then her father.

"You'll stay with us until you're ready to go," Gjertine said. "I can teach you what you need to learn until there's a school in Roslyn."

Ole unpacked his tools and spread them across the table to check that everything was there. Then he turned to his brother.

"I'll make a harness for your horse," he said. "That will be the first thing I do. But before I get started on anything, I want to see the countryside with my own eyes and not the way you see it, brother. We need to figure out where we're going to stake our claim, but it might take time, because wherever we settle, that's where we're going to stay until the end of our days."

Yes, said Hans, they should take a look around. They came to a free country. But they needed to give Hans an answer as to whether they would help harvest the potatoes.

Once Gjertine hung up their first real laundry since they had left Norway, they got in the oxcart and headed out.

"It's going to work out," Gjertine said.

"I need to get going, so I can earn money to buy lumber," Ole said.

There was lumber for sale in Webster, the Stavig brothers had told him that. But they had also said that the lumber was too expensive for people coming over without much more than the clothes on their backs. They would have to work a few years before they could buy beams. That was why new sod houses were constantly popping up, and some people even dug into the ground to make a root cellar, a *dugout*. You wouldn't freeze to death in one, even if you'd never seen anything so primitive. Ole wondered, Would they settle for a dugout to begin with? Or was a house of peat sod the answer? They had seen both types on the way. Primitive things, but a properly built sod house would keep you warm, and a dugout protected people when the terrible snowstorms came.

"We should make peace with your brother and stay with him over the winter," Gjertine said. "Then we'll build next spring."

Roslyn was no town. It was a cluster of homes by Lynn Lake. The town had been given its name by the first postmaster, who named it after his own hometown of in Scotland. There was a small café where you could buy food and beverages, run by an Englishman, with eggs and bacon for five cents.

When they returned, Hans and his mother had gone to bed. The next day they went out again, and the day after that they wanted to go out again. Getting around with the one ox was incredibly slow. Hans tried to cheer them up, and even loaned them his horse and cart to visit Webster. The people they encountered could tell they were new, and everyone wanted to give them advice.

"Scrape your shillings together so you can build a proper house," they advised. "Don't build anything makeshift. But if you have no money at all, you'll have to build with the stuff that's free."

Many of these small settler homes had sod roofs like the buildings in Norway, which required the roof to have a good slope for the water to run off, but not so much that the dirt slid off when the rains came. Flat roofs without sod needed little drainage and they saw many examples of those. Windows and other building supplies were for sale in Webster.

"I'll never build out of sod," proclaimed the saddler, who only moments before had been thinking of doing just that. "I'm going to build with wood."

"Yes, that's all well and good, but where would the money come from?" Gjertine asked.

They stayed in Webster for hours, writing down what everything cost, and then drove home. What Gjertine would remember from that first summer were the colors. It was the prairie's profusion of flowers and the brilliant blue sky. The lakes were infinitely blue on sun-filled days. And the butterflies, and the glorious plumage of all the birds, and the scents so new and dewy fresh every morning, the aroma of honey, the fragrant, drying grass. And the clothes people wore were colorful too. On rare occasions in Norway they would see colored cloth, but most clothing was dark gray or black, homespun. Here both men and women walked around in light blue pants and long, red shirts, with leather vests and cheerful hats.

At the end of that first week they traveled north again toward Sisseton. Many people said the soil was more fertile there than in Roslyn, but who to believe? The soil here is like Red River Valley, people said when they reached Sisseton. The clusters of homes on the prairie were competing with each other to become the most prominent town. They competed to get the railway and told stories about how splendid their town was compared to the others. In Sisseton there were thirty inches of black soil, folks said, and below that a kind of yellow clay soil. The soil there soaked up a lot of water and held onto the water so that it could tolerate long-lasting and extreme heat without damaging the crops. There were springs, creeks, and rivers. The lakes were rich in fish: black bass, several kinds of pike, and all the other fish you found here. People cultivated corn and wheat, and these two crops were definitely the ones you saw most of, but there were also people trying their hand at flax, barley, and rye, and the potatoes Hans Ås had invested all his money in. There were also several types of cattle grazing in the tall grass. They provided milk for butter that could be sold when the farmer and his family didn't need it. They heard that the wheat yield could be up to twenty-two bushels per acre, and each bushel was worth about forty dollars. That was a lot of money. A man who grew wheat on all his land could be left with an unbelievable sum of money! But before you could harvest, you needed seeds, and you needed to have several varieties, the saddler felt, in case one failed. There were sprouts and starts for sale, and many people tried cultivating the wild oats that grew. They bought some chickens and brought them home, where the saddler built a little henhouse by the northern wall.

They claimed 320 acres only a few miles from Hans and Ingeborg. They could look out and see each other, but didn't need to meet every day if they didn't want to. Then Anna and Peder Kjørsvika came and put down boundary markers on the north side of the land Ole and Gjertine had taken. There were a couple of small lakes, so there was no risk of being without water. That had happened at Slutåsen during some summer droughts, and the saddler did not want to go through that.

Gjertine traveled to Webster and registered the land in her husband's name. It wouldn't have occurred to her to do otherwise. But she insisted that the man keeping the records spell their name correctly: It shouldn't be "As," but rather "Ås"! And so it was that she came to spell her name differently than in Norway. She didn't want the Americans to keep pronouncing the G at the beginning of her name, which was exactly what they kept doing, so she from this point on she spelled it *Hjertine*, with an H, though not in the letters she sent back home.

Winter stood at the door, but they didn't know when the snowstorms would come. Was there still time to build?

They still had a few dollars left from their trip, and they equipped themselves as best they could, but they knew that Hans's enormous potato field awaited them.

The potatoes people grew in South Dakota were a big, coarse variety, dry and mealy. The potatoes could keep through the winter, Hans said. But the other farmers were betting on cattle, to be sure of having milk and meat throughout the winter. Gjertine and Ole and the children saw people harvesting wild hay and bringing it indoors. They reaped it and dried it on the ground, then brought it under a roof or in a stack where they cut it. Other folks were trying the usual varieties. They planted fields of timothy grass and clover, bluegrass and millet. Most farmers believed wild hay was cheapest and best.

3

The morning of September first, Hans brought in two horses in addition to the two he had to pull the hitch that would dig the furrows. Then Ole and Gjertine's travel companions, Anna and Peder Kjørsvika and their son, Anders, arrived. They were going to help as well. All Norwegians in the area who had a free hand had to help with Hans Ås's crop.

Gjertine was happy to see Anna. That was one aspect of life that she didn't want to admit, a bit of loneliness she sometimes felt in her life with her husband—regardless of how often they agreed, how often they found their way to each other at night, and how affectionately they spoke to each other.

They started early in the morning. Everyone except baby Edvard helped. A young girl who watched him spoke English, and this way, maybe, Edvard would be the first to master English. Olava worked like an adult. She would do anything to avoid being sent away. They tossed potatoes into wooden buckets and emptied the buckets into big crates that sat throughout the enormous field. Peder lifted the crates onto a cart and drove them to a root cellar by Hans Ås's house. From there they were delivered, little by little, to the shops in Webster.

Ole the saddler wasn't happy. He hadn't come for this. After one week he had had enough, and snapped at Gjertine after she spoke tenderly to him. Gjertine had asked him, Didn't he want to take off his shirt since it was swelteringly hot? He barked back that how he dressed was his business.

She said to him, "I am not trying to tell you what to do. I am showing you consideration, as you should for me."

Then he was quiet, and later he apologized.

Gjertine said, "I traveled halfway around the world to be here with you and to build a future. But I will not tolerate sulking, hitting, or scolding. Treat me the way you did when I came to you."

He said that he couldn't live without her, and that night he showed her a kindness, which transpired without sound. When Hans cleared his throat in another room, they realized that the former hotel wasn't soundproof. But they had to be allowed to touch each other, being husband and wife

Saddler Ole often had to be away from Gjertine now. As soon as the weekend came, he traveled to Sisseton to talk to the Stavig brothers about what kinds of hide to tan for leather to make good harness straps, and to pick out what he needed, which he bought on credit. He stayed until Monday and then was the first one out on Tuesday morning.

His brother Hans smiled, but it was not a good smile.

Hadn't Ole agreed to help his brother with the potatoes, since he was giving them a roof over their heads?

Gjertine straightened her back in the field then and said, "Ole needs to start on his own work. If he isn't a free man, he can't breathe. When he's away, I will extend my day and pick for two."

"The day isn't that long," Hans said.

There was a whole crew working Hans's potato field. The men drove the four-horse hitch to plow the furrows. The women and children ran behind, prying potatoes out of the sandy soil with hoes and tossing them into buckets.

When evening came, everyone went home but Gjertine. She used the hoe since there weren't any more plowed furrows. It wasn't as fast, but picking potatoes with a hoe is something she had done since she could stand up. In her mind she pictured the sky growing dark at Bortegard. But when she stood up she found herself below the dome of the prairie, the stars out.

She came inside after it grew dark, ate what she could find, and collapsed into bed. The next day she was out there at daybreak.

That's how it was on Monday, and she kept it up. After their breaks she was always the first one back in the field. She occasionally felt a little queasy, but when Hans approached, she hummed and sang. Hans had to admit that Gjertine was growing on him. He valued her for being such a hard worker. But even in the potato field, they did not get along. She almost pitied him. It seemed like Hans Ås wasn't comfortable in his own skin. For all his labor, he still seemed to stand on land that wasn't his. She couldn't do anything but tease him. When he leaned on the hoe and rested, she chided him: "You've got to keep at it, Hans! It'll be winter soon, you know!"

Then he worked hard, but when he sat down on a potato crate to rest he looked forlorn. What was wrong with him? Could a man be so be sorrowful because he didn't have a woman at night? It certainly looked that way.

When she tried to discuss this with Ole, he said that everyone had to forge their own happiness. Then Ole went to Sisseton again.

Gjertine woke up that night with severe abdominal pains: hard spasms or cramps, and she felt wet between her thighs. No one had even told her about things like this, but she knew right away what it was. In the dark she made her way out to a little creek and washed off the blood. She hid her bloody clothing under a big rock, then she washed herself again and walked back to the house. This was a private matter. Even Ole didn't need to know.

That morning she went to the field. She said she wanted to make a deal. She wanted to keep every tenth potato she picked, to eat and for seed potatoes, and Hans agreed.

Now it didn't feel so wrong. If she stuck with it, she might be able to do three bushels a day, which was about a Norwegian *tønne*. If she picked thirty bushels and kept one tenth of it, she would be left with three bushels for her family. Then they would be able to manage until next summer.

Gjertine Eriksdatter was there under the soaring sky on the endless plain of the prairie. She stood stooped over, picking potatoes in her brother-in-law's field, which stretched as far as you could see in all directions. And when the others called it a day, she stood there still, a tall Norwegian woman with a scarf on head and a dress that reached down to her ankles. Only occasionally, when she straightened her back, could she see the undulating prairie. She still thought that South Dakota was a land of milk and honey, even if the only thing visible as far as the eye could see was dirt.

4

It was a warm, dry, lush fall. When it grew dark Gjertine went home, but she wasn't afraid of the wild animals everywhere. As the nights grew darker the coyotes howled and ducks and geese migrated above.

When the evenings became chilly and they had to light the stove, she saw that the lack of wood was going to make things difficult. Hans Ås burned rock-hard bundles of stiff, dried native grasses the cows didn't like to eat, or pellets of buffalo dung they found on the prairie and that made a strange smell, or wood when they found it. Sometimes Santee men came selling wood. They said they had wood, and if they received payment up front, then they would just go fetch it. Gjertine found the men who came to the door handsome, but she didn't know if she could trust them. Gjertine didn't want to be tricked. So she used the English she knew with some words in Lakota. Then the men smiled and brought the wood, and she lit a roaring fire in Hans's woodstove so that the heat would make it to their rooms, which were farthest away.

5

The saddler went to Webster to acquire raw materials for a horse collar, and soon his first harness ready to show at the market at the Roslyn post office, where every Saturday the farmers came with their goods. There you found corn, wheat, potatoes, and rye, and could sell every kind of wares: linen, dried fish, plucked birds, and beef. Few Norwegians were growing corn; they didn't know how.

Saddler Ole didn't want to be his brother's farmhand, and he didn't want to spend the winter under his roof. But they didn't have any other option. Though it was cold, they kept to themselves in the two rooms Hans let them use, and they didn't join Hans and Ingeborg in the evening.

Once all the potatoes were brought in, Gjertine told Ole that though they still lacked just about everything, most of all she missed having stationary, and she wanted to write to her family back home in Norway.

The next time Ole went to Webster, he bought the finest stationary they had and a steel pen, which was what everyone used here instead of a quill and inkwell. But he came back with his harness; he hadn't gotten rid of it. When Gjertine asked what had happened, he only said there were enough harnesses in town.

What had happened to him in Webster? He refused to talk about it. Now he wanted to go around to the Norwegian farmers and show them the first harness he made in America. He figured that he needed ten dollars for it. It had taken him two weeks of work, and five dollars in materials.

Gjertine sat down by the small window, which let in a little light, and wrote to her brother Ola. She told him about the trip, by boat to England and from England to Quebec City, without hiding that it was an exhausting journey, but she also made a point to mention they had arrived in less than a month. Then she went to postmaster Russell's post office in Roslyn, and he stamped and postmarked the letter. It cost her ten cents. She promised in the letter that she would write to the others at Christmas.

6

Sara and Ola, who scarcely said a harsh word to each other (apart from that day when Gjertine came to announce that she was going to America), found their domestic tranquility ruined.

Ola received the letter from Gjertine on a day when he was clearing rocks from the field. It was a miserable, rainy day and he was wet all over, but he cursed to himself and vowed that he wouldn't give in until he completed a big section. Bastian Elisæus, nine years old now, was with him.

Bastian Elisæus could dig out rocks as well as any boy. It wouldn't be long before he measured up to a grown man, and he helped his father diligently, but his intellect didn't go as far. So when Ola asked the boy to run back to the barn and bring a pitchfork to load the rocks into the cart, Bastian Elisæus didn't do it, even though his father explained it several times. Then Ola lost his temper and hit the boy, who fell over and then ran into the woods.

Bastian Elisæus didn't come home until late that night. When he did turn up he seemed calm, but Ola was ashamed, and realized that he'd have to take steps to end an untenable situation.

His mortgage payment had been due on October 15, but Ola hadn't paid the money because he didn't have it. It was only a matter of time before the sheriff came to the door, demanding a foreclosure. Barring a miracle, the date of the foreclosure auction would be set, maybe even before Christmas, and Ole and his whole family would be driven off the farm without anywhere to go.

The prospects were unbearable. Ola went back out again to keep removing rocks from the soil, though it was bedtime. One stone was stuck, and Ola could not pry it lose. He grew so frustrated that he hurled his pry bar into the ground, where it stuck. He could not pull it out. He had to find his brother the next day to help him. This was how he told the story later, anyway, when it came time to defend his decision to sell the family farm.

7

It was a decision made in anger, but when the pry bar got stuck Ola took it as a sign. Higher forces were supporting his decision and this was the way it was to be.

There was a row.

"Is this why you carried me off here? And kissed me so long that I couldn't leave you?" Sara asked her husband.

"I can't get any more money to give to the bank," Ola said grimly. "If we don't leave, they'll take the farm away by force."

He had never looked so small and worn out.

Sara decided that she wanted to fight for her life in Norway. She took the steamer to Molde and turned up, unexpectedly, at Rekneslia. Sara spoke in a low voice as she explained what Ola was planning. Could Serianna maybe convince her brother to find some other way out of the situation?

Serianna accompanied Sara back to Bortegard at Hoem to talk to her brother, but the matter was decided.

In the winter he took his *faering* out, but his fishing efforts were a bust. The spring fishing hadn't been successful either—the herring had vanished. There was a country across the ocean that could feed its own children, and Ola wanted to be a citizen of that country. He didn't care if people said he was too old; he was only forty-four. True, that was getting up there, but he didn't always think the way others did.

His sister Gjertine had written to him. She and the saddler had claimed 160 acres from the American president. That was the equivalent of 650 *mål* of land. They were living with Hans Ås right now, but the saddler was making every effort to build a house of their own before the snow set in.

"650 *mål*, that's ten times what we have here!" Ola said.

"Ola, this is the land of our ancestors! You can't leave it," his sister Serianna said.

Ola shook his head and said, "That doesn't matter anymore, sister. We're in a new era."

Serianna looked around the kitchen in the home where she grew up and lived until she met Nesje. Would it end up in a stranger's hands? The farm tools and the chests that belonged to the family, some since time immemorial, would they go to other people? A hundred years of toil by their ancestors, and Ola was going to leave it behind?

Serianna felt how exhausted her body was from the grueling days of haymaking. They had barely enough fodder for three cows. They would never manage to feed more than a fourth, no matter how hard they worked.

Sara stood in the doorway with her back to her sister-in-law.

"What are you thinking about, Sara?" Serianna asked. "You're so quiet."

"I'm thinking that if we leave now, we'll never see these mountains again."

Sara went outside and sat on the hillside looking over at the fjord. She saw the cruciform church in Vågøy and the houses on the other side, and she said that she wanted to live on a hill like this in America, with a view of the water. But there weren't any fjords in South Dakota; Gjertine had been quite clear about that.

8

Serianna went to see her brother Erik the cabinetmaker, who had built his house and barn a stone's throw away, to see if he might be able to buy tickets to America for Ola and his family and in return reclaim the part of the farm that belonged to Ola. But the cabinetmaker couldn't. He smiled sadly. He had more than enough to handle.

Then he suggested something that at first upset Serianna, and then left her deep in thought. He asked Ola and Sara to leave one of their sons behind when they went to America, because Erik and Anne were childless. It would probably have to be the youngest, the one named Anton Edvard, because they didn't believe that Bastian Elisæus was altogether right.

Serianna was offended that someone would just say something like that. Only someone who was childless could not understand how strong the bonds between children and parents were. Sara said aloud that she'd rather die than leave one of her children behind.

But when Sara said exactly that, the cabinetmaker suggested to his wife that since Serianna and Nesje had three sons who were still children, maybe they could spare one? Erik was thinking of Anton Edvard, who was still so little that he wouldn't object, because he couldn't. Because eventually as children grew that's what happened: they didn't want to leave their mother and father.

Serianna felt something seize her, something more than fear. She had four children, but she didn't have any to give away. She returned to Rekneslia shaken and worried, thinking about what her brother had said. Nesje saw that there was something to this idea, but didn't bring it up until after the children were in bed.

"Ola has made up his mind," Serianna said. "He's leaving in the spring. He can't make the bank payments anymore."

Nesje realized that this wasn't the time to criticize Ola for his extravagant ways.

"Anne doesn't seem able to have kids," Serianna continued, "and Erik wants to have a boy, an heir. He wanted Edvard at Bortegard to stay in Norway with them, but Sara wouldn't hear of it."

"They wouldn't leave their own flesh and blood behind," said Nesje.

"So they asked if they could have one of ours," Serianna said.

"Well, we certainly don't want that!" Nesje said. "Our kids should grow up with us, shouldn't they?"

"Of course," Serianna said, incredibly relieved.

"But the idea was well intentioned," Nesje said. "They probably thought it would be easier for us that way too."

9

The residents of Grenville township were mostly Poles, and the Norwegians didn't interact with them very much for the first few years, even though Hans's farm was in Grenville. Eden township, a few miles farther south, was mostly populated by Germans. The Norwegians wanted to build their own church, despite the fact that the Germans were also Lutherans. Hans Ås was the chairman of the church committee, and he talked about it whenever he had the chance. It was a great cause, maybe the greatest he would encounter, he said. He wanted Ole and Gjertine to attend the gatherings held at his house, but Ole had thoughts of a house of their own; God's house would have to wait. He needed to put down at least one hundred dollars with the lumber man in Webster, and he estimated it would be another hundred on top of that before the house was finished.

"You'll have to borrow it!" Gjertine said.

"How can I borrow it? I don't own a thing! I have no collateral."

"You have everything you've made and your profession and your art as a saddler. Go to the farmers, whether they're Norwegian and live in Roslyn or German and live in Eden, and tell them that you can make them harnesses this winter, but that you need five dollars in advance for each one, because you have to buy the leather and the buckles and the bit. You can make twenty harnesses, can't you?"

"That would be one a week," the saddler said. "I'll have to work day and night."

"They say the winters are long here," Gjertine said, and she showed her strength. "Go to the Stavig brothers and get leather. Make the collars out of Douglas fir that you can get on credit in Webster, and then you'll buy a hundred dollars' worth of lumber. They'll have to wait until spring comes to receive the rest."

He couldn't contradict her, no matter how hard he knew it would be.

Two weeks later, Ole had collected a hundred dollars from the farmers in Roslyn, and a week after that he was on his way to Webster on the sleigh. The snow had arrived, but wasn't accumulating in big drifts yet. The air and the prairie landscape were mute and still, as if they were waiting.

10

When the first real cold arrived they had to beat their chests to warm up and wore mittens when they worked. But saddler Ole poured his foundation before temperatures fell below freezing. On that foundation he would build a little house, fifteen by fifteen feet, one room, with a little loft where the three biggest children could sleep. It was Douglas fir, already scored, so that the notching went quickly. When December came, they were still living with Hans. Some neighbors came and helped Ole with the notching: not Hans, and not Peder or Anna Kjørsvika, who had settled in the outbuilding at Lars Stavig's place and did not understand the rush.

They thought the saddler was overdoing it, and Ole wasn't the type to ask for help.

Ole worked on the house all day, and at night he sewed harnesses until he couldn't see his needle. Gjertine brought him food and acted as his assistant. The ringing blows of the hammer and the bite of the ax chopping and the squeak of a saw through wood were the most wonderful sounds she could imagine.

Once the roof was on she borrowed a sled and pulled the chest from her mother over to the new house and set it in a dry spot. The chest from the Romsdal coast, which Ingeborg had brought to Bortegard more than forty years earlier, was a kind of lighthouse inside the unfinished structure, a lighthouse that would show them the way through to the harbor. Gjertine thought that the chest carried what her mother called the song of youth. And so Gjertine always sang when she came to the unfinished little house on the prairie where the chest sat. It was a half-hour walk, but Gjertine wanted to show her husband that she was in good shape, and she didn't tell him what happened the night he was in Sisseton buying leather on credit for the harnesses.

II

The three biggest children were at the new house all the time. Olava assisted her father with nails and everything else. Sivert and Sanna lasted an hour before they grew

bored and went over to the Hustads', where they had play-
mates. Gjertine had little Edvard on her back, as usual. She
walked home again with the empty sled. Inside the dark
house, she walked right into Hans, who was going to do
some shopping.

"I have a question for you," he said.

"Ask whatever you'd like, Hans."

"What do you have against me?"

"I don't have anything against you, but my husband
needs to be a free man," Gjertine said.

"I arranged for this large floor plan so that we could all get
by," Hans said. "But all you want to do is get away from me."

"I did the work of two people this fall," Gjertine said, "so
our account should be even."

"Everything was done with the best of intentions," Hans
said. He stood so close to her that she could feel his breath.
Then he put one hand on her breast and pushed it, as if he
were weighing it.

"Hans, what are you doing?"

"I don't know what I'm doing. Why do you always walk
around with the top of your dress unbuttoned?"

He moved his hand off. He looked confused. Then he
touched her again, and she moved his hand away.

"Christmas is coming," Gjertine said, looking him
straight in the eye, "and we'll celebrate it together. But then
we're moving. Your mother is old enough now that she can't
keep house for you, and I don't think you should continue
looking after things on your own. You either need to get married, or you need to find a woman to tend your house."

"It can't be marriage," said Hans, and he was desper-
ate. Then he put his hand on her breast for a third time, and
Gjertine didn't move.

"What is going on with you?" she asked.

"I'm going crazy," Hans said. "Sometimes I think that I need to go back to Norway."

Then old Ingeborg walked in. She stopped short when she saw them, crossed herself, and began to turn around.

"What do you want, Mother?" Hans yelled.

"May God preserve us, one and all!" the old woman exclaimed. "But there's a woman outside asking for you, Gjertine."

"Now who's coming out here?" Hans said, and walked to the door, as if he wanted to chase the visitor away.

"Are you going to seduce my other son now?" Ingeborg asked Gjertine, and doddered out of the room.

"This place is a madhouse!" Gjertine said.

It was Karina Wold from Nordland, standing there with winter in her hair and on her cheeks.

"I'm looking for a position," she said. "I'd prefer to work in a Norwegian home."

Gjertine looked at Hans. She took a couple of steps back and didn't take her eyes off him. He gasped for breath. He wanted to speak, but no words came out. Only after a long time there came a gurgling sound.

"You're welcome here," he said, or something like that.

Gjertine put her coat back on. Then she abruptly turned from him and left. When she was out of view she shuddered.

Later that afternoon, Hans came up in the sleigh with his carpentry tools in a box.

"I'm going to help you get a roof up," he told his brother.

"What made you decide that?"

"I sent word to the others too," Hans said.

As Christmas snow fell in Grenville you could hear hammers striking, and after two days the roof was on. Peder

Kjørsvika was there, exercising his faith, as they called it. He had no fear of heights. He had a jaw full of nails and he hammered in each with a single strike of the hammer. The walls went up two days later, and after they installed a big woodstove, the saddler was able to fix up the inside. The windows went in, but Gjertine wanted to stay with Hans over Christmas, and as usual, Ole complied with her wishes. On Christmas Eve they ate porridge and sang a hymn. But because they were in America now, they would celebrate on Christmas Day. Why now? Tomorrow was the day the Savior was born.

On Christmas morning, Norwegians came in from many directions. The Stavig brothers and their legendary father, Lars, came from Nutley township. He was like a patriarch. Though he looked more like a grocer, he was their Norwegian Moses. The Hustads and the Kjørvikas came, and the Løseth family with their children and dogs.

It was such nice weather, no wind at all, that the Christmas guests weren't afraid to stay after dark, figuring they could drive home in the moonlight. So they fixed a meal in Hans Ås's house and shared what they had brought: dried fruits, pies, and cooked meats. They served dried fish and the Hustads brought four pounds of butter. But the highlight was a plum juice that Lars Stavig brought in a cask. They were so merry some believed it more wine than juice.

"It's like at the wedding at Cana," Lars Stavig said, "where the water was like wine!"

The mood was cheerful yet somber. There were enough people to sing Norwegian carols and dance around the little green bush Hans had brought inside. There wasn't a dry eye to be seen as they joined hands to dance around the Christmas tree. Gjertine made sure she was next to Lars, who had also heard of her. He may even have met her when she was a young girl.

"It's your fault, you know, all of this!" she said.

What was?

"That we all wound up here! I heard that you were going to emigrate the year I stood before the pastor in Vågøy! Now, twelve years later, here we are."

Lars Stavig wasn't chatty though. He was more interested in singing carols.

"It was in the Lord's hand," he said.

They stood waiting for Hans Ås to say which song to sing next. They were loud and restrained at the same time, as if they didn't really know how to behave. No one had brought any alcohol. Nor did anyone want to play cards on Christmas. Christmas was the children's holiday, and most of all they wanted the children to be happy. There were children of all ages. They had cleaned themselves up as best they could and put on the best clothes they had. Karina minded the children so that everyone else would enjoy the gathering. She knew countless children's games and rhymes.

Karina glowed with youthful, girlish joy. Everything had worked out, and Hans, too, had a twinkle in his eye. Yes, Uncle Hans was like a changed man, said Olava, who would be ten this Christmas and understood he was happy because Karina had come. But Ingeborg, the old grandmother, went around grunting.

"I suppose you won't button up your dress now either, not even in this holy Christmas season!" she said to Gjertine.

"No, I need more air than ever now," Gjertine said.

"You get air through your nose and mouth, not through your teats!" Ingeborg said, and then she went to bed in the middle of the celebration.

Gjertine didn't want to ruin the party, and Karina didn't know what to say to cheer her up.

"You can see into the future," Karina told Gjertine. "The only thing I don't know is if it frightens you."

"I can't see everything, but I did know that you'd come back from Webster," Gjertine said, "because a man who doesn't keep in touch for three years isn't worth keeping. I knew you'd come to that conclusion. And then I had mentioned another man who was available in the area. It's just a matter of putting two and two together."

What Gjertine didn't say was that Karina had arrived at a moment when she was thinking fervently of her.

"It's good that we have room so everyone can celebrate Christmas together," Karina said. "I said so to Hans today. I said, 'We should do this every Christmas!'"

She was a peculiar person, Karina. She sounded as if she had always been here, and as if she were the lady of the house, not a housekeeper. Gjertine couldn't figure her out. She didn't like that, and it made her anxious.

"Would you watch Edvard for a while," she said, and handed the boy to Karina.

She put on her coat and went out. There were little snow-drifts on the road; many sleighs had driven by that day. She stood with the vast snow extending in every direction, and she could hear singing. There was another round around the Christmas tree, children's voices chiming in.

And she, who always felt such strong joy when men sang and children were happy, felt she was standing at a precipice, an abyss that wanted to pull her down. She had to struggle to find her balance before she turned and headed back to the house.

Just then Ole came running out. She had never seen him like this before. When he couldn't find her inside, he had grown afraid.

"Where were you going?" Ole said. "I was looking for you."

"I just had to gather my thoughts," Gjertine said.

When they came in again, Hans was giving a little speech as the others stood around in a half circle. It was crowded. He paused briefly when Gjertine came in. He was talking about the church again.

"It will require us to sacrifice," Hans said. "Many people haven't gotten their own homes up, but it's high time we built a place of worship. Five hundred dollars would bring us a long way to our goal, if we also add in our labor and love. And we need a piece of land. Maybe one of us would see fit to donate some."

None of us have as much land as you and your mother, Gjertine thought.

"And we need to be on our guard, and make sure no shady characters come in to sow discord among us," Hans said. "Unfortunately that's happening in so many places among us Norwegians."

What was he getting at now?

Then someone cleared his throat, and it was none other than Lars Stavig. You couldn't really say that he was old. But in this group, he was among the eldest.

"You just said the truest thing that's been spoken tonight," he said. "You hit the nail on the head, Father. There has been far too much conflict among the Norwegian settlers about our views of Christianity," Lars Stavig said. "The flock of us Norwegians here in Roslyn, Sisseton, and Nutley is simply too small for us to tolerate any conflict! We need to stick to what the scriptures say, and we must have faith in what it says there, every letter. We can't just pick and choose what we understand and approve of. We must either reject all that has been preached unto us or embrace everything."

Gjertine noticed a little uneasiness in the small congregation. This probably wasn't the time? Shouldn't they be celebrating? Couldn't these discussions wait?

There was moonlight over the prairie when the families said their thanks. Their horses stood tied up by the barn wall. Only one family had sleigh bells. But there was a peace in the moon's glow over the prairie, and that one sleigh's bells sounded heavenly.

In January, Gjertine and Ole received a letter from Nesje. They hadn't been expecting one, and they certainly hadn't expected him to write so vividly about Molde:

The Swiss-style chalet in Humlehaven is light with luminous lamps. Paper garlands are strung between the leafless trees. The Christmas Day turnout at Molde Church was enormous. But things are quiet at the Alexandra, and there are hardly any guests at the new Grand Hotel.

Marshall County

I

Ola and his family prepared for their journey to America all winter. Ola rowed across the fjord to talk to Governor Hagerup, who asked him why a farmer who held title to his farm would want to take his children and leave his fatherland. Ola told him the truth: he had failed to pay the mortgage bank and now he needed to take action before the foreclosure auction was held.

County Governor Hagerup signed a document stating that Ola was leaving the country legally, that he was too old to be conscripted, that he would pay his debts by auctioning his house and home, and that the governor would be present when he did.

They had to sell most of their property to buy the tickets to America. And that's what happened. They sold their personal property and also the *faering*. Soon they owned only the clothes on their backs. Ola set aside two things: the pry bar he had rammed into the ground and his magnificent church saddle. No matter how heavy it was, he intended to ride on the prairie in that saddle. Sara did not contradict him. Why argue with him on small matters when she couldn't get her way when it mattered?

Sara tucked aside some silver spoons that she and Ola were given for their wedding.

They held the auction to see what they could get, but there were no credible buyers for the farm, so a second auction would be held. Ola and his family would be long gone by then, but Erik would handle the farm sale when there was a better prospect of a good price, since the buildings would be empty then and the crop sowed.

2

The biggest potato grower in Day County, Hans Ås in Grenville, drove his potatoes to Webster by sleigh all winter. It provided him a good income and made him arrogant, but something had also happened to the man. He bought a second horse and a wagon with high sides.

"I wonder if he's leaving Karina in peace?" Gjertine mused.

"My brother, the chairman of the church committee?" Ole replied.

"He is pious, but he is a man like any other."

"He's as pious as I am musical," the saddler said, and whistled off key.

"The question is whether he manages to walk on if her door is open at night."

"When a woman leaves her door open at night, that means she is," the saddler said.

They had been living in their house for a month. It was cramped, but they had a woodstove with an oven. The saddler had learned the English word for harness. Better sooner than later, he figured. Harness, he said, *harnesset eg held på med*. The harness I'm making.

He never was good at English. He cut the hames for the collar and for the decoration to be attached to the back of the harness out of Douglas fir, or oak when he could get it. He went outside when the weather permitted, so he didn't fill their one room with shavings and sawdust. He found a blacksmith in Webster with whom he got along, and that's where he got terrets, tog pins, buckles, and metal fittings.

They were more or less the same no matter where you were in the world.

Long after the children and Gjertine went to bed, Ole sat up working. The way he borrowed the money had been easy, initially, and he and Gjertine had moved in quickly, but it made Ole both serf and lord without a moment's peace. The light was so poor that his eyes burned, and Gjertine daubed them with herbal drops from a bottle, a remedy from Webster. Ole never had time to open a book, and the moment his head touched the pillow he was gone. This wasn't so popular with his spouse, but Gjertine *had* said that they shouldn't have any more children, though she was only twenty-eight, so there was no need to argue.

The winter passed quickly. The Norwegian farmers who gave Ole five dollars up front wouldn't leave him alone, though he'd said that he wouldn't be done until spring. Gjertine realized that if they were going to do any farming, it was up to her to see the grain sown and the potatoes set, and they would especially need to bring in hay.

When the snow was gone one Sunday in March, Gjertine went to see her mother-in-law on snowshoes. Old Ingeborg had been poorly all winter, so Gjertine went to cheer her up.

Hans answered the door in a state of distress.

"She tempted me with witchcraft," he said.

"Who tempted you?"

"Karina. Her door was open. I went in to her, I couldn't resist. What will the pastor say when he finds out about this?"

"'For better or for worse' is what the pastor will say," Gjertine said. "You'd better prepare for a wedding!"

"She ran when I said she cast a spell on me. I don't think she went far."

Gjertine went over to the farm where Peder and Anna had put up a little shack. They were living with Lars Stavig while busily working toward a place of their own. There sat Karina, tearstained, in despair.

"You have to go back," Gjertine said. "The wedding should be held the day before Palm Sunday, because the worst of winter will be over, and the pastor can come from Morris."

When they returned to the house, Hans dropped down onto his knee and asked her to be his bride and said he would be faithful to her for all his days. Ingeborg stood in a dark corner and crossed herself.

Gjertine witnessed the whole thing, but now Hans and Karina only had eyes for each other. Gjertine went on her way. For some reason, she felt discouraged.

The wedding was celebrated at the house. The Norwegians grumbled about their harnesses, which Ole the saddler still hadn't delivered. Ole was so tired after all the long days he had put in since Christmas that he could barely hold it together. But he didn't say much, and he did not give a speech for his brother, as many had expected. Nor did he dance, though a man had brought a fiddle. It wasn't until Gjertine insisted that he stood and danced with his wife, without smiling, his head held stiffly.

3

Ola, preparing to leave Bortegard, heard back from other emigrants what types of goods were lacking in the land of milk and honey. He brought his whetstone, several changes of clothes, cured meat and flatbread, and potato dumplings in a pail, like a fisherman. They packed the pail tightly full, and when the weather was hot a layer of mold grew on top, but you could scrape that off when you didn't have anything else to eat. Sara packed a silk handkerchief from her wedding, the silver spoons, her Sunday clothes, two pairs of shoes, and undergarments. Most of the things they brought were for the children. They had four children, with a fifth in Sara's womb.

Erik had his own *faering* and sailed his brother's family to Bud early May, 1887. Out on the fjord, Sara turned around one last time, and then she launched into a wail so heartrending that the children cried too. Ola watched with a small, ashamed smile, as if everything he had done resulted only in unhappiness.

Ola's family arrived in Kristiansund on May 18, 1887. The next day, they boarded the SS *Hero*, which took them to Hull. From Hull they took the train to Liverpool and from there they traveled on the SS *Nova Scotian*, which arrived in Quebec City in June. Thus began the long journey along the lakes by train to Browns Valley, Minnesota. It was ninety-five degrees when they stepped out of the train car, but they had survived. None of the children were sick, and Sara, four months along, hadn't had trouble sleeping. They looked at each other and smiled. Ola had fallen from Sara's good graces, but she trusted him and knew he would give his life for his family.

That's when they saw her: a tall woman in a long dress that reached to her ankles, the bodice unbuttoned at the top, like a traditional work shirt, revealing ample cleavage. There stood Gjertine Eriksdatter. She had come by horse and cart from Browns Valley in two days. A woman who turned out to be Hans Ås's wife was with her. Gjertine looked as if she had always lived in this foreign country, but when she saw them she cried out in the Romsdal way, saying it was "*fole fint*"— wonderful—to see them. Their luggage was on the cart, they headed out to Sisseton and Roslyn. They were to stay with Hans Ås to start, and Ola said that picking potatoes was not beneath him.

The saddler was in Roslyn. He was so busy that he hardly looked up when Ola and Sara and their children arrived having traveled halfway around the world, but Gjertine took the knife out of his hand. He had been cutting out a bellyband with it. Then they took a break to visit.

4

The 1880s drew to a close. The years passed so quickly that Nesje could hardly tell them apart. He worked long hours. He had spent his best years working the soil. With the scythe he was a grim reaper.

Reaping with a scythe is tiring work even if you're skilled. Hillsides are hard, and it's onerous to mow big fields. Nesje had worked the scythe his whole life, from when he was a young boy. He had mowed the Gørvell farm for forty years, worked his days for Leth in Reknes, and made hay on his own parcel. He had developed a method that let him cut a whole day and still have some strength in the evening. You couldn't waste effort. You had to find a steady rhythm, as he put it, so you didn't take those little five-minute breaks to catch your breath. It was this regular, wavelike pull that made the difference. You wouldn't get far without decent tools. That was why lead haymaker Nesje went along on those rare occasions when scythes needed to be replaced. He went to Brovold's Hardware Store first with Claus, and then with Adam Gørvell, to pick out the new ones. He tested the edges with his fingers, swung the scythes in the doorway to make sure there were no cracks in the steel, and held them to the light to check that the blade was forged correctly.

When he was a boy, he made the long scythe snaths himself in the woodshop at Kvam, but now there were good long snaths for sale in the mercantile. They were slim and strong and supple, the best ones made of knot-free birch. All you needed to do was be sure it was sharpened correctly. You couldn't leave the sharpening to anyone, which was why Nesje sharpened the scythes on the Gørvell farm himself. A scythestone could be synthetic, as long as it made the edge thin and sharp. When you honed, you used as much water as possible because the water rinsed the particles that came off the blade when you honed it. Best was when the edge was wet with dew, when you could wipe it clean with grass. When mowing on dry days, the haymaker brought water to the field, and as he rehoned throughout the day, he dipped the scythe blade in, or he could throw some water onto the whetstone.

The haymaker couldn't start cutting until this was done.

Only a fool would swing an unwhetted scythe, and fools never lasted long. Nesje had watched many admit defeat in the hayfield while he was able to keep going, hour after hour.

In his prime years, he looked forward to the day when the haymaking began, because then he knew when he would be done. Only then could he finally start on his own land. When the children were little, he would run off as soon as he had some food, and then at midday Serianna or one of the boys would bring him more.

Nesje mowed, cutting a wide swath, but he didn't bite forward into the grass very far with each stroke. He cut the edge of the grass in a wide arc and brought the scythe around more than ninety degrees to swing the scythe entirely through with the same heft and speed. You couldn't stand there hacking at it, and you had to follow the ground as closely as possible. That way you cut the whole straw, and the meadow would look like a living room floor. The height of the stubble showed who was inexperienced. You could sometimes see where Nesje mowed because he only left roots. He was a tall man, the right height for a long snath. He had the right swing, and in the summer his arms were like stone, so he could show them off in the evenings and earn the respect of his sons.

Even so, haymaking wasn't about strength. It was a way of being, he said. You had to be with the scythe in the right way if you were going to endure the season. If you swung hard you could bring the scythe through the entire forward stroke. And when you swung the scythe back, that return also had to be done in one big, uninterrupted motion, because otherwise you were done before noon.

You could see in the older haymakers this hard work had its price. Those who had spent a life in the haymaking field sometimes developed the shakes in their arms, so they could no longer write their own names or eat soup with a spoon. Gørvell assigned young men to the mowing, because they were the only ones who could keep up with Nesje.

Everyone saw a good haymaker had been there; everyone knew a thorough job had been done, so the work brought satisfaction. It wasn't just labor; there was an art to it.

In the morning you could use the dew, and the scythe became a predator's jaw that cut everything in its way. When the sun rose in the sky and the grass dried out, it was harder and all the more important to maintain that steady rhythm. When the afternoon shift began, and many napped, it was a matter of chasing Odin's sleep thorns from your arms and finding the power in your body again. An inordinate appetite came over you as you walked in the summer with the scents of dew and clover.

He had one ugly enemy, a tiny insect they called *smikke*, the biting midge. They came in the tens of thousands when there was no wind, tiny no-see-ums that bit everywhere and were especially drawn to the neck and scalp. So mowers wore wide hats and tied scarves around their necks, but mostly it was a matter of working up a sweat, which was thought to reduce the scourge of midges. Everyone worked harder when the insects were out, since their work distracted them. As the midges devoured them, they hummed and sang and worked harder. They wandered like flocks of singers on their way toward some destination. In truth, it was more a lamentation than a song because the midges bit so terribly. And you needed two hands on your scythe. As in a pilgrimage, great peace awaited them when they finished.

Of all the pilgrimage paths our Lord prepared, the one that runs through hay is most beautiful. You pace with the scythe until you reach the neighbor's fence, then you walk back. That route is the Lord's way. The midges are a work of the devil.

On windless nights Nesje tackled his own steep slopes, and the midges appeared when the sun went down, so by the time he eventually went inside, he was eaten up. He washed in piping hot water and even washed his hair with pine tar soap so the devil wouldn't feast on his scalp while he slept.

5

"How is the grass?" Serianna asked when he came home late, and he always replied that the grass was good, meaning it was growing well. Of course, when the grass was good, it was harder to cut. But haymakers wanted a good yield. In years when the meadows were easy to harvest, there wasn't much joy. It was rarer now for them to dry hay in the field. Now they hung it on racks and Adam Gørvell had a horse-drawn rake with big wheels, so he didn't need girls to rake anymore. The horse-drawn hay rake pulled the hay into piles they then hung on the wires of the racks. This was tough work done by men.

There was no longer the same contentment or playfulness to haymaking as there had been, or the same exuberance during meal breaks. People earned a higher wage now if they brought their own food. Serianna brought Nesje his midday meal, and she kept him company while he ate. When he was done she walked back up the hills to Rekneslia.

She wasn't an old woman yet, but she was forty.

The days passed in sun and wind in the fields at Reknes, and when the haymaking was done and they gathered for the celebratory porridge, Adam Gørvell didn't skimp. It was cooked in massive pots, swimming with rich cream. Sitting on the table in big wooden crocks was traditional buttermilk. After that the cured meats and flatbread came out, and those who knew no moderation could eat with depravity. As some of them left the table they would practically moan that they weren't fit to work. That's how it was in Nesje's day, and after the porridge the best was still to come, because he had two weeks off to bring in his own hay. True, first he had to put in his days mowing for Leth, because he had leased his hillside from him. But Nesje was only one helper on a team there. He ate his own food there and never stepped foot in the house. But as late summer arrived, and the rose hips and rowan-berries reddened, then the time came for the haymaker to harvest his own parcel. The nights were not as light, but the birdsong still came at four in the morning. In the years when Nesje didn't sleep well, he would sneak out to work at dawn and catch a nap after lunch. He was no stranger to a snooze in the hay. He would work even harder after a nap, because the work to be done increased every year as he made his place bigger. It wasn't until late in the fall when the crops were in that he could take a trip into town and hear what people were talking about. By then the haymaking at Gørvell's farm was a distant memory, though the toll still lingered. Those forty years were the best of his life.

6

In the early years something was off, but Nesje didn't notice. His work was his destiny, and his desire to do it was a priv-ilege. But it was gradually turning him into a solitary man. He wanted to fix that, fix the thing he had lost, but his work took most hours of the day, and he couldn't make his pres-ence felt the way he had when he was young. The friendships of his youth he made while strolling down Molde's only street, or while skiing in the winter, or on quiet evenings by the fishing lakes up in Moldeheia, were disappearing one after the other because he wasn't there. At first he didn't notice it. Nesje was an extrovert, but since he worked doubles and always felt he was neglecting his children, there was no room for friends. Nesje and Serianna rarely attended any gatherings or parties. No one invited them, but he didn't notice, and if he did, he wouldn't let it bother him. If, on a rare occasion, there should happen to be an invitation, he found some argument against going. And when it was too late, he breathed a sigh of relief. He was happier in his own home, and he had much to accomplish there. But there was something else, in addition to friends and acquaintances, he also lacked. He hadn't lain with Serianna for a year, and she wasn't showing any sign of wanting to.

"Hey?" he said in his gentlest voice as he lay beside her. "Hey?" he would whisper when she blew out the paraffin lamp, and he put a hand on her shoulder. But she responded, "Not now, not now, too soon."

And she removed his hand, gently, and rolled away.

7

Gjertine's second cow was calved on the land they called their own. They didn't have a fence up, so the cows were tethered and then moved when they had grazed everything in reach. Gjertine tended to her cows around the clock. They built a barn for the animals by one of the ponds, but when the summer came the pond dried up and she had to pull the cows, one by one, a long way to water.

Gjertine had hens as well, and a horse she rode when she needed to go to Roslyn or Webster.

Roslyn wasn't that big, and neither was Webster. Most people noticed the Norwegian woman who had settled on the outskirts of Grenville and who came to Webster once a month to shop. It was sixteen miles from Gjertine's farm, four hours to get there and four hours back again.

She wasn't plump—she worked too hard for that—but she had a strong body and a round, welcoming face, which frequently lit up with a smile when someone spoke to her. She worked hard to do what needed to be done, she rode her horse with confidence, and she got sweaty and hot. Men who saw her smiled and said to each other that she was quite capable, that one.

Gjertine visited the shops in Webster and watched new buildings. There was something new almost every time she took the wagon with the little black horse. She learned from the Norwegian grocer there that Webster had a short history. It had started in 1881 when a train station went in, right there in the wilderness, a station on a line that would continue on to Aberdeen. Three cars of emigrants were the first to arrive. There were no travel company agents, so the train cars shunted off to a side track to unload. One man named Sauer squatted on a piece of land to which the railroad company owned the rights. His friend procured lumber for a hotel he called the Baltzer House, which was the building Hans Ås later bought. The second man in town was named Ochsenreiter, which means "ox rider." He took on a man named Andrew Smail as his partner. The two names combined perfectly: Ochsenreiter & Smail. That had a ring to it.

E. D. Landon and R. H. Smith established the first brewery in Webster. Barse and Hutchinson opened a land office on Railroad Avenue. Then the town brought in A. C. Tuttle to start a newspaper, the *Reporter and Farmer*. In 1882, the Prior House was opened, and by 1884 Webster was able to boast of a variety of shops and establishments. J. C. Bush had a livery barn and Dr. Harris opened a drug store. The Norton General Store was founded, and then the saloon opened. Then someone arrived named John Prendergast, who became postmaster. When he first arrived he was a tinsmith.

Gjertine preferred to go to the new Farmer's Hardware when she was in Webster. They could help her with what she needed on the farm, which she ran on her own. Olava, too young to go into service, helped her watch the younger kids.

8

Three weeks after Ola and his family left Norway, his brother, Erik was summoned to the auction at Bortegard. County Governor Hagerup came to make sure that everything was handled properly. They had to let the farm go for a thousand kroner, even though that was only half its value. Erik received enough to cover Ola's debt, but there was no money left to send.

The buyer was a man from farther up the fjord. His name was Elias Hansen Svenøy, but people soon switched to calling him Elias Hansen Hoem, as was the custom in Norway when a person moved to a new farm or village.

Elias and his wife, Gjertrud, had a single son. This son was given the name Edvard, which was fashionable at the time, and, as the son of a man named Elias, the last name Eliassen.

In the fall Erik and Anne traveled to Molde to attend a mission meeting. It was really an excuse for a trip to town. They weren't Readers, but it was interesting to listen to a meeting like this, attended by people who had spoken with Africans and convinced them to bend their knees to Jesus.

The meeting was all well and good, but after they arrived in Rekneslia, where they were going to spend the night, Nesje noticed Erik talking to the boys and saw that he favored Anton Edvard in particular.

Once the children were in bed and it was quiet in the loft, it was only a matter of time before the topic came up, as if in passing—yes, it might even first have been mentioned as a joke that there sure were plenty of up-and-coming farmers here. Erik said that Anton Edvard in particular seemed to have a good attitude about this and that. There may well be a working farm available in Frænen someday, Erik pointed out. But it was late now, and they ought to sleep on it.

Nesje lay awake late into the night. Serianna noticed, and he explained what was bothering him, and then she couldn't fall asleep either.

Nothing was said the next morning. The guests put on their best clothes and walked to church. When they came back, there wasn't much time before Erik and Anne left to take the steamboat home. In the end, Nesje just had to say something, so he asked if they really wanted his youngest as their heir.

Erik said that if they did, he would have to come join them as soon as possible, and as far as Serianna was concerned that settled it. She couldn't send her baby away. Then Erik and Anne said, "No, no, if the parents refuse . . ." and went to catch the steamboat. Nesje and Serianna didn't have a chance to talk until everyone went to bed. They agreed that sending Anton away was out of the question.

But a few days later, it was just as clear to Nesje that he couldn't simply reject the offer outright. This might be the kind of lost opportunity that his youngest would hold against him later. But there was no way to ask the boy what he wanted; he was still a child. No child with a good life wants to leave his parents.

Without knowing where things stood, they saw their relatives again over Christmas, and by this point Nesje was more amenable to the idea. He humbled himself and asked if the offer for Anton Edvard was still good. It was, but they needed to know what the answer would be soon, the cabinet-maker replied, because there were other candidates under consideration. Serianna was stunned that her husband brought it up. She thought they had turned it down once and for all. But now Nesje asked for a deadline, and he and Erik agreed that it would be decided by the first day of summer, which according to the calendar would be April 14, 1888.

Serianna cried. Couldn't they wait until he was a few years older? Couldn't they wait until he was ten?

But there was no putting it off. Well in advance of *Sommermål*, they sent word to Frænen that the boy would arrive by Midsummer, so that he could start at the new Hoem.

Goodbye and Hello

I

On June 17, 1888, Nesje turned fifty, and Anton Edvard, who shared his birthday, turned seven. They didn't usually give each other presents, but they did wish each other a happy birthday and ate supper together, something there wasn't always time for. Fifty years was a round number, after all, and a seven-year-old is done with the first part of childhood, where playing is as important as one's obligations. The rest it, as we know, is not child's play.

So Serianna lit a candle at supper, though it could hardly be any lighter during the "nightless days" of the midnight sun.

There sat Eilert, almost twelve, and Kristine, nine, and the parents on either end of the table. Though they had said that everyone needed to be home by eight o'clock, Bastian Georg wasn't there. He was in town somewhere. Nesje was sad that his eldest didn't show him respect on this special occasion, and then he said they should start.

As they had helped themselves to the porridge, Bastian Georg came home, and they could tell that something had happened he didn't want to talk about. After he finished he got up from the table without waiting for the others. That affected the mood. Nesje could see how tightly pursed Serianna's lips were.

As his mother cleared the table, Anton Edvard asked if he could speak with his father in private.

Nesje said, What was on his mind that the others couldn't hear?

No, he wanted to talk to his father alone, and Serianna said they should go outside and have a conversation, man to man.

"You have to help me," Anton Edvard pleaded.

"Help you with what?" Nesje asked.

"Help me get out of going to live with Uncle Erik. Please, Papa."

It was a heartbreaking moment as his son stood before Nesje and begged to be allowed to stay home. Then Serianna came outside. The summer evening, which had just been so glorious, turned bleak and gray.

Nesje looked at the boy, then at Serianna standing beside him with her face hard and unyielding, and looked back at the boy again, seeing eyes full of tears. It was as if Nesje's voice came from somewhere else. He only had one way out: "Your mother knows what's best for you," he said, afraid his heart would stop.

"Am I really going to stay there all my days?" the boy asked.

"What do you mean by 'all my days'?"

"Am I going to live and die on the back of those mountains?"

"Well, that depends on which side you look at it from," Nesje said. "The people over there think they live on the front side."

"The sun doesn't shine behind the mountains! For twelve weeks of the year!" the boys complained.

His mother told him that, and she had grown up there.

"Well, that means the sun does shine for forty weeks," Nesje said, but the words left a bad taste in his mouth.

"When you grow up," he added, "you'll get to decide where you want to be."

"How am I going to leave?" the boy said. "If I'm even going to go, I mean?"

Nesje thought he had a marvelous idea: "If you ultimately decide that you don't want to live on that farm," he said, "there is something in Throndhjem called the School for Non-Commissioned Officers. Some of your ancestors went there!"

The boy bowed his head and walked around the house, over the rocks, and on to town. Nesje wanted to run after him, but Serianna stopped him. Nesje sat down on the bench behind the house he'd built with his own hands. In a flash he realized that he was losing a second son. Hans had left when Serianna came and had barely been back since he had moved to Throndhjem. In fourteen years, Hans worked his way up from errand boy in Throndhjem to store manager in Kristiansund, but he didn't have time to visit his home town. If a store manager is in charge of his own hours, Nesje thought, why doesn't he come?

But this was about Anton Edvard now. Since the decision was made, and the boy was resisting, Serianna thought it best to make quick work of it. The next week she packed the clothing her youngest son would bring into a sack that she could carry over the mountains. They would go on foot. Since they would be gone for a few days, her daughter, Kristine, would also come. The two older boys could look after themselves.

Serianna and the two youngest children walked into the woods and took the path that led over the mountains to Åndal in Frænen, then hiked over the shoulder of Mt. Jendem to Hoem.

They came down from the mountain to a little spring, the one people called Sælebotsikla, or Health-of-the-Soul Brook, which flowed where the church road came down from the mountain. Serianna was not as youthful as she had been, and her hips ached after the long hike. She bent down and drank.

"You two drink too," she told the children. "Whoever drinks from Sælebotsikla will live to a hundred."

The boy hesitated.

"I don't want to stay here until I'm a hundred," he said.

"After your confirmation you can go anywhere you want," his mother said, "even America."

"That's where I'm going!" the boy said. "I'm going to America and I'll turn a hundred there."

He bent down and drank. His sister drank too.

"I'm going to live until I'm a hundred too," she said. "But you're still going to live longer than me, because you're younger than I am."

They walked toward their destination. They walked past the house at Bortegard where Serianna had grown up and lived until she was thirty. Ola and Sara had lived there with their five children. Now another family had moved in. Serianna didn't look; she didn't want to put herself through that. She had that big bag on her back, and the children ran free, first behind her, then ahead of her, but now she took them by the hand. She walked with the poise of a queen, but she slowed, as if she didn't know if she was doing the right thing.

"Why are we going so slowly, Mama?" Anton Edvard asked.

"I just want to a look around. This is where I grew up, and this is where you're going to be."

Her sister-in-law Anne met them at the door. The cabinet-maker was in the cowshed. He came in and they ate supper, but the conversation between the sisters was halting, as if they both disliked what was happening. Anton Edvard thought the food tasted funny, he said, and no one seemed happy about that.

"Get used to it," his uncle said.

"It's about bedtime," Serianna said.

Anton Edvard thought it was strange to go to bed when it was still light out, but he went.

At seven in the morning, Serianna was ready to leave. Her brother gave her cheese and butter in exchange for her son. Serianna and her brother had always got along with each other, but now nothing felt right. It was a short goodbye. The weather was rainy. They stood in the yard and got wet.

"Go inside and sit down by the window," Serianna told Anton Edvard. "Then you wave to us and we'll wave to you for as long as we can see you."

Anton Edvard thought they would see him longer if he stood outside the house than they would if they were watching him through the window, but he did as his mother said, taking a seat by the window and waving until they were a few stone's throws away. His sister was walking backward, and his mother too. They waved and waved. Then suddenly they turned around. They couldn't see him anymore. He stood up and wanted to go outside. His uncle stopped him.

"What would you like us to call you?"

The boy looked confused. "My name's Anton," he said.

"Well," his uncle said, "you have another name. You're also named Edvard."

"We'd better call you Edvard," his wife agreed. "That way we won't mix you up with Anton at Nordgarden."

"Can you go out and move the horse's stake, Edvard?" the uncle said. "Do you know how to do that? Bring the ax over there. You just knock the stake into the ground. You are seven after all."

"I can do it," said the boy with the new name. He took the ax and headed for the door.

"What's this I see?" the uncle said. "Are you wearing shoes, in the middle of summer?"

"It rained. The grass is cold. Why, is it wrong to wear shoes?" the new Edvard asked. "Surely I can wear shoes if I want?"

"You listen here!" the uncle said. "From now on, I'm the one who's going to be keeping you in shoes, and I don't want you wearing them out over the summer. You can put your shoes back on in the fall after the first frost!"

Then to his wife, Erik said, "It's terrible how they're spoiling kids in town, letting them walk around in shoes all year 'round."

Anton Edvard took off his shoes and went outside to move the horse's stake. Another boy was standing on a little hill above the house. They approached each other without speaking. They stood together at the edge of the meadow above the house. It hadn't been mowed yet.

"Want to race through the grass?" asked Per Andrias from Nordgarden.

"I'm not allowed to do that," said Anton Edvard. "I learned that already."

"You're not allowed to run through the meadow?"

"Not before it's mowed."

"That's the weirdest thing I've ever heard," Per Andrias said. Then he ran through the meadow and darted back to his house.

That afternoon the uncle stood scowling at the trampled footpath through the tall grass. Per Andrias was coming. Anton Edvard suspected that something was about to happen that he might not be happy about.

"Who ran through this meadow?" his uncle asked.

Per Andrias pointed at Anton Edvard, and didn't say his name, just pointed.

"I told him not to do it," Per Andrias said, "but he wouldn't listen to me."

That evening, Anton Edvard's uncle beat him.

"I'll teach you to unlearn those town ways," the uncle said, whipping the boy's bare backside with a willow whip. Anne tried to put herself between them, but the uncle said, "I must chasten him diligently, it says that in the scripture!

*He that spareth his rod hateth his son; But he that loveth him
chasteneth him diligently!"*

"I suppose that's true, yes, but he's not really your son."

"Who else is going to punish him?" the uncle yelled.
"You mustn't contradict me, and certainly not where he can
hear it. *Let the women keep silence in the churches.*"

"This is no church," Anne said, and left.

The uncle let go of the boy and the boy pulled up his pants.

"You should love me and obey me as if I were your father,"
his uncle told him.

"I already have a father," said the boy who was Edvard.

"I'll teach you to be impertinent!" the uncle yelled and
picked up the whip that he had tossed aside. But there was
no more whipping. It was as if he had regained his compo-
sure. Later that night, Anton Edvard saw his uncle sitting in
a chair and crying without a sound, but the boy never found
out why. His aunt Anne stood with her back to him, washing
the dishes.

2

Ola decided to claim land in Marshall County, in the hills
by Buffalo Lake, which had previously belonged to Fort
Sisseton, but was now open for settlement. The area opened
because the US Army no longer used the fort. The hunt for
land in South Dakota had started eight years before Gjertine
and Ole arrived. By the time Ola reached Sisseton with Sara

and their children, there was little left in the central part of Roberts County. Much of the land in the area was part of the Sisseton-Wahpeton reservation, which belonged to the Santee Dakhóta. The eastern border of the reservation ran southwest from Lake Traverse to Lake Kampeska, three miles west of Watertown. This created a triangle delineated by Big Stone Lake, Grant County, and the reservation. This reservation, which was called the Lake Traverse Indian Reservation, was a homeland for the Sisseton Wahpeton Oyate, the Santee Dakhóta people. The reservation was comprised of portions of seven counties, but most of the reservation was in Roberts County, South Dakota.

On a clear autumn day, Ola was on his way toward the hills where he had put down his markers with Ole and his two sons, Bastian Elisæus and Edvard, now eight and six. He wanted to decide where to build their house. He planned to dig a dugout where they could winter. He hoped to build a house of wood next summer and move the livestock into the dugout. Sara and the girls would stay with Gjertine until he could put a roof over their heads.

Ola had asked Sara to find the twelve silver spoons his parents had given them for their wedding. Sara knew right away that this would be the last time she'd see those spoons, but what could she do?

She had handed her husband the silver spoons, one by one, and he packed them into a cloth sack that he carried on his chest.

When Ola and the saddler and the two boys were halfway to the hills of Buffalo Lake, Ola saw smoke rising from a small Dakhóta village. He asked the saddler and the boys to wait, because he wanted to speak to the Dakhóta—and he wanted to do it alone. The saddler thought this was risky, maybe dangerous, and what would become of Sara and the children if anything should happen to Ola?

Ola said the words that would become something of a motto for him in America: "When the white man acts like a human being, the red man also behaves like one!"

So there they stood, Ola's two sons with the saddler, watching Ola walk toward the Dakhóta village. They saw him stand outside a tipi for a good while, before someone flung the bison hide aside.

Among the Norwegians, only Ola could say what transpired. What was he doing? Ola later claimed that he got along so well with the Dakhóta because he studied their customs. Most importantly, he said, when a door was closed, you waited outside. You announced yourself and waited to be invited. Then you sat down, but only when you were asked to, and you always sat on the left side of those who were already there, and always closest to the opening, while the residents sat farthest in. He said a large family lived in this tipi: nine children, the mother and father, and a grandmother who had been most interested in white people. Ola's Norwegian accent was heavy and his English limited, but the family in the tipi understood why he was there. They hesitated before meeting his request halfway. Ola wanted to buy a tipi, or enough buffalo hides for a tipi. They were reluctant to give this to a white man. After all, white people had disdain and then some for Native customs, thinking it would be better for them to live in houses.

But when Ola showed them the silver spoons, something happened. They asked if they could borrow the silver spoons and feel them. According to Ola, they stuck the spoons in their mouths and then split their sides with laughter at this utensil white people ate soup with. The man of the family, who Ola said was one of the handsomest men he had ever seen, was still disinclined. The man didn't take his eye off his guest, not even while he discussed the matter at length with his mother. He did not seem unfriendly, but he did not smile either. When Ola spoke in his heavy Norwegian accent, the man nodded thoughtfully but shook his head. His wife was so beautiful, Ola later said, and she nodded and laughed and agreed with on everything. The grandmother, on the other hand, wanted to help Ola because, he thought, she understood he needed a roof over his head, and she gave him credit for observing Dakhóta etiquette.

The grandmother launched into a monologue, and Ola couldn't claim that he had understood every word, but he thought he got the gist. The grandmother reminded her son that it was the women who decided inside a tipi and that she was the matriarch. When the question of being permitted to buy a tipi was asked inside a tipi, it was the women who should respond. The beautiful wife agreed with the grandmother, Ola said, and then she said something in a sharp tone to her husband. Then Ola blurted out *cogito ergo sum!* And the man seemed to concede, and he responded *cogito ergo sum.* Ola had learned this expression from Pastor Jervell when they once had a discussion about life's great questions. Ola didn't really understand what it meant, but the Dakhóta people did. And with that there was agreement.

"*Cogito ergo sum!*" the Dakhóta family exclaimed in unison, and laughed heartily.

It was arranged. The family followed Ola out and showed him to a tipi, not so large, which lay rolled up under a small rocky overhang, and Ola was permitted to take it in exchange for his silver spoons. The man was helpful and even carried the heavy tipi over to the cart where the saddler and the boys were waiting. Bastian Elisæus looked at his father for a long time then, and Ola interpreted this to mean that his son had a great deal of respect for him. Edvard laughed in delight. They got the tipi stowed in the prairie schooner.

But the man followed them, a few paces behind. Ola turned around several times, thanked him for his help and bowed low, repeating his perpetual *cogito ergo sum*, but still the man followed, walking quickly and steadily, pointing and saying something in Dakhóta which Ola couldn't understand.

On the hilly slopes where you could see Buffalo Lake twinkling in the distance, the man grew more enthusiastic. Ola wanted to stop by a small lake there, but the man took the lead and gestured for them to follow him.

The man led Ola a good way up the hill. He stopped in a ravine where some cottonwoods grew, pulled aside some branches that were lying there, then he dug down with his foot, and suddenly there was water sparkling. There was an underground stream there, which presumably ended at the little lake. There was another lake a bit farther up.

Ola looked at the man. After that he looked at his boys, and he cleared his throat. When he spoke, his words were primarily directed at Ole. It was as if Ola were calling a witness when he announced: "Here," Ola said. "We will live here."

He would no longer use the name Bortegard.

"*Cogito ergo sum!*" the Dakhóta man said with a smile of farewell, and walked back the way he had come.

Ola had found his place to live on the prairie west of Fort Sisseton. The prairie was almost treeless, which made the glory of the flowers all the greater. Swooping over the countryside were pelicans and prairie geese, ospreys, swans, cranes, light geese, hawks, crows, woodpeckers, blackbirds, marsh hens and prairie chickens, snowbirds, and wild canaries. Butterflies of all colors whirled over the hills, with prairie grass so tall you could stand in it and not be seen. The saddler realized that this cottonwood grove was where his brother-in-law would stay.

There was a view in every direction. There were big lakes to the south, and to the northwest they looked over the magnificent Buffalo Lake. Prairie hills extended all around in big, rolling movements.

Saddler Ole might have felt jealous if he were the type. This landscape was a paradise for a farmer who had had to leave his farm in Norway, but most especially it would turn out to be a paradise for the sportsman and hunter.

So they put in their marking stakes, which announced that Ola from Norway had claimed this land, and they would later register this with the magistrate in Bitton. The buffalo for which the lake was reputedly named were no longer there, the only reminders a few skeletons. Pronghorn and elk still roamed the prairie, and they saw foxes, coyotes, wolves, beavers, skunks, and rabbits.

For a long time they would remember the moment Ola walked over to his wagon for the shovel he had brought all the long way from Norway and the pry rod that he had driven into the ground. He thrust that same rod into the prairie, and it went right in. Then he started digging on a ridge not far from the cottonwood grove.

"What are you doing, Ola? Are you checking the soil quality?" saddler Ole asked.

"I'm digging a *dugout*!" Ola said. "Whatever the Norwegian word for that is! I know how to do it!"

And he did. He had seen many of them on his travels through Marshall County.

"Don't you want to eat some lunch first?" saddler Ole asked. They had been driving for several hours.

"I'll work up a sweat, and then I'll eat my lunch," Ola declared.

Ole stood for a while and watched his brother-in-law, then grabbed his shovel. Bastian Elisæus and Edvard went to go pick berries with a wooden bucket, and Ole showed them where to look. Strawberries, blueberries, and wild cherries would be a nice treat with their supper.

When evening came, they had dug out about three hundred square feet, one cubit deep. The prairie soil was light and dry, almost sandy. Then it was time to set up the tipi, and Ola cut thin cottonwood poles he stuck in a circle and bound together near the top. The hide was old and worn, but would be home for Ola and his sons that fall. The girls and Sara, who was pregnant and in her sixth month now, would stay with Gjertine and Ole. It was cramped there, but they were welcome.

The next day the saddler returned home to fetch more of Ola's equipment, and the two boys went with him. For two weeks, Ola dug on the prairie. He did not work quickly but in a regular and unbroken rhythm, from the moment the sun hit him in the eye until it set. Then the big man slept in his tipi with his loaded blunderbuss within reach, listening to the unfamiliar noises as he grew drowsy. It took him a month to visit his wife and tell her she could come join him. By then he had made an opening on the east side of the slope for a door, and he was covering the roof opening with ash wood.

Ola brought his household possessions to the dugout, including the luggage from Norway and the farm tools he had picked up in Roslyn.

When Ola dug down far enough to have room enough to stand inside the dugout, he built a sod wall with doors and windows into the eastern slope of the hillside, where his turf hut had a large opening. He built this wall two cubits thick with two different layers of sod. No one had told him to make the sod wall so thick, but Ola wanted to feel secure. Ola supported his double-layered walls with willow and birch poles and filled the space between the two layers with wet, boggy soil or mud. Ola knew the English word *sod*, and he found it funny because it reminded him of the Norwegian word *sodd*, a type of soup. Maybe the soup connotation gave him the idea for the insulation layer. At any rate, there was Ola's first house on the prairie near Buffalo Lake: part dugout and part sod house.

Ola had had the foresight to buy an oxcart with sealed edges and that came in handy now, because he and the boys had to load that insulating mud into the cart from a creek a stone's throw away, then drive it back. He scooped up big wads of muck and packed it into the space in the middle of the double wall so that it was sealed and the two walls adhered. He hurried to finish before the rains came, but he wasn't clumsy about it. He had learned from the experience of building the house in Norway he had left behind. Next he put the roof timbers over the dugout, fitted them tightly together, and over those spread birch bark the way he covered the house at Bortegard, the difference being he didn't have a layer of boards. He stuffed moss and prairie grass between the timbers so that the bark roof was watertight. Then he put a layer of turf, grass side up, on top.

He knew it was one of the best days in his life when he went to Fort Sisseton to buy a door and window from an old sentry hut that had been torn down. Ola went to the fort to "introduce himself," as he put it, and although his English certainly wasn't good enough to chat with them, he met the civilian crew who remained, emptying the barracks of their furnishings. Ola managed to negotiate three beds from the officers' quarters, along with a table and chairs. They stacked these off to the side so that he could pick them up in a few trips.

As rainclouds came gliding in from the west and the sky darkened, Ola drove one load of furnishings each day from Fort Sisseton to his sod house by Buffalo Lake. Those at Fort Sisseton thought it right for some cooking pots, plates, and other utensils to benefit a settler, and so Ola's dugout was furnished more quickly than many settlers' homes. It was November when Ola was ready for his family to move in. When the saddler Ole drove Sara and the four children out, it was again one of the memorable days in Ola's life. He stood on the hillside with his hand on the doorknob. He had long ago decided on his opening line, borrowing it from the Norwegian version of "Good Christian Men, Rejoice": *Træd ind, om her er smaat!* Ola said. Come in, even if it be humble!

Sara reacted as he hoped, clapping her hands when Ola showed her the beds where the children would sleep two by two to keep warm, and the big, proper bed that had belonged to the commander at Fort Sisseton, Ola said.

3

After they ate and praised the furniture, which was sturdier than what they had in the old country, it was time for the saddler to go. Ola sent his wife and daughters and sons out to pick berries. He had noticed plants heavy with all kinds of berries only a stone's throw away. They carried them back in baskets and buckets and pails. When he brought home a cookstove from Fort Sisseton they could make preserves and pickles and bake bread. Best of all was Ola's blunderbuss. He killed two geese in a single shot, and they had hours of plucking and salting. A day later he shot a runaway ox that came thundering along and threatened to trample the fragile roof. He sold the hide to his brother-in-law; that was how Ola earned his first dollar. He cleaned the carcass and butchered it as he had in his homeland.

Ola had to buy potatoes from local farmers. They could get through the winter with about three *tønner*, about twelve bushels. He mowed huge quantities of prairie hay and stored it to dry, because he thought the wild cattle would come to the dugout when it was snowy and there was no food for them. Then he could capture them, milk them, and tie them up outside. That was as far as Ola had gotten before the fall storms set in, but he felt confident that they would get through the winter. This was a hard place to live, this sod home, but once you got into it, it was remarkable what you could accommodate. Eventually, he bought a sheet of canvas that he hung on the wall to make it cozy inside. The bison hides from the tipi became their rugs in the dugout. They didn't cover the whole dirt floor, just the area by the table and the stove that kept them warm.

Most everything came from Fort Sisseton, though they had bought some things in Britton. All they had from Norway was a coffee mill, a mortar, and a copper kettle. That Norwegian kettle was like a small, luminous memory that showed them the way to go if they were going to be victorious.

4

That summer the US government surveyed the land that had previously belonged to Fort Sisseton and was now available to settlers, and immigrants could go to a land office and pick up a map of the land they might want to register when the time came for that. The land had to be registered by the end of 1888, when the survey plats were returned from Washington to the new land office that was to be established in Grand Forks. Ola and Sara made it there with plenty of time to spare.

They all went to Britton, and the money for their work in Hans Ås's potato field came in handy. Sara, heavily pregnant, walked into the courtroom in Britton. Relying on facial expressions and hand gestures, she managed to register their land near Buffalo Lake, as an official took pity on her when he saw that she was going to have a baby soon.

The land Sara registered was the northern quarter of section 4, town 157 north, range 157 west. The court clerk asked her name, and he wrote her into the registry as *Sarah Holmes*, which was the best he could do.

Sara did not have a strong wish to be the registered land owner, but when Ola heard about it, he said that it was entirely right, her reward for having come to the Dakota Territory with him. He, who had to leave Norway because of his mortgage at Norges Hypotekbank, had borrowed money from other Norwegians and gone into debt to procure bedding, salt, and sugar to make it through the winter.

And thus the days passed until Christmas. Ola chopped

down cottonwoods in a grove near the house and cut them and split them so Bastian Elisæus and Edvard could carry the wood inside, but it took time for it to dry. In the meantime they burned prairie grass.

Perhaps Ola was luckier than usual. The frost set in abruptly in October, so that the walls of the dugout froze, rock-hard, and didn't thaw until the spring. There was every reason to be grateful this happened before the winter storms began. Between the frost and the dugout's hefty dimensions, Ola's dugout did not collapse the way many others did. It was snug and warm on cold days, and in the spring sun it was cool and pleasant.

That did not keep Ola and Sara from worrying quite a bit about the winter. They weren't as familiar with the weather or its signs as they had been in Norway. They didn't have ancestors to rely on. Newspapers from Sioux Falls didn't reach them until they were a week old, by which point the weather forecasts were long outdated.

Ola spent some weeks hunting with two of their neighbors. They rounded up wild oxen and shot them with their blunderbusses and other firearms, and carved them up and divided the haul before returning home to salt the meat. He was able to travel again to Roslyn with the hides and sell them to his brother-in-law, who wanted all the hides and leather he could get, and then some. Ole was safely installed in his own house, but he did nothing but work, making harnesses day and night for the countrymen who had paid him up front.

Ola came home with goodies as Christmas approached: raisins and rock candy, coffee and tea, and two bags of wheat flour for fancy baking. Sara with her big belly stood at the cookstove waiting for the bread in the oven to finish baking. It was the week after Christmas when she felt the first labor pains. She let everyone know, and then she went to bed.

There was no midwife, only a neighbor lady from the nearest farm two miles away, when Sara had her fifth and final child just before New Year's Eve, 1888. It was a girl and they decided to name her Marit, or Mary, as people said here, because they were thinking of Mary from the Bible. But then the storm struck.

5

The warning was when mild weather set in at a time of year when everyone expected freezing temperatures. It was their worst winter, that first one. Two months of freezing temperatures followed the first frost in October, but, happily, it never grew warm enough for the dugout to thaw. The snow grew deeper and deeper, week by week, through December and January. Then the cold commenced. Just before New Year's a stream of arctic air flowed in over the Midwest and settled into all the valleys like fog. In cold like that, the senses become heightened and then dulled. The cold is like a knife or a flame that cuts and burns any skin that suffers exposure.

On the prairie, the cold was worse in January. On January 11, the folks in the dugout by Buffalo Lake saw sundogs in the pale blue sky, three colored spots that followed the sun. It was twenty below zero and had snowed the night before. The snowflakes flew in airy drifts, light as feathers, and the sunshine bounced like gold off Buffalo Lake. Suddenly, in only a few hours, the temperature rose by twenty degrees, and they said that spring must be on its way.

Ola was surprised when he stuck his head outside that morning. He preferred to relieve himself under the open sky. The warm air hit his face. And then Sara came and stood beside him and sniffed the air. Did Ola think spring was coming? No, he said, and he didn't like this. There was something unnatural about this sudden heat. Something else was surely to follow.

So far everything was peaceful and quiet. He chopped wood until late in the morning and he carried it inside.

Then there was lightning and thunder. Ola yelled for everyone to come inside, and then the blizzard hit. He only just managed to close the door behind him.

6

Many have said the blizzard of 1888 came with a roar, like a train at full speed. The snowfall didn't arrive in waves; it came as a flood of snow. The air churned.

Ola reinforced the door with some planks that he placed crosswise and drove in with big nails. Then the devil began to wail and yowl, but they had heat in the stove and firewood stacked on all sides.

For four days the blizzard raged over eastern South Dakota. When the storm finally stilled, it took a long time to get out. Ola's door opened inward, as was the custom, so he didn't have to break it. He then spent hours shoveling through the seven-foot snowdrift amassed outside. The snow was piled in deep banks. Eventually, the neighbors came and told them about all the animals and people who had frozen to death in Sisseton and throughout the territory. This came to be known as the Children's Blizzard because more than two hundred schoolchildren froze to death in those four days.

The snow stuck until late April. The critical spring season began dangerously late. Ola planted oats, wheat, and potatoes in the smaller fields he plowed. He had the most faith in cattle, because there was so much grass. He fenced in a big area with barbed wire, and with that came the end of the time when Native people and white people could live side by side. Barbed wire prevented Native people from riding across the prairie. They had to stay on reservations and avoid the land that white people had taken.

7

Hardly any place in the world boasted as big a difference between winter and summer as the Dakota Territory. In the summer of 1888, Ola harvested his first grain crop. The wheat towered like it never had in Norway, and the corn, although with this he had no prior experience, was tall and green, as large flocks of birds flew across the sky. His family had managed in the dugout that first winter. He would wait through yet another year before he could build a house. Ola's harvest was so large that he offered up his goods at the Britton market and bought two horses for the spring plowing. He plowed a big field.

The children ran along the edge of the field watching the corn grow. Sara planted potatoes. The soil here was suitably dry and the weeds less troublesome. In the summertime the days ran together. It was light everywhere, and they rarely saw their neighbors, all of whom—Norwegians, Swedes, and Germans—were busy with their own farms. Every once in a while they would stop by to borrow farm tools or to discuss when threshing time might come. The Norwegians from Romsdal were talking about the new threshing machine. Could they afford to go in on a machine like that?

Sara and Ola exchanged looks when people talked about such things. They didn't smile but they weren't opposed. They couldn't yet afford a threshing machine. They needed a proper house and a roof over their heads. That was at the top of their list. For the next few years they were going to have to thresh the old way, beating the sheaves with a flail to separate seed from straw and grain from seed. They would winnow the grain to remove the chaff, and winnow it again before they milled it with a hand-powered grinder they would borrow from Ole. This was never-ending work they never did in Norway, where almost every village had a water-powered mill. But they were thrilled by how much more the same crops produced here than they had in the old country. Though the winters were long, and they endured stretches where they didn't go outside for weeks, Mother Nature was more generous here. Before the snow arrived, they worked night and day, but when the snow fell in late October or early November, life was different than it had been in their previous life together. They could relax and care for their children, and Ola and Sara loved children. When the children said something memorable, they would look at each other and smile. They smiled at the thought of how they came together, and as the children gradually grew up, their mother told them how their father had stolen her away, scooped her up onto his horse's back, and ridden her away to Bortegard.

But as he neared adulthood, Edvard wanted to know why they had emigrated. It seems that the parents might not have told the truth about this. Instead, Ola made up a story about how the blue people, as folks called the mound dwellers, trolls, and hob-thurses, had traveled over the ocean before them.

Very early one morning, he said, Ola had set out on the fjord, Frænfjorden, and he was pulling a long line with multiple hooks. There was no wind to speak of and not much swell, and the fog was so thick he couldn't see land. Instead of making a fool of himself by rowing off in the wrong direction, he let the boat sit near some islets in the middle of the fjord until the fog burned off.

That was when Ola saw them, the blue people. Twenty to thirty underground spirits, males and females all mixed together, hulders, hob-thurses, small gnomes, and goblins, all dressed in blue and their skin a bluish hue. The underground dwellers were gathering to travel to America.

He called to them and asked, "What are you up to, blue people?"

"We're going to America," the eldest blue male yelled back. "Because this country is no longer a place to stay! Merchants and horse traders and barbers have taken all the power in Norway, so blue people can't stay here anymore."

Then they climbed into their boats and rowed away. That, Ola told his children, was when he knew he needed to leave. He didn't want to be ruled by merchants and barbers either.

Off the Rails

I

A tall, slim Norwegian woman was on her way to Webster with an old horse and a cart that had seen better days. There weren't many women driving around alone in those days, but this one didn't care what people thought or said. She went out on all sorts of errands that her husband didn't have time for. He was still making harnesses at a record pace, and he needed to maintain this furious pace if he was going to have anything left to show for his work. So his wife ran the farm, and she was the one who went to Webster once a month.

Gjertine longed to become familiar with this foreign land, but the language stood in her way. The children were learning English from the postmaster's daughter and knew much more than she did. She tried to lure them into sharing new skills and new vocabulary, so that she, too, could make herself understood.

The old horse kept his own pace and he wandered a bit from side to side, so she tugged the right rein to keep him on the road. Webster was in its seventh year and the streets were paved. So much growth since Gjertine had arrived! The area around Webster was one of the best agricultural regions this side of the Mississippi. It was 230 miles to St. Paul, Minnesota, a trip that took weeks with a horse and carriage, but by train it was no more than three or four hours. The town had a population of a thousand, and a thousand farmers had settled in the surrounding area. There were big and small houses to be seen everywhere between the tallest buildings, including the Congregational Church and the grammar school on the east side of town.

Ochsenreiter & Smail sat on the south side of Main Street and sold not only hardware, but also machine parts and harnesses. Each type of product had its own department, and there was a stable where the customers left their horses.

This was where Gjertine went. Her first visit came after she had already lived in Roslyn for two years. She went to the harness department. She had seen ads in the *Reporter and Farmer*, and even though she didn't understand everything the ads had said, she had the impression that Ochsenreiter & Smail was advertising harnesses for the laughable price of five dollars apiece. If saddler Ole took less than six dollars, he made nothing.

Gjertine wanted to know how they could sell their harnesses so cheaply. She tied up her horse and went inside. The smells of leather and oil struck her. Hanging up there weren't ten or twenty, but maybe a hundred harnesses, alongside riding saddles, reins, and bridles. The prices weren't marked on each individual harness but on a large poster in the middle of the room. She walked over there and saw only that the prices matched what a farmer in Roslyn told her. Five dollars for a shiny new harness, straight from the Brookings Ltd. factory. It was a mass-produced harness, everyone knew that, but as she studied the seams and the padding on the inside of the collar, Gjertine had to admit that this was just as good as anything saddler Ole could make. And he couldn't have done it for that price. This would lead to death by starvation in six months.

A perky store clerk approached. How could he help her? Gjertine responded the way she almost always did when she was in a store: "Just looking."

He gave her a smile that said this was exactly how they lived, people studying their wares to discover something they couldn't live without.

But weren't these harnesses ridiculously cheap? Five dollars? It turned out that the price had come down from eight dollars to five in the past year. They brought the goods in from a harness factory that sold harnesses all over the Midwest. He couldn't guarantee that they were making a profit on the harnesses, but it paid insofar as farmers came back when they needed other things as well. He knew that among the Scandinavians, there was at least one if not multiple saddlers, and one man was even making harnesses. Ochsenreiter & Smail couldn't sit idly by and watch that happen. Maybe they would even need to lose a few dollars? At any rate they kept their prices low until that saddler, or saddlers, realized that the battle was lost. This was how progress happened. Competition brought out the very, very best in every way. Did she maybe know this man? "Ma'am, are you not a Scandinavian yourself?"

Yes, that she was. But did she know this Norwegian, who was apparently both handsome and skilled? Those were incidentally valuable qualities, the clerk said, in God's own America.

"He is my husband," Gjertine said.

The clerk's face changed colors, and then he laughed nervously. But, ma'am, that can't . . . what a coincidence! Yes, well, not so surprising that the saddler's wife was interested in the goods other people were producing. He was certainly a remarkable man, this saddler, but he couldn't compete against machines! Was she asking where these harnesses came from? The factory was located in Sioux Falls. If her husband wanted a job in the harness factory, they might well have a place for him.

But of course she wanted to live in the best part of the Dakota Territory, didn't she? There was no danger that Scandinavian harness makers and saddlers wouldn't have enough to live on. There was always wear, which meant there was always tear, and a place for people who could repair what broke.

She thanked him for the encouragement. As she had said, she just came to look. She should use the time she had, he said, because her husband would be curious about what she had to tell him.

The clerk got down a few harnesses so she could study them more closely, and hung them back up with great care when she was finished. It was often mentioned among the farmers that the clerks at Ochsenreiter & Smail were unbelievably attentive and accommodating. You didn't leave the store without your wishes fulfilled. But Gjertine had only one wish and one prayer: for it not to be true that her husband was outdone by machines, and now she knew that exactly what the situation was.

After she untied her old horse and stood on the street, she didn't know what else to do. The newsroom for the local *Reporter and Farmer* was next door, so Gjertine went in and subscribed. Then she went to the big grocery store, Kertlogg & Co., which stocked everything from sugar and flour to bales of dry hay. After that, incredibly late, she set out for home. She didn't stop when she passed Ed Smail's big lumber yard, where Ole had acquired the lumber for their house and turned himself into a drudge, a peon in the process. She didn't stop to look at the church, which might have offered her a quiet moment. There was even a ring by the church door where she could have tied her horse if she wanted. She moseyed away toward Roslyn without hurrying. Some part of her dream was shattered, and she needed new reasons to have left all the old behind and come here.

She could think of no reason to keep everything to herself when she came home to her husband and children. Ole heard her out without any interruptions, without tears. He had known for a while. He had chosen not to mention anything to her, the woman he lured to America.

That fall Ole was out in his brother's potato field again after he and Gjertine had harvested their own crops. He figured it was time to reconsider. Ole wanted to get out of the saddlery business and wanted to earn money some other way. Farmers still came wanting him to make them custom harnesses, but in most cases he said no. Those who wouldn't back down and who believed it was best to buy a harness made by a Norwegian had to pay ten dollars, and once the potatoes had been brought in, saddler Ole once again sat under a paraffin lamp, bent over his leatherworking tools. On the rare occasion he took a break, it was as if he stared into the darkness within him. At another table, under another small oil lamp, Gjertine sat and read the *Reporter and Farmer*. The newspaper provided her not only with information about what went on in Webster, but what was going on throughout the entire United States. For the first time, Ole would be able to vote in the American presidential election, and Gjertine told him how to vote when the polling place opened at the post office in Roslyn. The Democratic incumbent, Grover Cleveland, was trying to win a second term in office against the Republican candidate, Benjamin Harrison, a former senator from Indiana. The economy was flourishing and the country was at peace, but Cleveland lost to Harrison, who was on the side of industrial factory workers and who wanted a high minimum wage that Cleveland had claimed would harm consumers, who he believed deserved low prices.

2

By the time June of 1889 rolled around Ola determined that the prairie where he had settled was better suited to grazing cattle than to farming. A lot of dirt disappeared when he plowed, after the prairie winds set in. He would do better plowing the eastern slopes where the wind wasn't as strong.

He bought heifers and fattened them up. He had an ox he had sometimes hooked up to a plow along with his good horse. The prairie soil was hard to turn over, and the ox and horse were a mismatched pair that didn't always want to pull at the same speed. So now the ox could make himself useful and cover those five heifers. It was almost too much of a good thing. The next time it might lead to inbreeding, but Ola was planning to slaughter the calves one or two months after they were born, so they would never have a chance to reproduce, and then they would have food in store for the winter. The heifers could be outside until late in the fall, but Ola didn't believe a word of the tall tales about how they could be left outside all year round. True, wild cows could retreat into the forests when the storms were at their worst, but there were hardly any forests here. Ola's heifers grazed inside the barbed wire fence, and there was nothing to provide them with shelter.

3

One June day, Ola and Sara were on the road with two horses, traveling through the sounds and smells of the prairie. A heron shrieked overhead, and an eagle circled far above in widening loops. The butterflies dominated closer to the ground, ahead and all around them, swarms of every conceivable color and pattern. Ola and Sara moved through the middle of this billowing, fragrant, rushing life of midsummer, and the prairie's beauty reminded them of all they had to thank the Lord for.

Ola was almost fifty, but he felt young and strong. Sara was a few years younger, but life's toil had left its mark on her. How did she dare go out without her children? There wasn't anyone else at home who could watch them, was there? No, but Edvard-on-the-prairie was almost seven, and he was uncommonly wise. Sara had no choice but to go, because she and Ola were on their way to Fort Sisseton for an auction that day.

Fort Sisseton was not so far away. From the hills where they lived, they could just make out the lakes. But it still took several hours to get there on a road that was no more than a bridle path, with tall prairie grasses on either side.

They eventually arrived. The buildings at Fort Sisseton were still in perfect condition, both outside and inside, but the soldiers had filled in the moat before leaving. Only a handful of men were left to run the auction, which included eight hundred pounds of potatoes, two big stacks of lumber, a desk from the commander's quarters, a long watering hose, and a telegraph line that had formerly been stretched from Fort Sisseton to Webster.

Not very many people came. Fort Sisseton was too far for most people to travel to. It was more than a day's journey to the town of Sisseton, and several hours to Britton. One Britton merchant came to buy the potatoes.

In a different and better world, Ola and Sara could have used these potatoes for animal fodder and sold more of their own potato crop in the fall. But the lumber was what they came for. There wasn't that much, only five stacks: just enough for one house with two rooms and a loft where the children could sleep.

The four men in charge of the auction were in a hurry and didn't care if potential bidders were still en route. The desk went for five dollars, which was a steal. Next came the stacks of lumber. A lieutenant called for bids, but there was some confusion about whether the lumber was being sold all together or in separate lots.

Sara stepped forward and yelled, "Fifty dollars."

"Fifty dollars for what?"

"For one stack!" Sara said.

"Why don't you take it all?"

"One hundred dollars!" Sara said.

"Sold!" the first lieutenant yelled, and with that it was over even before it had begun. The other auction goers protested, but the lieutenant simply moved on to the telegraph line. Who in heaven's name would be interested in that? For some reason or other, Sara thought about her sisters and parents as she went up and paid. She walked up to the first lieutenant and counted out the bills for him. This was all the money they had, but the lumber was theirs.

Then the auction was over, and they needed to transport the big stacks of lumber to the farm. They loaded up an enormous load, but even so they could only manage less than a quarter of the entire amount in one trip. So, Sara grabbed the reins and said, "God bless you, Ola! You'll have to stay here so no one steals our lumber. I'm sure I'll manage to get it unloaded. These logs were heavy to load, but they'll be easy to roll off."

Ola remained at the fort as Sara drove away. But when she made it home, she realized she needed to go to Roslyn for more help. Ola slept by his stacks of lumber with his muzzle-loader by his side. No one was going to steal these logs.

Two days later, Ole and Hans came with horses and carts to pick up the lumber, and they spent three days moving it.

It came in handy now that Ola had added on to his house back in Norway. He knew what he was doing, and before the snow arrived they had a roof over them. The cows had the dugout to themselves.

4

On the other side of the earth, seven-year-old Anton Edvard sat doing his homework in the cabinetmaker's house. It was November and it was raining. It grew dark far too early at this time of year, and he wondered if he should take a blind man's holiday and light a lamp.

Erik and Anne had seen to the cowshed while they could still see their hands in front of them, and now they sat resting in the twilight. Anton Edvard could no longer see to read the homework he was assigned, and he asked them to light the lamp so he could find his way in the book, as he put it. He was reading the new Nordahl Rolfsen reader because his mother had taught him to read before he left Rekneslia, which was why teacher Røshol assigned him the new reader even though, strictly speaking, he was too young for it.

But Erik said they needed to save the lamp oil. You won't get far in this world if you don't exercise thrift, he admonished, and Anton Edvard should have done his reading while there was still enough daylight. He would just have to do it in the morning, right, Anton Edvard? That's how we do things around here. Anything that doesn't get done by nightfall, we do the following day!

They were at him to call them mother and father, as well. He was supposed to forget that he came from somewhere else. But he was so strongly opposed that he had his way in the end. He used their first names, and he didn't call them uncle or aunt, either, not even the local versions of uncle and aunt, *fabbro* and *moste*, which most of the other children used. He called them Erik and Anne.

5

During the depression of these years, when the wage for day laborers dropped by thirty øre, Nesje knew he had to return to his old job for Trolla Brug. It was time to dismantle the old stone hearths that lingered on in so many houses and to install woodstoves with built-in ovens. The new stoves saved wood and produced a stronger heat than any fireplace could. And there were so many amazing stoves available now! All kinds of crown stoves, and tiered stoves, and all of them slimmer than ever.

Nesje traveled around the Molde region. He walked and rowed, and took the steamboat when there was no other way. He sat and talked with people in the dusky half-light. He showed them catalogs he got from Hans in Kristiansund, and drawings of new models. He explained how to install them. People clapped their hands and laughed when he showed them the most modern types of stoves and ovens. There was one he called the "crane fly," that was number 59. Number 16 reminded the men of a woman's breast. Yes, perhaps there was something suggestive about it? But the one that sold the most was model number 202, because it had a water chamber on the side. You could tap hot water out of it any time it was lit. What a relief it was for people who had babies and young children to always have warm water!

Nesje, a tall, serious man with refined features, wore his hat and his double-breasted jacket when he was out on his calls. He whipped his hat off his head before he reached the front door and he knew to say goodbye when people ran out of things to talk about. He shook hands when he arrived and when he left, and generally comported himself like a man who knew his own worth.

Serianna laughed in delight when she heard about all the orders he received, but she quickly realized that once everything was tallied, he was left with too little.

Nesje found reasons to travel to Frænen to sell stoves, and that way he checked on his son, Anton Edvard. Nesje noted how the boy continually made himself useful. As soon as Anne came inside after milking, he went out because he needed to bring in water from the well, and this was a job he did in the dark. Nesje noticed it was dark there, even after the sun rose, which was exactly what Anton Edvard had said when he begged to be allowed to go home to his parents.

Anton Edvard got up to go to school. To deaden his stinging pain, Nesje walked the boy to school. Oh, how desperately he wanted to wrap his arms around that little body when they parted by the schoolhouse gate, but they weren't in the habit of displaying their emotions that way, so the father and son shook hands. Then Anton Edvard walked off toward the school without looking back. His father called out to him, and then the boy only turned around and just raised his hand in greeting before slipping in the schoolhouse door.

The father walked along the cart road, between the rocks, over the marsh puddles, and along the rocky knolls all the way to the good natural spring by the foot of Mt. Jendem. There he slaked his thirst and washed his face before setting out on the long hike over two mountain ranges. He didn't reach home in Rekneslia until late.

6

Eilert did well at school. Bastian Georg was no blockhead, but was more restless than his brother. He was in the sixth grade at Kvam School and he wanted to be confirmed as soon as possible. So he attended the confirmation class in Molde and not in Bolsøy, where he belonged, because that was too far when he also went to school. So he went to Molde Church, yes he did, but the Word of God did not appear to make much of an impression on him. Eilert, on the other hand, was with the Sættem family all the time, said his evening prayers, and wanted to live a pious life.

Kristine was nine, and a prodigy when it came to reading and mental arithmetic. When she wanted to impress her father with her talents, she held her book upside down as she read. Serianna said she couldn't have them walking around poorly dressed at Kvam School, so she made sure everything was in decent shape and clean. But when they came home from school they took off their good outfits and put on work clothes, and she sent them outside to help their father, who spent every available waking minute working on his parcel of land.

Nesje had let his beard grow longer even though it was taking on gray streaks. He looked like a patriarch, people said, far older than his years. He blackened the toes of his shoes with coal from the stove and decided he could afford a bit of mustache wax from the barber Raknes, which was lavender-scented and was a comfort on gray days.

7

They harvested the last of the potatoes the same day the assessor came and raised the appraised value to twelve hundred kroner. This year, 1890, Nesje harvested six *tønner*, about twenty-four bushels. He walked to town with the milk that evening to spare Serianna the trip. But after he had delivered the milk, still warm from the udder, to the customers' doors, he did not go home as planned nor by the way he always took. He parked his pushcart under a tree in Boybakken and strode right into the bar at Brændevinssamlag, the trading partnership that held the exclusive right to sell alcohol in town. He didn't have much in common with the men who hung out there, but the conversation might be interesting. In here, people talked about the defeat of Johan Sverdrup's government and the new prime minister, Emil Stang. None of them had the right to vote, of course, because you needed to own property before you could, but these were well-informed people, and as time went on Nesje found it so interesting that he felt he owed his friends a round of aquavit, so he quietly ordered back behind the bar and then brought out several bottles of brewery owner Dahl's beer, because the aquavit needed a chaser.

But suddenly the *skilling* from both his jacket pockets were gone, even though he was sure he had had two kroner left. He pulled out his pocket watch and then headed home, convinced that he needed to go to confession and confess what he had done. It was completely dark and the road was difficult to navigate. It wasn't until he was up at Rekneshaugen that he remembered he had left his handcart behind and had to go back and get it.

Up the hill past the Sættems' house it was tough going, even though he didn't have anything on the cart other than empty milk pails. He felt discouraged in a way he hadn't felt for many years, and that discouragement sent him fretting about his life: the land he was farming, the soil he was cultivating. When he was pouring drinks, he thought, he saw himself as he really was, and what he saw did not look so good. Suddenly it was clear to him that he was never going to achieve the prosperity of good times he dreamt of in his youth.

Serianna could tell right away what kind of a mood he was in, and she also realized that the milk money had been spent on liquor. Where was the rest of it? There wasn't any money left? Unbelievable! She brought him into the bedroom so the children wouldn't see him and put him to bed.

8

Nesje did everything he could to improve their situation. He negotiated a new suit for Bastian Georg to wear for his confirmation. It had been fifteen years since he had bought himself a suit. He couldn't afford it, but the tailor was patient and content to let him make the final payment at Christmas. That was the last suit Nesje bought. Nesje never said, and never let it show, that deep down he thought he was a different kind of person than those he shared the field with. He came from a long line of men who did things right, men who didn't take shortcuts, men who had fulfilled their obligations to society by putting on a soldier's uniform. He hadn't done that, but he still felt different from his fellow workers. They didn't read books, didn't go to the library, didn't wash their hands before and after meals the way he, the son of a midwife, did. It was as if there were an invisible air of refinement about him. That was why he didn't have any close friends besides his wife.

Those he shared his circumstances with were of another sort than he was, and those he considered his equals did not share his circumstances.

He stood in front of the mirror to comb his hair, as long as he had hair to comb. When his hair thinned he combed the wisps over his pate to conceal his baldness. He bought pomade on rare occasions and mustache wax, but eventually he let his beard grow so long that his mustache and his beard grew together into one. People noticed his upright posture. He almost always carried something or other when he walked from town up to Rekneslia, but even when he pulled a handcart along behind him or walked with a milk pail in each hand, he tried to walk just as straight as a second lieutenant, with the posture of his ancestors, who had been noncommissioned officers, every one. At the same time, he would bow deeply to anyone who outranked him. He tried to instill that in the two sons who still lived at home: that they must be proud but not arrogant, humble but not unassuming, bold but not cheeky, self-confident but not haughty, steadfast but not stubborn, yes, Lord knows it all. The haymaker's wisdom was the wisdom of moderation. He was a person who did not draw attention to himself or put himself down, a person who took what was right but wasn't greedy, a person who was good to his word even if everyone else wasn't.

When summer came, the price of milk went up because the two hotels, the Alexandra and the Grand, used every drop they could get for their summer guests. Many of the cotters went to the hotel entrances with their milk when their regular customers didn't want to pay the new price. But Nesje always took his milk to the furrier Jacobsen and the bank manager Isaksen and the other regular customers, and he let them pay the price to which they were accustomed and tried not to remind them that there was a summer price for milk.

On the rare occasion he needed a horse, he had firsthand experience with winter and summer as different seasons. In the summertime the horse folks charged twice as much. Serianna thought he came home with even less money in his hand than when he left. But Bastian Georg ran errands for them and carried luggage for summer guests, and wasn't afraid to stick out his hand and accept payment.

It was great help to Nesje that the boys were learning how to support themselves. And he gained courage this summer. He had scored lumber the previous winter, and before the haymaking he built a pantry on the north side of their west-facing room and installed a door and a window. The room was sealed and wallpapered, the ceiling and floor painted. The walls of the east-facing room were also sealed. Eilert was in charge of the putty and plaster and paint work. And as if that weren't enough, Eilert also painted the exterior of the house and repaired windows. In the loft he set up a tile stove with an oven that his father got from Trolla Brug at a significant markdown. Nesje praised Eilert for his tireless dedication, but it wasn't easy to get close to him. He worked long hours, as if he wanted to stop something from happening.

What was going to happen?

It looked as if the haymakers would soon become redundant in the Molde area. The new horse-drawn haymaker machines were becoming widespread. They had been too expensive for many in the beginning, but you could hear them humming on a July morning and people asking themselves, "What now?"

9

In South Dakota, automated production had rendered saddlers redundant. The saddler would be forgotten, Ole said.
There were no harsh words between him and Gjertine, but
they knew something had changed between them.

Nothing happened from one day to the next, from one
week to the next. But the conversations gradually faded
between two people who had been everything to each other.
Would they find their way back to each other?

Ole found some hunting friends, and they hunted small
game for pelts to sell to the Stavig brothers, who now had a
general store in Sisseton. They trapped skunks and mink,
voles and beavers. Ole and his buddies wore snowshoes and
skis to check their trap lines in the winter and tried to figure
out how the Dakhóta caught their small game. The tribe were
outstanding trappers and supplied the dealers with more
pelts than the farmers did.

Eventually, once he acquired a good gun, Ole started
hunting bigger game like moose, which you might occasionally
encounter, and deer, and even prairie dogs. In the spring he
did farm work with Gjertine and the children and figured
out what would give the best harvest. In the early days on
the prairie, Norwegians mostly stuck with varieties of grain
they were familiar with, but they gradually became more
audacious.

Large farms, like Hans Ås's, were soon producing such
large potato harvests that the prices fell. Then it hardly paid
to produce anything other than what you needed for your

own consumption. So they planted oats and rye, and eventually they harvested seed from wild oats and planted that.

Ole didn't hunt in the spring. He didn't want to disrupt the animals while they were birthing their young, not even with snares or traps. The trapping was done in the fall, after the farm season was over, and in the winter. Gjertine couldn't do anything but encourage him, which meant that she couldn't say anything but yes to his going away for so long at times that he had to spend the night with other Norwegian men.

They didn't all conform to the standards Gjertine had. A few of them kept liquor on hand and Ole didn't turn down the occasional dram these days. Gjertine had changed since her youth, when all types of human and earthly pleasures were repugnant to her. She now believed that a dram could be a valid refreshment for chilled menfolk who had been outside all day. But there other things that went with the alcohol. Yes, there was card playing. Did Gjertine have anything against cards? No, but she did think it was a sin and an embarrassment when people played for money. Because gambling never resulted in more money! Ole said that when his hunting buddies started talking about playing for money he bowed out. But didn't he still get in on the action once in a while, for a hand or two? Yes, and when he did, he had completely unexpected and unparalleled luck, slapping the ace on the table and raking in four or five dollars.

"The ace, the ace!" he yelled.

There was no point in lying to Gjertine about what he had been doing. She saw right through him. When he came home after his hunting trips, she would curl up against him at night, sniff him, smell him, and ask, "Have you been drinking whiskey? Have you been playing cards?"

"Yes, indeed I have," Ole said, knowing she would find out anyway.

"But didn't you promise me that you wouldn't do that?"

"I promised, but I wasn't able to keep my promise!" he said, wanting to caress her.

She punished him by turning her back to him, but she thought she was mostly punishing herself this way, sochanged her mind and turned back to him again. And after he fell asleep, she lay there looking at the ceiling in the little room they had to themselves, and images of her home country came to her. But it wasn't Slutåsen that she pictured in her mind's eye. She had almost forgotten that place. It was Bortegard, her childhood home, the house, the two *stabbur*-style storehouses, the barn, the view of the fjord. Sometimes when she woke up from some dream or other, she thought she was back there again. Sometimes it was so real that she had to share it with Ole. She couldn't be the only one.

"Ole, are you asleep?" she might ask, and he was easy to wake up. Just the sound of her voice was enough to rouse him.

"No, what is it?" he said.

"I had a dream that I was up in the storehouse loft," Gjertine said, "where we were first together."

"That took some time," said he who had once been the saddler Ole. "It took a long time before I was able to come to you."

"Don't leave me again," Gjertine said.

"How could you think to say something like that?"

"Sometimes you're so distant that I could almost believe you were thinking about another woman."

"You're starting on that again?" Ole said.

"No, I'm not starting. But it was stupid that we didn't wait for the full two years to pass before we got married."

"You wanted to be a Midsummer bride. Did you forget?"

"We could have married the following summer!"

"No. You really need to stop," said the former saddler, who wanted to go back to sleep.

"I know it's hard that you can't practice your trade," Gjertine said, scooting closer to her husband.

"I'm not complaining," Ole said. "Sometimes when I'm out in the woods hunting, I think that harness work trapped me in a life of hard, boring labor. I worked from dawn to dusk, into the night, and it wasn't enough. I don't want to talk about it. I'm not a saddler anymore."

"You'll always be saddler Ole to me," Gjertine said, running her hand down the back of his neck, because he had turned away from her to go back to sleep.

"Aren't you getting up at dawn to tend the cattle?" he asked her.

Yes, she was. And when she woke up and he was still asleep, she didn't wake him but fed the children and got them off to school before she ate a crust of bread and dressed to go to the cowshed. The little pond that was the reason they had chosen this spot froze, and it was quite a challenge to find water for the animals. When the ice melted and the countryside was clear again, the little pond shrank down to almost nothing. You could put in as much of an effort as you wanted, but most of the time it didn't matter. Was it all arbitrary, or was everything in the Lord's hands?

It was a strange spring. Ole wanted them to devote all their land to grain, and she didn't contradict him. Once the wild oats and the wheat were in, he went off again to hunt the forests around Watertown. She was left on her own with everything. It was draining. Gjertine wrote to her siblings, but she didn't tell them that everything was different than she had expected. Serianna read out loud to

Nesje. And Nesje wondered why little Gjertine, who had always been so matter of fact, had so little to say about herself.

10

Things were quieter in Rekneslia. Bastian Georg was apprenticed to the tailor Reistad, and he didn't come to see his parents every day. Eilert, still at home, was confirmed in Bolsøy Church on April 5, 1891, and was looking for a job. He had an offer to start as an apprentice baker with Ole Schistad, and he had sought that apprenticeship himself, but when it came down to it he didn't seem particularly interested. But the baker Schistad wanted an answer, so Eilert accepted, though he added that he had to help his parents with the haymaking, so he couldn't begin at the bakery until August first.

Ole Schistad thought it was odd that the teenager tried to dictate when his apprenticeship would begin, but in the end he went along with it. He saw how hard the Nesje family worked up on the slope.

Nesje certainly hadn't asked Eilert to stay. He wanted his son to be able to support himself when he moved on, but he did admit it was an advantage having him at home to help with the harvest, which couldn't be tackled until Gørvell's fields were mowed and Nesje had completed his contractual mowing at Reknes. Nesje cut the hillsides, and no one could keep up with him, but Eilert brought the hay indoors and showed his strength when he did. His father and mother stood watching as he drove the hayfork into enormous haycocks, scooped the load upward, propped the hayfork on his shoulder, carried the heavy load up to the barn, and tossed the hay in. Eilert was their great hope for the day when they could no longer do this. Bastian George did not see himself as a slave to the soil, he had said, and they wouldn't force him, careless as he was with both money and tools. They talked about how enthusiastic Eilert was all summer.

But it wasn't easy to know what was going on in Eilert's head. He spent a lot of time on his own and did not spend time with friends the way Bastian Georg did. Eilert never attended dances or games. Nesje had never been much of a carouser, but in his youth he attended Saturday night dances and enjoyed the occasional drink. Eilert didn't dance, and he definitely didn't drink the strong stuff. In the evening he liked to go to the Sættem house and talk with people. That was where Eilert sought spiritual guidance, and Nesje couldn't say he liked it. But he couldn't control a boy who was confirmed and thus an adult.

One evening the father saw his son more lost in thought than usual and, since it was Sunday, decided to talk to him. At first Eilert didn't want to say what was on his mind. But since his father insisted on knowing what was weighing on him, he gave in and fetched a letter he had received from his Aunt Gjertine in America. Nesje hadn't known anything about the letter. Why hadn't Serianna mentioned it? In the letter Gjertine said that Eilert was welcome in their home in South Dakota, if he wanted to go through with his plan to travel across the ocean. The family in South Dakota did not have any money to send, however. He would have to save that himself.

There was something about the tone of this letter that gave Serianna pause, which was why she had waited to discuss it with Nesje until they had time. At least that was the explanation she gave when Nesje asked why she hadn't shown him the letter. Gjertine had explained that she'd been sick a fair amount this winter, but she hadn't said what type of ailment. Her sister was usually verbose, providing detailed descriptions of all the amazing things that life in America had to offer, but there seemed to be a lot of difficulties. The saddler had to be away for weeks at a time and Gjertine would wake up at night, terrified some misfortune would befall them. What sort of a tone was this from her brave, lighthearted sister, who at her own confirmation had reprimanded the pastor?

The only thing Gjertine hoped for now was that Eilert would come over there so he could work on their farm his first winter until he found something for himself. Gjertine had been left alone with the farming as the saddler had more than enough with his hunting and fishing.

"Didn't the man go there to make harnesses?" Nesje asked.

In the letter Gjertine explained that for the Norwegian settlers on the Dakota prairie, life was mostly a continuation of the lives they had lived in Norway. The vast distances on the prairie meant that the road to market was too far to travel routinely. Only in the fall, after the busy season was finished, could they travel to Webster and offer goods for sale. The rest of the year they were subsistence farmers, living off their own crops and what they got through hunting and fishing. They ground their own grain with hand mills mounted on wheels that were pulled from one house to the next, along roads that were nothing more than cattle paths.

There could be many reasons why Serianna hadn't mentioned this letter to Nesje. Maybe he would be angry when he saw Gjertine trying to lure Eilert over there. Or maybe the letter could be used as evidence that things were not going as well with the Norwegians in the Dakota Territory as people were led to believe.

Eilert's Exit

I

Nesje felt anger rising in him, but then composed himself, even if he was convinced that Serianna was up to something he interpreted as a plot. For the second time in his married life, Nesje walked to town and drank. He told anyone who would listen that times in America weren't so great anymore, whereas it seemed like they were having some good years here at home. When he returned home that night, he was not steady on his feet, but Serianna, who had come home and found out that Nesje knew about Gjertine's letter, didn't find fault with him. Eilert went down to the Sættem house. It pained his father that he went for advice and solace there, and he thought about going down there to bring him back, but if he did that, after he had been drinking, his son would cut him off completely. Serianna was convinced of that.

Nesje didn't go, choking down his humiliation, but when Eilert came home he asked the boy what they had decided at the Sættem's place.

"We didn't come up with any definitive answer," Eilert said. "We prayed for God's guidance."

"But did they advise you to go?"

"I'm not going anywhere until I have money for a ticket, but I'm sure I'll be able to scrape that together if it's God's will that I go," Eilert said.

Eilert began his baking apprenticeship with Schistad, and he flourished. Nesje even thought he had given up on his silly emigration ideas, and they didn't discuss it any further.

It wasn't until the following summer, just before he was to leave, that Eilert told them he had a ticket on the Allan Line from Throndhjem, and he would be leaving Kristiansund by steamboat on June 17, 1892, his father's fiftieth birthday.

This was the third of Nesje's sons to leave his parents' home, and the first to set out in search of a home on the other side of the ocean.

2

"He'll be on his way soon," Gjertine told her husband. Ole had no idea what Gjertine was talking about. He figured she had told him about someone or other who was leaving Norway. Yes, well, there were so many leaving these days. Many even traveled back and forth between the New World and the Old.

Gjertine and Ole sowed the whole farm with grain, potatoes for their own use, and hay to keep a couple of cows over the winter. The milk that they didn't drink themselves they gave to the calves.

"Are you leaving again?" Gjertine said sadly when she saw her husband take out his fishing rods. He took off whenever he saw a chance.

"We'll thank the Lord in the winter for the fish we caught in the summer," Ole said and then kissed his wife.

He kept a tiny little homemade boat, hardly more than a canoe, by one of the lakes on the reservation. He could drag the boat somewhere on his own if he needed to. And now he sometimes met hunting parties from Minneapolis and Sioux Falls who rented space at Fort Sisseton now that the military no longer used it. He was hired to show rich people where the good fishing spots were and to look after their equipment. So, he was a hired assistant for people with money. They didn't pay him all that well, but he earned a few extra cents to show them where the fish would bite, and that came in handy. He even bought himself a new jacket. He figured it was important to dress the part, so the people who hired him weren't ashamed.

"Isn't that jacket going to be too hot?" Gjertine asked him. Something struck her when she saw him, ready to leave.

"If it is, I'll take it off," her husband responded casually, "but it'll be good to have when it gets dark."

"You're not going to sleep under the stars, are you?" Gjertine asked.

"Not unless we don't catch anything big. Then we won't stop for the night."

"And there's supper when you get to the fort?" Gjertine asked.

Yes, he figured there would be.

"And when will I see you again?" Gjertine asked.

"You'll see me when you see me, right?" Ole said, gave his wife a smooch, then left.

After a while, it struck her again. Something was very off, but what was it and how could she stop it? Had the struggle to feed her family made her neglectful of the one necessity? As she moved toward the future, had she strayed from the path that leads to the realm of heaven? On how many days had their uncertain prospects darkened her heart? How often did she forget there was someone who could quiet their worries?

Could a person who had believed as fervently as she once had apostatize? Was that even possible? And what was going on with her husband? Had he grown tired of her? Did he think she had duped him when she convinced him to travel over the ocean?

Gjertine felt shaky. She couldn't hold a pot in her hands, much less a cup. She couldn't stand. It was as if an abyss opened up before her. She went to lie down in bed. Her heart was throbbing wildly.

Sivert came in, and the ten-year-old realized right away that something was going on.

"What is it, Mama?" he said. "Should I yell for Papa, so he comes back?"

"No, no," Gjertine said. "Just let me rest a while and everything will be fine."

Her whole body was numb. She wasn't sure if she had slept or swooned, but when she came to she could tell from the shadows it was late in the afternoon. She was still numb but wasn't shaking as badly, and set out supper. When they sat down she asked little Edvard to say grace, and he did, at such a fast pace his siblings laughed at him. Only after the three youngest were in bed was she able to cry. Olava, almost an adult, sat with her and stroked her hair. At some point or other Gjertine had won Olava over, and she no longer thought everything her father said and did was beyond reproach.

"Why has he gone?" Olava asked, standing at the window with her back turned. "That hunting party hardly pays him anything. Maybe he just does it for the fish?"

"He said he didn't know if they had their cook with them this time," Gjertine said. "He said he might have to do the cooking."

"You don't think the cook is why he ran off so quickly?!" Olava gasped, spinning around in fear. "He wouldn't dare! What an awful thought. It makes me sick!"

That thought transported Gjertine many years back in time, to when Ole's sister Ane worked as a serving girl at Bortegard and told her about Ole's nighttime hijinks.

"I don't think he's doing anything behind my back," Gjertine said.

"No, because he isn't," Olava said.

"No, I don't think he is," Gjertine said. "But your father is a handsome man, and funny, so there are a lot of women who find it easy to forget that he has a family and obligations and responsibilities. Can't we talk about something else? Eilert will arrive soon. Maybe he'll arrive before the summer heat."

"Is he going to stay here?"

"Where else would he stay?"

"Oh, I don't know," Olava said, blushing.

3

The horse-drawn coach plodded away from Molde, heading toward Kristiansund along Fannestrandsvegen, as this part of the road was called, through the long avenue of maple trees that had been planted a hundred years earlier. Every now and then you could see a tree that had been planted more recently. The new maples were like stalks while the old trees were so thick that a man couldn't wrap his arms around them. To Nesje it was a visualization of time passing, and a shiver ran through him as he asked himself how big around the new maple trees would be when he saw Eilert again.

Nesje had borrowed a horse and buggy from Lars-at-Gørvell. The farm manager was a man who showed compassion when it mattered. Eilert didn't say much on the way there, and his father didn't know what to say either as they drove along the muddy, neglected road through the summer landscape. His son sat so close to him in the buggy that he could have put his arm around his shoulders, but he didn't do that. Eilert sat and stared at the mountains across the fjord, his face turned away. Was he cold, or afraid he might cry? He stared as if he were seeing this countryside for the last time. But this couldn't be the last time he would see the mountains, nor the last time his father would see him! He had to earn some money and come back home. Nesje couldn't bear the thought that his son would stay there for good. Eilert wasn't even seventeen; he had a whole life ahead of him. And Nesje figured on living twenty or thirty more years. True, many of Nesje's peers had found their places under six feet of soil, but he planned to be around for a long time.

He figured that since Anton Edvard had new parents to take care of, he couldn't expect too much from him. And he didn't have much confidence in Bastian Georg. Eilert was the considerate one, so it was hard to picture him being away forever. He had better calm down and give the boy some good advice to take along on his journey.

"If you should experience the worst," the haymaker told his son, "and you run out of money, you mustn't assume that is simply the end of all happiness."

"No, right," Eilert said.

"But you should always keep a little bit of money in reserve, which you don't touch until you're genuinely in need."

"Yes."

"In challenging circumstances like that, it's usually best to head out into the countryside, to a rural area, because that's where you'll find food most easily. And when a person is looking for work, it's easier to find a helping hand there."

This was certainly true, even if you couldn't call it wisdom.

"When you need to sleep with others at night," Nesje told his son, "it's usually best for the guest not to talk about his own people, but rather listen to the people who have taken you in and given you a bite and a bed."

Obvious, perhaps, but he considered it better said than unsaid.

"But misfortune is not the biggest trial," Nesje told his son. "It can be an even bigger test when fortune comes knocking, if you come into good money. Because that is the test of whether a person can steer clear of amusements and parties and hide away the extra money, so that you have something to tide you over when times are leaner."

"I haven't been prone to running off to parties," Eilert said wryly.

"That's true," his father agreed. "You've always demonstrated your natural abilities, and I know you'll be able to bear both calamities and distress. But if it should turn out some day that it looks like there's no way out, then you should take fresh courage, because the situation can only improve. When you reach bottom and you can't go any lower, and then the result is good—then everything is well. And the last thing that you mustn't forget, even if you forget every other thing you've been told and learned, is that you don't go out into the world alone."

"That's true, Father."

"Because there is someone up there, accompanying us on our journeys and showing mercy to us in our need."

Nesje did not make confessions of faith like this very often, but this happened all on its own, he hardly needed to think. These words were born of his own deep pain. The sight of his son as he said goodbye to his mother—he could not erase that sight from his mind. What was this? Why was his son looking at him with such amazement? True, he had to admit that the profound truths coming out of his mouth were not things he had learned through his own life experiences; these were truths that came from another time and another place, suddenly there for him. His son had searched and found solid footing, but what about him? Sure, he was a Christian man. He had his childhood faith, but he wasn't born again, as they called it now. He had not converted; he was no Reader.

"You mustn't say anything that you don't stand behind," his son said, and Nesje thought that sounded harsh. What in the world did he mean by that?

"You're going to have to explain what you mean by that, boy!" Nesje said. "I stand behind what I've always stood behind."

"It's not very often that you mention your faith in Him up there," Eilert said. "To me it seems like you mostly have faith in your own strength. But if you turn to Him above now, then there is nothing about this departure that gives me more joy than that."

"It may well be that we also have our grounding, those of us who don't go shouting about it," Nesje said, a bit choked up. He was reminded that Eilert, with his gentle disposition, still had a hardness about him.

Then it hit him. His son was setting off into the world, and what was the most important thing his father could send with him? Bible passages that he needed, Eilert would be able to find on his own. But there was something that wasn't in the Bible and that might be good to call on in such a time, and that was how a normal person can staunch the flow of blood.

He hadn't forgotten that he had sworn to keep it to himself. He couldn't break an oath in which he had sworn by Jesus's name. He only knew that it was a long way between midwives in America, and out on the prairie most people had to make do with the neighbor ladies. He had read that in the newspapers, and he thought that at least in Norway things had progressed to the point where midwives attended to mothers when babies were born. He himself had had a mother who walked on her own two feet all the way to Kristiania to attend midwifery school, before coming home again and helping a thousand babies into the world.

"When you're alone and can't get ahold of a doctor or a midwife," Nesje said, "it's important to know how to staunch the flow of blood. There are some words to say that make the bleeding stop. I've seen it with my own eyes, because it happened when you were born."

"You've never mentioned this before," Eilert said.

"Your mother had a painful and difficult childbirth," Nesje said, "but the right words were spoken, and the bleeding stopped."

"What are the words?"

"I can't tell you that!" Nesje said, and now there was desperation in his voice. "I swore that I wouldn't tell anyone, because if people who would misuse these words learn of them, they lose their strength. But it was none other than Gjertine who spoke the words, and she is the one you are going to see! When the day comes that you leave her to find your own homestead, you ask her if she can teach you."

Eilert stared at his father in amazement. Then he decided to let the subject drop.

They boarded the steamship that would take them to Kristiansund, where the next steamship awaited. In Kristiansund, they asked Hans for a place to stay, and he had a room they could sleep in and two living rooms besides, that Hans. It had been five years since Nesje had seen his eldest son, but the reunion couldn't deaden the pain of Eilert leaving. Hans had been married to Bertine for many years now, but this was the first time Nesje had met her. When Hans married her in Throndhjem, he hadn't invited his parents. True, Serianna wasn't his mother. Maybe it was because he didn't think they would get along well with the bride's family? At any rate, there was no choice but to just put up with it. Either you were invited to a wedding, or you weren't.

Nesje told himself that this woman was by no means a bad wife for Hans. She was welcoming to her father-in-law. She proceeded to inquire after everyone in the family. Nesje found her to be a stately lady. She didn't really do very much. She set out food for them, but a maid came and cleared the table after they ate, and a little later she said with a smile that surely the Nesje men had things to discuss among themselves, so she said goodnight and went to bed.

Nesje and Eilert slept in the same room that night, but Hans was so distant. He had important business, it appeared, and although he was thirty-two he behaved like a middle-aged man. He said goodbye to his brother as they left the house, declining to accompany them to the wharf. Did he not see the waves of pain and anguish running over his father's face? His third-eldest son was leaving him, bound for a country on the other side of the world.

They reached the wharf two hours before the ship was scheduled to depart. They watched as everything was loaded aboard. It felt like forever until the departure. There was a new pain every minute as the moment approached.

Things had never before felt as serious as they did now. Time was standing still for Nesje when the ship's bell rang, a first time and then a second.

Two boys came up the street with a handcart full of luggage, presumably belonging to a man talking with the captain, so they didn't depart until all of his things were aboard. A boy stood beside the man, holding his top hat because it was hot. He was probably one of the klipfish kings, taking a trip to Bergen. Both he and the ladies with him, in their big hats, looked like they had all the time in the world. They knew the steamship wouldn't leave without them. Once that last trunk was hoisted aboard, Nesje's young son would just run up the gangway. Now the bell rang a third time. Nesje wanted to hug his son, and in the end, he did. Nesje ran after him to stop him, and then they hugged each other and cried without a care as to who saw them.

"Goodbye, in Jesus's name," Nesje said.

"Yes, in Jesus's name! Give my best to Mother and little Kristine and to Anton Edvard, whom I didn't have time to see. And to Bastian Georg, yes, to Bastian Georg!"

"Don't be discouraged and don't bear worries in your heart," his father said. "You're setting out into the world in search of happiness, and someday this day of sorrow will become joyful, because our grief is turned to joy."

He said this, but the moment was like a dream, a fever dream. The hardest thing to face, the greatest obstacle to believing the words that came out of his mouth, was the endless labor he performed, without happiness—the incessant days as a hired laborer on the big estates and every dawn and every evening that he toiled away on his own steep scraps of land.

"May I see you again in this life," Nesje prayed. But his son gave no clear answer.

"That is my hope, if God wills it," was all he said.

The steam engine fired up, sending big clouds of smoke billowing out of the smokestack, and began to run. The ship shook. Foam bubbled from the stern and the hawsers were cast off. Eilert hurried aboard on long strides. He went to the lower deck, third class. There he stood and watched everyone gathered on the wharf as the steamship pulled away. Nesje saw his son with a serious childlike face below a black hat. He stood waving a handkerchief, but when Nesje couldn't see him anymore, the tears welled so that he had to stumble off to find his horse. It took him a long time to find the right street.

4

The day after, once he returned the horse and buggy to Gørvell, he made his way again over to Rekneshaugen, where a pavilion and flagpole had been erected so people could sit, even in rainy weather, and enjoy the view of the Romsdal Alps and know that they were in the most beautiful town in all of Norway. Molde, the City of Flowers. Nesje turned his back to the view. His eyes were on his home, and he thought the whole thing looked plainly poor, though it was high on the hill, free and clear. The house wasn't particularly big. It could almost be considered a cabin, and the barn, well, could it even really be called a barn? There was one small outbuild- ing with room for two cows and four sheep. Maybe that was why that good boy of his decided to leave and go so far.

As Nesje climbed the hills, it struck him for the first time that this was a long and difficult climb, and he stopped to catch his breath, and the rest that he took was so long you would think he didn't want to get home. He stood there, mid- way, and thought about how to describe his final moments with Eilert to Serianna. He couldn't let her know his heart was breaking.

He came up to the house, reached for the door, and stood in the doorway shielding his eyes from the light. She stood up from the table and he saw that she was an old woman, this woman who had been sitting at their table with a wreath of silver around her head. She came over to him and took the jacket he held and hung it on a peg. As she took it, she rubbed his arm and shoulder. Her touch was more than gentle, and heat surged through him. They were together, for better and for worse, that was what the pastor had said when he had married them almost twenty years earlier. He walked over to the table and sat in the chair opposite hers, and when she found him a plate and a cup of milk she settled in to hear how it had gone. But as he searched for the right words to describe the day, in almost minute-by-minute detail, he realized it didn't take any effort to hide the pain and desperation that had settled over him like a raincloud. Instead he focused on the fairy tale–like aspects of his final journey with Eilert through the Norwegian summer. Yes, the pain was gone. It had been a triumphant journey in which the father and son were together and felt the bond of love between them, so strong and steadfast. The Atlantic Ocean between them was not a division but rather a connecting link on which ships would shuttle back and forth bearing greetings between them.

No, Eilert hadn't traveled away from home, he had traveled to the country that God had promised to those who took the initiative, those with faith. Eilert followed the ways of the Lord and fulfilled God's mandate be fruitful and increase in number and fill the earth. Nesje was confident that his son would find his way because he carried his good heritage from a modest and God-fearing home. Serianna thought Nesje was getting a little carried away, but she otherwise agreed with him. If the world was ever to get on an even keel, the capable people couldn't sit at home with their parents—they had to go out and do useful work and be good examples to those around them. Oh, it was as if the trip to Kristiansund would never end. He had to tell her about everyone he saw. Who was out and about, traveling on the back roads around Midsummer. And the birdsong over Osmarka, he had to tell her about that. And the ornamental shrubberies all along Fannestrandsvegen, the floral beauty all around him the whole way. He described the strange night they spent at Hans's place in Kristiansund, when his eldest son kept coming in to see if there was anything they needed but wouldn't sit down to talk. How was it that Hans was such a stranger to his own family? It was as if he couldn't remember his brother Eilert, or as if his brother were somehow irrelevant. Nesje described their night in the room, when Eilert slept noisily and while Nesje scarcely closed his eyes. He described how his son stood on the wharf like a man, Nesje said. He was a grown man among others, going into the world. Strong and resolute, but remember how he scampered aboard and waved as the ship left the dock.

However hard it was for them as parents, for Eilert this was *right*, because it was too cramped for him here at home. Eilert wouldn't spend all his days trudging around on leased land as they had done. And when the Lord arranges things so well for young people, parents shouldn't get in the way. They couldn't think about what would bring them the most joy. True parental love asked what was best for the children, and how could they find a living to support themselves and their families.

Yes, yes, yes, Serianna sat and ran her hand over the tablecloth, as if to remove some invisible crumbs. It was all true, just the way he said it. She didn't disagree with him on a single point, but she couldn't deny that her mother's heart was crying.

Nesje was still wearing his good clothes. He didn't need to do anything more today, but once he ate, he changed into a work shirt and old wadmal and followed her to the cowshed. Serianna was well past fifty now, she who always bragged that she was younger than he was, but he could see a bit of dowager's hump as she stood calling the cows with her *kulokk*, the lilting herding call she always used. They heard twigs snapping, and the cows emerged from the woods. He tied them to the cowshed wall so she could get the milking stool and pull the milk out from their teats under an open sky. The milk streamed into the pail. He went into the cowshed and found it stifling and stuffy.

Since he couldn't afford to hinge the windows, he thought he might take out the whole window to air the place out. As he did this, he could smell the scents of summer, and he savored the lack of wind and heat because they meant his son would have good weather on the first leg of his journey.

He emerged from the cowshed as Serianna was pouring the last pail through the strainer that stood atop the pail by the wall, so that the milk ran through the sieve cloth into the pail. The moon shone over the Romsdal Fjord. Kaiser Wilhelm's ship, the *Hohenzollern*, was moored in the fjord, and they could hear music. Maybe they were having a ball. Maybe the young ladies from town, or those among them from the upper class, had come aboard to dance with sailors. Fundamentally, his was a good life, as the Lord intended it, Nesje told himself, but sometimes there are complications and we know great suffering. It is good that we don't live forever, and that there is one who can ease our loss and sorrow.

The evening arrived at the end of this strange day. What should he do now? Read the Bible, maybe? No, he couldn't rally himself. He remembered that he had been sent the latest price list from Trolla Brug and pulled out the little brochure. The nice woodstove, "No. 208," was up to fifty kroner now. That was the one Ola had bought for thirty-five kroner seventeen years ago. And they had come out with so many nice models. Stoves and ovens were constantly evolving. There were American-made brewer's pots he would have liked to own. A twenty-gallon pot cost only forty kroner. The waffle iron was up to two kroner now. It had been one and a half when he bought his. He used to have all the prices in his head. Now he thought it best to bring the price list with him so the customers could see with their own eyes what everything cost at Trolla Brug, or Throndhjems Mekaniske Værksted as the company was now called, though in Nesje's mind it was still Trolla Brug.

Serianna came out after cleaning her milk sieve and rinsing the pail. She stood beside him, his silent companion. He sometimes felt strangely unfamiliar to her, but grief drew them closer together. In the days that followed they showed each other a quiet regard, because they knew they were each carrying their pain without a word.

5

Nesje went to town several times without having any errand to call him there, because spring came late and the haymaking on the Gørvell farm was postponed. He wasn't loafing around, but he took the time to chat with people. Everyone knew his second son had emigrated to America. Molde was a small town. Really, it hardly qualified as a town, though it had held that status for a hundred and fifty years. The population recorded in the census was well under two thousand souls.

He received comments from all sorts of people: recognition and admiration, he thought, from people who felt it wise of Eilert to emigrate. Time after time Nesje offered details. Eilert wasn't traveling into the unknown, Nesje explained, he was traveling to his mother's people, which was to say Gjertine Ås and her brother Ola and their spouses, who had claimed land in the Dakota Territory. Gjertine and Ole Ås were in Roslyn, and Ola and Sara were by Buffalo Lake, a day's journey from Sisseton. Nesje put the stress on the last syllable in Sisseton, which was what he did with all his words. Near the town of Sisse*ton,* with emphasis on the last syllable. After that many people in Molde pronounced it the way Nesje said it. Nesje was a man who expressed himself well when he wanted to, and when for the fiftieth time he told the story of how Eilert and he had parted ways, his voice took on a solemn tone: We parted ways in Kristiansund, he said. In his retelling, the With Wharf in Kristiansund also took on a fairy-tale luster, and when he described how they embraced each other, there were some who had a hard time holding back their tears.

"You'll see, he'll come back after he's made a few kroner," people said. Because it did sometimes happen now that young people went over just to work there for a few years and save up some money. Those who traveled with their whole family were rarely seen again, but young people without any obligations, they might go back and forth; some even made these trips several times.

Nesje listened to them and sometimes agreed, though he didn't like the talk about dandies returning with gold teeth and silver-handled walking canes. Eilert would never deck out himself so tastelessly in anything like that! But then people talked at such length about all the young people who came back that he began to wonder if it might happen with Eilert too.

"You'll see him here in the doorway again before we know it," he told Serianna. "At any rate, it's certainly plausible that he'll return home before the century *runs out!*"

More and more he lately fell back on expressions like these, which he picked up from the *Romsdals Budstikke* and other newspapers he came across. He collected and saved them and sprinkled them into his conversations. The century, it was going to *run out* in eight or nine years, although there had been some debate on how to count it. The nineteenth century couldn't be considered over until the sun slid into the ocean at the end of 1900, which meant there were eight and a half years more. Eilert had left the nation of Norway in the year of our Lord 1892, before he turned sixteen.

6

The frost came to the hills around the house in Kringsjå earlier than usual, and it was high time to bring in the potatoes. The crisp fall arrived with the sun low, and with this change came prolonged contemplation. A day before the frost, the first letter from Eilert arrived. He described his long journey from Ellis Island to Minneapolis, and the train ride to Sauk Center, and the journey from there by train to Webster, only three or four miles from Roslyn. *The Indians welcomed me!* Eilert had written, and they read his letter many times, and cried and laughed because he'd arrived safely to his own people.

But why hadn't he written about how Gjertine and her family were doing? Serianna found this more than conspicuous. That did not bode well. Nesje thought it meant more letters would arrive soon. He must want to describe his own trip in this one and let them know that he had arrived safely. That must be it.

When they went to bed he noticed that Serianna was upset. He knew well that it was best to leave her be when her mind wouldn't settle. But in this situation, when they could thank the Lord that Eilert had made it safely to Roslyn, he had to know what was troubling her.

And this time she didn't mind sharing her thoughts with him.

"What if he never comes back?" Serianna said. "What if we never see him again?"

"How can you think that?" Nesje said. "Don't you know everything is in the Lord's hand? And we certainly don't deserve such a sorrow as to never see Eilert back home again."

"But what if he meets a woman and marries her, and then he settles down and has children and grows livestock? He might not get away until the children are big and he can get people to help him with the farm!"

"He remembers us and will do what he can to come see us," Nesje said. "Now you must put these thoughts to rest and thank God for his having arrived there safely."

"I don't doubt that he'll do his best to come back to us," Serianna said, "but sometimes life is harsh. There could be an accident, or misfortune, or storms in that unknown country, and then he'll have to take care of his wife and children like everyone else."

"I think you're too gloomy now," Nesje said, and he tried to be firm without being severe. "If everything goes wrong, well, just trust in the words of God the Father that one day we'll meet again in heaven."

"But will we even recognize each other in heaven?"

"What are you saying?!"

"Is there any certainty that we'll recognize our own loved ones when we get there? Couldn't it be that friendship and acquaintance and guilt all wind up in the background so that we don't care about any of it, because we are all God's children and praise him forever?"

Her thoughts frightened him. If someone other than Serianna had said something so preposterous, he would have considered it the most extreme free thought. But she was mourning two sons now: Anton Edvard, gone to Frænen, and Eilert, gone to America.

Maybe most of all she was grieving the third, Bastian Georg, who in a way had left them, though he was still there. He no longer confided in them; he no longer told them what he did. Bastian Georg, so rebellious and grudging, made them feel as though he despised them and their poverty, that he blamed them for being unable to offer their children a better life. This may have hurt most of all. They knew their other boys had their parents in their hearts, and in that sense would always be with them.

Nesje sympathized with Serianna. She could be gruff and snippy, but when things got tough, she only had him.

I mustn't cut her short or scold her, he thought. She's discouraged, but she's making sense.

"I don't know what to do besides pray," he said.

"You go ahead," said Serianna, "but perhaps you can do that silently."

That's how it was, never fully the way he wanted it. Here he had been trying to bring her some peace, with the words of the Lord's Prayer, but she couldn't be bothered to listen.

"I can feel you praying, even when you pray silently," said Serianna. "I know you so well that I can even feel which exact prayer you decide on, every time."

Then he prayed slowly and earnestly, and without a sound. But when he came to *Thy will be done on earth as it is in heaven*, he heard gentle snoring. She had fallen asleep.

Finally he, too, fell asleep. That night he had a dream. He saw a big mountain, shaped like Store Venjetinden, the mountain he saw as a child. It was a big mountain with snow on top, with a green, birch forest further down. His children came down from this mountain, one by one, on a path that switched back and forth. He first spotted them when they were way up, and he couldn't tell for sure if it was them. But then they came out of the forest to stand in front his window. There was Hans in all his reserved decorum, as if they had never truly known each other, and Bastian Georg with his dark smile. Then he saw kindhearted Eilert, and never had the father seen his face look so bold and happy. After Eilert came the apple of his eye, little Kristine, and she looked sad, yes, and perplexed, as if she didn't understand what the point of this meeting was. The last was Anton Edvard from Frænen. He looked serious, but there was no ill will in his eyes.

His feet couldn't hold him up, so Nesje couldn't walk to them and hug them, but he could greet them. They called to him that they were all doing well, and that they could only stay a short while. He replied to them that he certainly understood, and that he was grateful they had thought of him.

The dream ended with a vision of himself, walking up the hills to Kringsjå. He walked up and up, until finally there were only white clouds. The white clouds surrounded a heavenly meadow where he walked and swung his scythe in a strange, golden light. He didn't know who he worked for, other than the Lord, who would provide for him even in the everlasting. The Lord had him do what he did best: making hay in heaven. That was the work he enjoyed the most, swinging the scythe. He saw that he was smiling in his dream, and he knew that when the sunny days were over, his children would come and be with him for all eternity.

When the morning came and Serianna opened her eyes, he told her: "Last night I dreamt that I will be a haymaker in heaven too," he said. "So there's no chance that Eilert won't recognize me."

AUTHOR'S POSTSCRIPT

Haymaker in Heaven is a novel based on vague memories of people who actually lived. I knew only one thing about Gjertine Eriksdatter: that she opposed the pastor who was to confirm her, telling him that he wasn't teaching correctly. I saw her grave in Roslyn for the first time twenty-five years ago. Knut Hansen Nesje, who goes by Nesje in this book, I know from my father's stories, but the vast majority of his life story, here, was artistic creation, and the same is true for his wife, Serianna. The dates are taken from parish registers, and information about life in South Dakota and Molde from newspapers and a number of other sources. Since my early youth, I've thought I would write about these people who struggled to make a living, who knew grief and privation, but who also entertained big dreams that life would some day be better.

EDVARD HOEM
Oslo, October 12, 2014

Paul Audestad

Edvard Hoem is the author of *Haymaker in Heaven*. One of Norway's most celebrated literary writers since his breakthrough with the Critics' Prize–winning novel *The Ferry Crossing*, he is an accomplished translator, the author of more than a dozen acclaimed novels, and a four-time finalist for the Nordic Prize.

Libby Lewis

Tara Chase is the translator of *Haymaker in Heaven*. Her translations from the Norwegian, Danish, and Swedish include work by Jo Nesbø, Per Nilsson, Lene Kaaberbøl, and Agnete Friis. She lives in Seattle.

milkweed
editions

Founded as a nonprofit organization in 1980, Milkweed Editions is an independent publisher. Our mission is to identify, nurture and publish transformative literature, and build an engaged community around it.

Milkweed Editions is based in Bdé Óta Othúŋwe (Minneapolis) within Mní Sota Makhóčhe, the traditional homeland of the Dakhóta people. Residing here since time immemorial, Dakhóta people still call Mní Sota Makhóčhe home, with four federally recognized Dakhóta nations and many more Dakhóta people residing in what is now the state of Minnesota. Due to continued legacies of colonization, genocide, and forced removal, generations of Dakhóta people remain disenfranchised from their traditional homeland. Presently, Mní Sota Makhóčhe has become a refuge and home for many Indigenous nations and peoples, including seven federally recognized Ojibwe nations. We humbly encourage our readers to reflect upon the historical legacies held in the lands they occupy.

milkweed.org

Milkweed Editions also gratefully acknowledges sustaining support from our Board of Directors; the Alan B. Slifka Foundation and its president, Riva Ariella Ritvo-Slifka; the Amazon Literary Partnership; the Ballard Spahr Foundation; *Copper Nickel*; the McKnight Foundation; the National Endowment for the Arts; the National Poetry Series; the Target Foundation; and other generous contributions from foundations, corporations, and individuals. Also, this activity is made possible by the voters of Minnesota through a Minnesota State Arts Board Operating Support grant, thanks to a legislative appropriation from the arts and cultural heritage fund. For a full listing of Milkweed Editions supporters, please visit milkweed.org.

Interior design by Tijqua Daiker and Mary Austin Speaker
Typeset in Arno

Arno was designed by Robert Slimbach. Slimbach named
this typeface after the river that runs through Florence,
Italy. Arno draws inspiration from a variety of typefaces
created during the Italian Renaissance; its italics
were inspired by the calligraphy and printing
of Ludovico degli Arrighi.